LOVE LETTER LOST

a sweet romance

HILLARY SLAUGHTER

To Mom and Dad.

Thank you for helping me chase this crazy dream. Love you!

Trigger Warning

This work of fiction speaks vaguely of past verbal and physical abuse that does not occur on the page.

Chapter One

My fingers fumbled as I secured the door lock, then the dead bolt. The rattling sound of the chain sliding into place brought an odd sense of satisfaction and relief as I sank onto the floor, my back against the door. I shook my head as my escape registered.

A brown ball of fur shoved her face into mine, forcing me to laugh as I attempted to push away the wet, persistent tongue.

"No, Ruby. Just because I wouldn't let Bruce kiss me, doesn't mean you get the honor."

After a few more attempts, the dog took the hint and curled up in my lap, accepting chin scratches instead.

"I'm guessing the date didn't go well."

I looked up to see Audrey, Ruby's owner and one of my roommates, watching me from the hallway that led to her bedroom. Her long black hair was piled on top of her head in a messy bun I wished I could copy. That combined with her workout clothes meant I was probably preventing her from attending yoga at the rec center. But I was not opening that door for at least another twenty minutes. Bruce could have followed me from the car, ready to claim his post-date hug. Or worse, a kiss.

"Why do I always attract the weirdos?" I groaned.

"What happened this time?"

"It started with—"

"Wait," Chloe, my other roommate, called from her bedroom. She surfaced from the opposite end of the hall a few minutes later, her pixie-cut brown hair sticking up in disorganized spikes that somehow made the hairstyle cuter. "Mallory, you can't start the post-date retelling without me. Just let me save my assignment."

As Chloe disappeared back down the hall, I nudged Ruby from my lap and stood.

"I do not envy her taking college classes," I said.

Audrey shrugged. "At least Chloe's set to graduate within a reasonable amount of time. It took me several years longer than planned to get my degree."

"Can we skip the detailed date recap and go straight to the ice cream?" I asked as I followed Audrey to one of the worn blue-plaid couches I'd gotten second-hand from my parents. Despite the couches having been in our apartment for over a year, they still smelled of my parents' basement: wood polish and Febreze, two scents that followed us no matter how many times we moved.

"Nice try, Mal. But if we're going to truly commiserate, we need all the details."

Chloe appeared a few minutes later and sat on the loveseat diagonally from Audrey and me. Ruby hopped onto the couch next to Audrey and settled on her lap.

"Okay, spill. And I mean all the details. If there was hand-holding, I want to know." Chloe leaned forward, elbows on knees, her chin resting in her hands.

Chloe's petite size and eager expression reminded me of my fifth graders, causing a twinge of sadness as I remembered today had been the last day of school. Not only had I had to say goodbye to my students today, but now I had the memory of yet another disastrous date to grapple with.

"The short version: it started with his over-inflated ego and ended with me running from the car. There was no hand-holding, thank goodness."

Audrey nodded in sympathy. "Dang! I hoped this one wouldn't end up on your List. What's the long version?"

I sighed, slouching deeper into the couch.

"Let's see…I maybe said two words during the drive to the bowling alley. He was too busy telling me about how he was up for another promotion and that his video game scores were at an all-time high. He complained about all the bowling alley balls, claiming they were inferior. He had to catalog each shortcoming for me, explaining how they paled in comparison to the one he owns."

"Then why didn't he bring his?" Chloe asked, a question I'd posed to Bruce after his continued complaints.

"It was in storage and too hard to get at for anything short of a play-off game. On the plus side, Bruce is good at bowling. In fact, he promised that if I got my priorities straight, I could be good at bowling someday too. Of course, if it means I have to compete with Bruce's trash-talking ability, I'll pass."

"Please tell me dinner afterwards was better," Chloe said.

"Not really. Bruce spent the entirety of dinner yelling at a tennis match on TV. I started to worry we'd be asked to leave. He got very…heated."

My roommates blinked at me in silence. As I looked between the two, a sign I'd placed on the entertainment center caught my attention: Count Your Blessings. While intended as a decoration for the Thanksgiving holiday, I'd left it out in an effort to bring more positivity into my life, a New Year's resolution I was working on with mixed success. Thinking quickly, I added a few positives from the date, ticking them off on my fingers.

"It wasn't all bad. Bruce held the door for me, the sandwich I had for dinner was good, and the restaurant served Dr. Pepper."

"I thought your mom liked him," Audrey said. "Didn't she say he was 'perfect' for you?" Audrey made air quotes around the word *perfect*.

"I'm pretty sure she set us up because we're both single, Bruce is connected to one of her book club friends, and she loved the idea of teaming up with her friend to plan the wedding."

"Where are you ranking this one on your List?" Chloe asked. Our lists of worst dates helped us find humor in the slew of bad dates we'd recently experienced. Occasionally, we went on good dates that left us hopeful about our chances of someday having a healthy relationship. My date with Bruce was not one of those dates.

I tapped my finger on my chin, considering. "I think Kevin, the guy who took me axe throwing and kept telling me how fast his pet snake could eat me while comparing me to his ex-wives, still holds the title for my worst date ever. But Bruce might be second place."

"Kevin? I thought the guy who wouldn't say a word to you the entire date and then made you walk home was in first," Audrey said.

"What about the online guy who wanted to go night hiking up American Fork Canyon?" Chloe asked.

"I never actually went on a date with Night Hike Guy, seeing as I didn't want to be murdered. Silent Guy gets an honorable mention, but I still have nightmares about Kevin's snake."

I rested my head on the back of the couch and stared up at the ceiling, grateful I'd taken the time last year to remove the old popcorn effect. The smooth, white finish that greeted me was much more pleasant to look at when pondering my dating quandaries.

My phone buzzed, and I looked at the screen. I had five texts from my mother, no doubt asking about my date. I assured her I was fine and promised to tell her more later before shoving the phone back in my pocket. I needed to process the day a bit more before adding my mother's anxieties to the mix.

"I know everyone means well with all these date setups, but I think I'm declaring this summer a no date zone. I need a break."

"Attracting weirdos is better than attracting jerks," Audrey whispered. I looked over to find her hugging Ruby to her chest, the dog staring back at me with liquid brown eyes that seemed to concur with her owner.

I reached over and gave Audrey's hand a squeeze.

Last summer, Audrey and I had had near identical dating experiences. Audrey had dated her last boyfriend, Lyle, for nearly a year, to the point that she had been anticipating a proposal. But a family emergency had come up, and Audrey had dropped everything to go home and help her mom. It had been the beginning of summer, so she'd taken leave from work, promising Lyle she'd be back as soon as she could. Three weeks later, Audrey had come back, expecting to find Lyle waiting for her with a hug and the reassurance everything would be okay. Instead, she'd found him at his apartment kissing her former best friend. At the time, I'd been her shoulder to cry on promising that everything would work out for the best, blissfully unaware that my fiancé had also had another woman in his life.

About a week after Audrey had made her discovery, I'd decided to surprise Matt with an early wedding present. I'd shown up at his office to find him sitting in his car getting cozy with the new receptionist. I'd thrown the wedding present, a framed engagement photo for his desk, at the car, scratching his shiny black Lexus. I'd then driven home, canceled the wedding, and sold the ring online. That money currently sat in a savings account, waiting to fund my dream side-hustle: property management. Purchasing the fourplex I called home from my dad would be the first step.

Chloe broke into my thoughts. "You've sufficiently spilled your guts. I vote for ice cream! It's my turn to buy, and I think Ben and Jerry's is on sale."

I put in a request for something loaded with caramel and chocolate but bowed out of going to the store. Between the terrible date and saying goodbye to my students, I needed a moment to change into sweats and unwind.

While they drove to the store, I slipped into my room and dug out my bright blue joggers with pockets and my favorite t-shirt which read: "I teach children, what's your superpower?" I'd just settled back onto the couch to wait for the promised ice cream when my phone buzzed with a text.

I glanced at the screen, expecting another message from my mother. Instead, my lips stretched into a grin when a message from my cousin, Livvy, greeted me. Livvy was getting married next week, and as one of her bridesmaids, I received near-daily panic-driven texts verifying details. Curious to see what had Livvy stressed this time, I opened the message and began to read.

LIVVY: How would you feel if I told you a mystery-man from your past was about to make a reappearance in your life at my wedding?

This was too good to pass up. I considered how to respond before settling on the obscure.

ME: Is it Seth? Please, tell me it's Seth.

LIVVY: Who's Seth?

ME: That kid who used to live down the street from you. He had a neon green bike and he smelled like grass stains.

LIVVY: No. I haven't thought about that kid in years. I think he moved before junior high. Also, how do you smell like grass stains?

ME: It's like fresh cut grass but mixed with BO. I give up. Who?

LIVVY: Ridge Matthews.

I froze as I read the words. Of course it would be Ridge.

Chapter Two

I FOUND MYSELF LOST in memories: Friday evenings playing night games, the damp air filling my lungs, summer days floating the Provo River with the smell of sunscreen lingering in my nose as my legs went numb from the cold water. I could picture Ridge in high school. He'd had short brown hair, bright blue eyes, and an infectious grin. He'd used his smarts and confidence to win student body elections, though being on the basketball team hadn't hurt either. Ridge had been my cousin Kyle's best friend growing up, and because Kyle's twin Livvy and I were close, I'd spent a lot of time with him over the years. We'd watched movies, hiked to waterfalls, set off fireworks, and countless other exploits in our time together. I'd grown up all over the Wasatch front, but between family parties, where Ridge had always been welcome, and sleepovers at Livvy's house, we'd become friends. I'd even thought we could be more, but Ridge had shattered that hope.

The slamming of the front door pulled me from my thoughts.

"We got you something with caramel, but they had some new flavors we thought we could try together. This one involves oatmeal cookies and sounds divine." Chloe walked in, a plastic grocery bag in one hand and a pint of ice cream in the other. Audrey followed behind her at a slower pace as she bent to pick up Ruby.

"Sounds good," I said as I slipped my phone back into my pocket. I'd respond to Livvy later. Tonight was for ice cream and girl talk.

"What movie should we watch?" Chloe deposited the ice cream on the scratched-wood coffee table, a thrift shop find I'd been meaning to refurbish, before flopping onto the loveseat. "I'm thinking something with Tom Hanks, though I wouldn't be opposed to Ryan Reynolds."

My phone buzzed, another text from Livvy filling my screen.

"You guys pick. I need to grab a blanket." I slipped into my room and sat on the bed as I read the text.

LIVVY: No pressure, but I feel like that revelation deserves more than radio silence.

I paused, considering my response. I couldn't ignore her, but I needed to make sure my reply came off calm and as if my first heartbreak reappearing in my life didn't faze me. After all, I had enough to worry about between home renovations and helping Livvy keep her sanity during the wedding. Not to mention a new apartment complex was being built down the street, creating competition for renters. I didn't need high school drama resurfacing.

ME: It's been a long time since I've seen Ridge, but I think it'll be good to catch up. What's he been up to?

I thought that should appease her without sounding too eager. I snagged the grey fuzzy blanket from the foot of my bed and headed back out to watch the movie.

Back in the living room, I grabbed my ice cream from the bag and sat on the opposite end of the couch from Audrey, propping my legs on the coffee table and draping the blanket across my lap. "What movie did you pick?"

"We decided to keep it simple and watch a home renovation show. That way, we won't miss anything important while we talk," Audrey said.

I smiled, knowing they'd made that decision for me. I loved home improvement shows, more than most movies, and would much rather unwind to the sounds of hammers and nail guns than another one of Chloe's romcoms. It was likely the side-effect of having a dad who flipped houses on the side. While it had resulted in a lot of moving, it also meant I'd learned how to tile a bathroom before I'd learned to drive.

"Sounds perfect." I took a bite of ice cream and let the sweet caramel cover my tongue before swallowing. The cold made me shiver, and I pulled my blanket tighter around me. I was perpetually cold despite it being close to 100 degrees outside, but ice cream was well worth the additional chill.

The sounds of the TV show host explaining her latest project filled the room for a moment before Chloe spoke. "I still can't believe you almost got asked to leave the restaurant. He must *really* love tennis."

Her incredulous tone made me chuckle, triggering a laughing fit from all three of us. Our conversation moved into more dating horror stories, and my spirits lifted considerably as we commiserated with each other. The comfort of that moment broke only once as Audrey relayed the details of her first kiss. It involved bumping noses, a piece of gum, and her little sister witnessing the entire thing.

"Luckily, my other high school kisses weren't nearly so bad." She shrugged. "Though I was convinced I would find my love in high school, we'd graduate college, marry, and live happily ever after. I was way off."

At the mention of high school, my thoughts returned to Ridge, my heart hitching for a moment as I remembered his easy smile and ready laugh. Taking a deep breath, I pushed the memories away. He was a part of my past, and I was determined to keep it that way. I had enough scars from the past to deal with.

I reflexively pulled out my phone to glance at the time, hoping for a distraction from my memories. Instead, I found a text from Livvy.

LIVVY: I'm not sure what he's up to, but he asked about you.

Chapter Three

Saturday, I woke to sunlight, plans to help Livvy move, and twenty texts and three voicemails from my mother. *Thank goodness for sleep mode.*

Deciding that I couldn't put her off any longer, I selected her number from my contacts and hit call. I settled back against my pillow and pulled the green bedspread my grandmother had made for me up to my chin. I fiddled with the yarn ties as I listened to the phone ring, finding comfort in the worn blanket that had moved with me from house to house throughout my teen years and college.

Maybe I'd get lucky and Mother would still be asleep. I could leave a message and avoid the interrogation.

I wasn't lucky.

"Mallory! I'm so glad you called. I know you texted last night to say you were back from your date, but when you didn't say anything else, I started to worry." I heard a rustling sound and then my mother's muffled shout to my dad, "She's fine, Paul."

I sighed, acknowledging this was my punishment for ignoring her the night before. I should have called her after the date, but I'd needed the break. I propped myself up on my pillows and braced for what lay ahead.

"Hi, Mom... I mean, Mother," I said, when she paused a moment to take a breath. After reading some random parenting blog article, she'd decided I was too old to keep calling her "Mom" after I graduated college. When I refused to call her Barbara, we settled on "Mother" as a compromise. It still felt weirdly formal, but it made her happy, so I played along. "What are you up to today?"

"I was about to grab my keys and drive down to check on you. Make a weekend of it. You know, maybe take you shopping for an outfit for your next date. Something with color."

I forced a laugh, not sure how serious she was. "Good thing I called. I would hate for you to drive all the way down here just to turn around and go back. I'm helping Livvy move. And then painting my room." I had no plans to paint, but if it kept Mother away, I'd do it.

"I guess we'll have to go shopping another time. I'm sure your wardrobe needs sprucing up. Anyway, how did the date go? When's your next date? Isn't Bruce perfect? From what Dana said, he sounds—"

"Mother." I broke in, knowing she could ramble for hours if I didn't intervene. "Breathe. We went on *one* date."

"I know. But you've been single for so long, and he sounds nice. There's no way the two of you didn't hit it off." Her voice grew louder with her excitement, and I was certain if my roommates were awake, they could hear every word from the other room.

"Here's the thing—"

"Just wait until I tell Trudy Oscarson. She'll be green with envy. It's been years since she's gotten to plan a wedding, what with all her kids married except for Debra. Anyway, once you're married, it won't be hard to convince Bruce to move up here. I'm sure we can find a place in the neighborhood. And—"

"Hold up, Mother." I practically yelled into the phone. "It was one date."

"It can't hurt to be prepared, Mal-bear." I cringed at her use of my childhood nickname. I hated it, but she kept using it despite my requests she stop. "What harm is there in a little daydreaming? I mean weddings are pure magic and I've dreamed of yours since I found out I was having a girl. Where I didn't get to plan one last year, I was hoping this year would be the year. Not to mention, I've always dreamed of having you kids close."

"There's a bit of harm, especially when it leads to rumors and questions from extended family about my nonexistent fiancé." Which would undoubtedly be followed by comments about my former fiancé.

"But honey, you're dating someone now. Dating leads to engagement which, in most cases, leads to marriage and a forever home with kids. It's really not that big of a leap." Her thought processes left me dizzy and out of breath despite decades of experience. Not to mention we both knew that "forever homes" weren't a guaranteed part of her formula.

"Enough." I did shout this time, my face flushed and my hands shaking as I attempted to slow my bulldozer of a mother. "Bruce was not my type at all. There will be no second date or any of the other things you just listed." I gritted my teeth, each word coming out like the clack of a nail gun.

"Oh." She finally broke the silence with the quiet, hurt-filled word. "You didn't have to shout."

I sighed, pinching the bridge of my nose so hard it hurt. My mother's ability to jump from one extreme emotion to another was legendary, and I was a professional at triggering it, especially since the accident over a decade ago that had transformed my mother's hovering tendencies from bearable to suffocating.

"I'm sorry." I stared up at the ceiling, noting that it could also use a fresh coat of paint. At least there was something in my life I could fix. "I'm just frustrated about a few things and took it out on you." My biggest frustration was my mother's efforts to micromanage my life, but I wasn't about to explain that to her.

"I just want you to be happy." She choked the words out, and I knew I'd be getting a text later from Dad wondering what I'd said to make Mother cry. Hopefully, he'd see the humor in the situation and help me see it as well.

"I know." I decided we needed a change of topic. "Did Dad tell you the flooring guys are coming in two weeks?" While Dad owned the apartment building I lived in, he'd given me complete control over renovations in all of the units.

"Yes. I'm glad the two of you are making progress on your little home improvement project."

My home renovations were more than a "little" project, something she should understand after helping Dad flip homes for years. They were my ticket into property management, though now wasn't the time to remind her of my plans. It would just make us both angry, again. Instead, I spent the next few minutes trying to make her feel better with promises of future shopping trips and discussing details for Livvy's wedding.

By the time I hung up, I was exhausted, but I needed to get moving if I was going to help Livvy.

I pushed out of bed and quickly dressed for a day of physical work, wearing a t-shirt from a school fundraiser and a pair of faded sweats.

My phone dinged as I headed to my car. I glanced at the screen to find a text from my brother. Chris was three years my junior and only texted me for favors or my birthday. Since my birthday was still six months away, I was curious to see what Chris would ask for today.

CHRIS: Hey, sis. Quick question.

ME: Hi, bro. What's up?

CHRIS: You're still single, right? Mom keeps saying you are, but I wanted to double check.

I rolled my eyes and considered how to respond. The fact Chris had to ask proved how little attention he paid to my life.

ME: Last time I checked...

CHRIS: Great. I have this friend Sheila wants to set you up with. Want to double with us?

What is it with my family? I wondered as I stared at the words filling my screen. My mother must have called Chris and his wife, Sheila, after we spoke. I stuffed my phone into my pocket. It was the third time in a month that someone from my family had tried to set me up. It would be humorous if I wasn't so frustrated. Just because Chris had married and moved down the street from my parents, the perfect distance for my helicopter mom to check in daily, didn't mean I would follow suit.

Why can't they leave my romantic life alone? Between work, roommates, and managing the apartment complex, I didn't have time for love, and my family needed to accept that. Maybe if I signed up for the property management course I'd been eyeing at the nearby university, they'd believe me the next time I said I was busy.

I was climbing into my car when my phone started ringing, and this time Livvy's smiling face filled my screen.

"How's the future Mrs. David Okada doing today?"

"In need of a huge favor. How are you?"

I paused. Livvy was never one to beat around the bush, but this was a whole new level of direct. "I'm fine." I spoke the words slowly, afraid of what might come next. "Just about to drive over."

"Thank goodness! Mom's out running errands and Dad's disappeared and I really need someone here to keep me company. My motivation is dying. Save me!" The whine in Livvy's voice testified of her desperation.

"I'll be there soon."

I slipped my phone into my pocket, turned up my favorite country music station, and pulled out of the parking lot. Maybe if I hurried, Livvy and I would finish early, and I could spend the rest of the day painting. Maybe once I finished this first remodel, my family would finally take my dream seriously. And maybe the sky would turn purple and a young George Strait would walk into my life professing his undying devotion and serenading me while I renovated homes and became a millionaire. If I was going to dream, it might as well be big.

Chapter Four

I PULLED UP IN front of Livvy's parents' house, wincing as my tires found the curb. At least this time I'd managed to only nudge it. I didn't need to pay for another tire alignment for my older-than-dirt green Hyundai Sonata.

I climbed out of my car and started up the driveway, smiling at the house where I'd spent so much of my life. I took a deep breath, the scent of roses and fresh cut grass filling my lungs. A movement across the street caught my eye and I paused, turning to see a guy walking towards me with a wave.

My hand raised instinctively but froze when I registered who was crossing the street: Ridge. My heart stuttered as I took in his changed appearance after having not seen him for over ten years. His hair was long on top, his shoulders more filled out than the gangly teenager I remembered. Laugh lines hugged the corners of his eyes, eyes that were the same teasing blue I'd tried to forget.

"Ridge."

"Hey, Mal. Long time no see." He stopped in front of me with a grin and a shrug, though I could also see hesitation on his face and in the way he hung back from me, not offering a hug or a handshake.

"Funny what happens when you run away and ignore someone. You tend to lose contact." The words tasted bitter on my tongue, but I couldn't push them down. They'd waited too long for escape.

Ridge took a step back, surprised by my response. His hesitation only lasted a moment before a grimace stole across his face and he responded.

"You know, communication is a two-way street. But heaven forbid you should have any ownership in what happened."

"In what happened? You mean the fact that—"

"Ridge, you ready?" A woman called out and we both looked over to see Ridge's mom, her hair in the same chin-length bob I remembered from high school, waving toward the car in the driveway. "We don't want to be late."

"Be right there," Ridge called before turning back to me. "It's been...a surprise to see you, Mal." He waved and walked away, leaving me gaping after him for a moment.

My awkward position standing in the driveway finally registered, and I shook my head, forcing myself up the steps to the front door. Between Livvy's text yesterday and running into Ridge today, I felt off kilter as I grappled with the blast from the past. Hopefully, helping Livvy pack would provide a much-needed distraction.

Aunt Jenna and Uncle Ken's house had been built nearly forty years earlier, and because of our constant moves, it was the closest thing I'd known to a forever home. I'd watched as they'd transformed their house into a quaint, welcoming cottage, complete with a wraparound porch and brightly painted shutters. The sight always brought a load of memories to the surface, most of which involved Ridge. I couldn't believe I'd just seen him and that he'd been so hostile. What did he have to be angry about? I wasn't sure I was ready to see him again at the wedding. Also, why was he here? Sure, he had been close to Livvy's family, but the last I'd heard, Livvy hadn't spoken to him in years. Not to mention he was living out of state, though his mom still lived across the street from Aunt Jenna and Uncle Ken. I had no idea what could have brought him back to Utah.

Tamping down thoughts of the past, I knocked on the teal door before pushing it open, not bothering to wait for someone to answer. Instead, I called out a greeting as I stepped inside.

"Downstairs!"

I followed Livvy's voice into her room in the basement, passing piles of boxes and miscellaneous items as I went.

"You only have one room in this house, right?" I asked as I rounded the corner into her bedroom. She'd had the same room her entire life. The pink walls and tan carpet had witnessed many sleepovers, pedicures, and talk sessions. It was hard to believe we were now both fully functioning adults with Livvy's wedding happening in a week.

I found Livvy stuffing books into a box, her dark hair escaping its ponytail and her glasses sliding down her nose.

"I have so much crap. There are all of the gifts from the shower and then Mom decided to clean out her stuff and give me everything she was getting rid of, not to mention nearly 30 years' worth of stuff adds up." She gestured around the room, indicating half-full boxes covering nearly every available surface.

"It looks like a demo zone. Are you sure I'm the one conducting major renovations?"

"Very funny. Trust me, it was worse earlier. I've gotten a lot done already." Livvy pushed up from the floor and walked over, throwing her arms around me in a tight embrace. I fought back a sneeze as I breathed in dust along with the musty smell of sweat. "Thanks for coming. This is going to be a lot more fun with help."

"Where do you want me to start?" I eyed the closet, still packed with random items, wondering what Livvy had already accomplished. At least the work ahead would provide a welcome distraction.

"If you want to tackle the drawers in the closet, that would be great. Just throw everything into a box and I'll go through it later. Or I'll throw the box away. At this point, either option works."

I grabbed an empty box and moved to the built-in dresser. Opening the first drawer, I had to stifle a laugh at the brightly colored horses that greeted me. "Really, Livvy? You still have all your My Little Ponies? I thought you would have contributed these to the toy bin for your nieces to play with." I held up one purple horse whose mane had seen better days.

"While I love my nieces, these toys are for my children. Besides, I'm pretty sure those are collector's items by now. They're probably worth a small fortune." Livvy looked up from her spot next to the bed, surrounded by a handful of bins.

"More like you *spent* a small fortune buying them. Currently, the only thing they're collecting is dust." I loaded the toys into a box and started on the next drawer. This one contained an odd mix of old makeup and jewelry. I smiled when I saw a pink and green friendship bracelet I'd made for Livvy back in our preteen years. "Have you cleaned out your room ever?"

"Yes. But you never know when something will come in handy."

"I frequently find myself wishing I'd held onto my junior high Lip Smackers collection." I held up one of the giant pink tubes of lip balm. "You never know when you're going to need some"—I glanced at the label—"sugar plum to spice up your goodnight kisses with David." I puckered my lips at Livvy and made kissing sounds.

"Shush." Livvy threw a pillow my direction and I laughed as she missed, the pillow landing in one of the open boxes instead.

"Now the extra noise makes sense," a loud, laughing voice said. I looked up to see a petite woman with thick black hair and a giant grin leaning against the door frame.

"Aunt Jenna!" I walked over and wrapped her in a hug. "How are you?"

"I'm great. Though I do need to borrow the future bride for a minute. I need some direction on what to do with some boxes I found in the garage."

Livvy groaned. "I thought I got them all. I'll be right back."

Aunt Jenna and Livvy left me in the room, and I got back to work on the dresser. After packing a drawer of old t-shirts, I found myself committing to a deep clean of my apartment as soon as I finished painting. I opened the last drawer, a smile filling my face when I spotted the photos and yearbooks inside. I picked up a few of the images and began thumbing through. A picture of 10-year-old me and Livvy with matching braids, our arms thrown around each other, was at the top of the stack. Most people were surprised when Livvy and I told them we were related. From my straight blonde hair, tall frame, and fair skin that only went from pale to burnt in the summer to Livvy's dark wavy hair, petite frame, and naturally tan complexion, we couldn't appear more different. But she'd been my best friend for as long as I could remember. I was grateful she would be staying in Orem for a few more years while David finished his master's degree. I wasn't ready for her to move away yet.

I shuffled through more pictures until one of Livvy and me in formal dresses, a guy to either side of us, caught my eye. My breath hitched in my chest as I looked into the familiar blue eyes of my date: Ridge.

Unbidden, memories of that night filled my mind, my heart aching as I relived senior prom a decade earlier.

Ridge had asked me to prom after his original date had bailed. I had been thrilled, spending hours with Livvy searching for the perfect dresses, mine a deep green and Livvy's a soft pink, and planning our elaborate hairstyles. That night had been magical. Ridge and I had danced and talked and laughed, and I'd known it couldn't get any better. As we'd left the dance, Ridge had reached for my hand and led me to the car.

"I'm not quite ready to call it a night," he'd murmured. "I think we need to do a bit of stargazing first."

We'd driven to a nearby park, settling onto the swings, our hands intertwined as we rocked gently back and forth and gazed up at the sky.

I'd sat there happily, soaking in the feeling of his hand wrapped around mine. Eventually he'd stood up, pulling me to my feet. The momentum had propelled me into his chest, and when he'd pulled me closer, I'd known what would happen next. Our lips had met and I'd given into the wonder of my first kiss. It had been fireworks and butterflies and magic all rolled into one unforgettable moment.

Looking back, I realized that the kiss had been more about hormones and teenage angst than actual good kissing technique, but it had shifted my world. I had thought everything would change. My crush on Ridge would no longer be unreturned. I had proof. He and I would become a couple and follow the path to happily ever after.

I pushed away memories of the rest of that night, memories I refused to think about even now. Memories of screeching tires and flashing headlights. That night had changed more than my romantic dreams, thanks to the car accident I did my best to pretend had never happened. After that night, Ridge had never called. He'd never texted. He'd simply disappeared, finishing his high school diploma online and running away to a job in Florida. Suddenly, the friend who had been a staple at family functions had just been gone. He hadn't responded when I'd tried to contact him. The only proof I had that prom had even happened was in dance pictures like this one and the memory of a first kiss that had shattered first my world and then my heart. I hadn't seen him since, until today.

The sound of a stair squeaking signaled someone's approach, drawing me back to the present. I looked up as Livvy peeked her head into the room.

"Those boxes are going to take a bit longer than anticipated. You good by yourself for a few more minutes? Also, Dad's out picking up drinks. Do you want anything?"

"I'll be fine, and I'd love some Dr. Pepper with blackberry and lime."

"Deal. I'll be back."

Livvy disappeared once more, leaving me alone with the ghost of my teenage broken heart. Usually, that night felt far away. Now it felt like yesterday, all the pain of rejection hovering closer to the surface than I cared to admit as I fingered the faint scar that ran along my right arm just below the elbow, a physical reminder of that night. With everything that had happened with Matt, I would have thought my first heartbreak would have faded away, replaced by more recent events, and yet there was something about first love that left a mark even time couldn't erase.

Trying to avoid digging up more painful memories, I piled the remainder of the drawer into the box. As I pulled out the last yearbook, an envelope fluttered out onto the floor. I set the yearbook in the box and reached for the envelope, surprised to find my name written on it in a masculine hand that looked oddly familiar.

"Mallory, drinks are here," Livvy called down the stairs.

Not wanting to lose the letter among everything else scattered around Livvy's room, I carried it up the stairs, curious to know what it contained.

I stepped into the familiar kitchen decorated with framed recipe cards and faded produce wallpaper to find Livvy searching through a pile of papers at the table, two 44-ounce cups sitting next to her.

"Wow, you really want to keep me motivated if you're providing the biggest size possible." I laughed, reaching for one of the cups and glancing at the label before taking a swallow. The Dr. Pepper, combined with a zip of lime and the tang of blackberry, was exactly the pick-me-up I needed to power through the remainder of Livvy's closet.

"Joke all you want, but if this is what it takes to keep you a happy worker bee, I will provide all the Dr. Pepper you can drink. I just wish I had thought to keep some slushy ones in the back of the fridge for extra motivation." Livvy looked up and gave me a wink before her eyes locked on the envelope in my hand. "What's that?"

I shrugged before showing her the front, my name scrawled in the familiar handwriting that I couldn't place. "This fell out of one of your yearbooks. Any idea what's inside?"

Livvy paled as I watched her for a reaction.

"It's nothing. Just a, uh, note that I must have forgotten to pass along. Silly me! Oh well, it's too late now. Might as well throw it away." She reached for the envelope, but I pulled it out of reach. Something about her reaction wasn't adding up.

"In that case, I might as well take a look. Maybe go for a walk down memory lane." I slipped my finger under the flap, tearing it open to find a single page of lined paper filled with the same boxy handwriting from the envelope. I glanced at the bottom to discover the sender, my heart freezing at the name: Ridge.

"Livvy, what is this?" I gasped out, my throat constricting from the sudden discovery.

"A letter." She sat oddly still and straight in the kitchen chair, not looking at me.

"I can see that. Why do you have a letter from Ridge that's addressed to me?"

Livvy sighed. "You were never supposed to find that."

I stood, waiting for more. Livvy finally pushed to her feet and began pacing, gesturing to the letter in my hands.

"Ridge wrote to me, a couple years after the accident. He wanted to apologize, to reconnect and make things right, but he didn't have your address, so he asked me to give you that letter. But you'd just started getting your life back together after all the surgeries. You were finally starting college and talking about dating again, and I didn't want him to ruin that. So, I kept it from you."

"Ridge tried to contact me, and you didn't say anything?" The quiet words hovered in the air between us as I digested Livvy's words.

"I thought I was protecting you."

"Who said I needed protecting?" My voice came out hoarse as I stepped away from Livvy. I needed air and space.

"Mal, wait—"

But I didn't hear the rest of what she had to say.

I didn't remember leaving the house, let alone climbing into my car and, yet, somehow I made it to the park down the street from Livvy's parents' house. I turned off my car but didn't climb out, not wanting to be interrupted by the family with kids playing on the nearby playground.

Before I could question myself further, I picked up the letter from where I'd tossed it on the passenger seat and began to read.

Dear Mallory,

Hopefully you'll read this letter and not just throw it away, though after everything that happened on prom night, I don't deserve it.

I've been working construction in Florida for the last several years. I love the beach and the friends I've made, though I could do without the humidity. I'm finding my way, away from my dad and all his expectations. Funny how much he used to harp on me, given everything that happened.

But that's not why I'm writing. I have something to tell you, and for some reason, a letter felt like a better option than email and I don't have your number any more. I think it's because email is instant. If I don't get a response through email, I know you've gotten it and that you're ignoring me. But with a letter, there's always a chance it will get lost, that the post office will make a mistake, which I think will make your potential silence more bearable.

Mal, I like you, maybe even love you. I have for a long time. Probably since the first time I saw you plunge off the Rock into Provo River without hesitation. But after the accident, knowing I was responsible, and then dealing with my dad afterwards, I panicked. How could you ever forgive me? Especially when I couldn't forgive myself. Now, I realize I should have stayed, but back then, I didn't feel like I could handle your rejection. It's crazy what time and space can do for a person.

I'm visiting home in a month, and I wanted to ask you a question. Will you go on a date with me when I get back? I want to apologize, to make things right, and I think this is the first step.

I hope I hear back from you, but if not, I understand. (Sorry I'm sending this by way of Livvy. I don't have your address and figured she would get it to you.)

Sincerely,

Ridge Matthews

My breath caught as my thoughts swam with this new information. While I always chose to end my walks down memory lane with the kiss, there was more, so much more. As we'd left the park, another car had run a stop sign, hitting Ridge's car on the passenger side. Ridge had received only minor cuts and scrapes. I hadn't been as lucky, as the scar on my right arm reminded me. Weeks later, when I'd finally recovered enough to get my head on straight and start to venture back into real life, Ridge had already left. Dropped out of school and run away to Florida. He'd changed his phone number and pushed me out of his life completely.

Tears stung the corners of my eyes, but I pushed them back, refusing to cry about that night again. It had taken me years to completely let go of Ridge. I'd dated other guys and done my best to forget about prom, my first kiss, and the accident, but some memories never fade. That night was imprinted on my mind, always followed by the same questions: Why? Why had he kissed me? Why had he rejected me? Why had he left? Why couldn't I let him go? In some ways it haunted me even more than catching Matt cheating on me.

Now that I'd found this letter, a new set of questions rang through my mind. What did this mean? Why hadn't he reached out one of the countless other times he'd surely visited Utah? Would I have wanted him to?

I don't know how long I sat there, lost in the past, processing the letter from Ridge. Eventually, the heat began to register as sweat ran down my back, and I started my car. It was time to go back to Livvy's. I needed answers.

Turning onto the street, I stopped at a stop sign, checking before pulling out. I started to move forward but slammed on my brakes at the sight of a car barreling out of a nearby neighborhood. My car stayed still for only a moment before it unexpectedly shuddered and rocked. I'd been rear-ended.

Chapter Five

"Great." I muttered. I glanced in my rearview mirror to see two women in a small blue sportscar directly behind me. I flipped on my hazard lights and moved to the side of the road, the other car following.

Just what I needed on top of this emotional day. At least it wasn't my fault, not that anyone would believe me when I told them. My minor driving mishaps had become legendary among my family and friends. As if they never bumped into trash cans or light poles on occasion. Of course, it didn't help that every minor incident sent my mom into a panic with memories of the accident in high school.

I dug through my glove box, past paint chips and flooring samples, and found my proof of insurance before grabbing my phone and hopping out of the car. Both women were out of the car, one examining the damage, while the other stood with her arms crossed over her chest, glaring at me.

The women looked similar, with long blonde hair and striking green eyes. Their clothes and hairstyles hinted at money. They were of similar height and build, though the one glaring at me was clearly younger.

"What is wrong with you?" The younger one yelled as I approached, her high-pitched voice quickly traveling the distance between us.

"Excuse me?" I stammered, stunned.

"Slamming on your brakes like that. You could have made it. Now Daddy will never buy me a Tesla. He'll take this as proof that I can't handle it."

"I'm sorry, but—"

"You should be." The sound she made reminded me of a strangled yell.

"Now hold on, Ella." The other woman stepped forward, placing a hand on the younger girl's arm. "You're the one that rear-ended her."

"If she," Ella waved towards me with a flick of her hand, "hadn't slammed on her brakes, this wouldn't have happened." She jerked away from the other woman and turned to me. "Tell me you have insurance."

"I do. I hope you have it too." I folded my arms to hide the insurance documents until she produced her own. "Just give me your information and I'll be on my way."

"That's not how this works. The *victim*," she emphasized the word with a grimace as she pointed to herself, "files a claim and needs the insurance from the responsible party." This was followed by a gesture in my direction.

I had no idea where she was getting her information from, but there was no way she was the "victim" in this case. I straightened and, channeling all of my anger and frustration of the day, prepared to respond when the other woman stepped between us, her hands spread in a placating motion.

"Ella, you're being ridiculous. You rear-ended her. You are not the victim here."

"But Amber—"

"No. You are not going to throw a fit and bully this woman for your poor decisions." Amber gave me an apologetic smile.

"But you know Daddy will never buy me a Tesla now!" Ella huffed out, folding her arms in front of her chest and glaring at Amber.

"Then maybe you should have listened to me when I said you were too close to the car in front of us. Also, Daddy's not going to buy you a Tesla while you're still in high school. You know my car"—she waved to the blue sports car with a dented bumper—"was a *college* graduation present."

I watched the two sisters stare each other down, unsure of what I should do. It didn't feel like the right time to ask for their insurance information, and yet, I needed to get back to Livvy and the discussion I'd run away from.

Abruptly Ella turned on her heel and stalked to her car, jerking the passenger door open. While I waited, I pulled out my phone and took pictures of the damage on both cars, making sure to capture her license plate, just in case.

Amber relaxed her stance, giving me a sheepish grin. "Sorry about that. This is her second car accident this year, and our father will not be happy."

"I get it. Thankfully, it's a minor incident, and no one was hurt."

"Here." Ella returned, thrusting the papers in my face, and I grabbed them before handing her my own. We both took photos and then I handed her documents back.

"Thank you." I forced a smile, hoping to leave on civil terms.

She snatched her papers and threw my documents into my face. "You'll be hearing from my lawyer." She gave the parting shot before climbing back into her car.

I stood stunned. She put my sassiest fifth graders to shame.

"Sorry again." Amber gave a small half-wave before climbing in the car. Once she was situated, the duo drove away, leaving me on the side of the road. If it hadn't been for Amber's civility, I would be wondering if I'd somehow been sucked into a cheesy TV teen drama.

Breathing deeply, I walked back to my car, grateful the sisters were already gone when my toe caught on a rock and I stumbled a bit, banging my shin into my bumper. I rubbed the sore spot, muttering words my mother would be ashamed of. I called my insurance agent and relayed the needed information before pulling back onto the road and driving to Livvy's parents' house, preparing for another confrontation.

Chapter Six

I PARKED IN FRONT of Aunt Jenna and Uncle Ken's house a short time later. I was surprised Livvy hadn't called me in a panic. I had several missed texts and a phone call from Mother, but nothing from Livvy. When I got out of the car, her silence made sense.

Livvy stood in the front yard talking to a tall guy with curly brown hair, definitely not her black-haired fiancé, David. As I got closer, I registered familiar bright blue eyes from my run-in earlier in the day, only this time he wore an infectious smile that had been absent this morning: Ridge. My heart plummeted, sending my pulse racing. I'd thought I would have more time before seeing him. I wasn't prepared for this moment, with its combined sense of anticipation and dread. The words from his letter ran through my mind. He'd broken my heart. I couldn't just let him waltz back into my life as if nothing had happened, and yet, the events of prom and the accident had happened over ten years ago. Should they continue to dictate my actions?

I froze on the sidewalk, debating how to proceed. From all appearances, they hadn't seen me yet. I could slip back into my car and drive a lap around the block, give myself some time to mentally prepare for the conversation ahead. Maybe I'd stop for a soda since I'd left the one Livvy had bought me on the table in my rush to read the letter alone. If ever there was a moment for Dr. Pepper, it was now, and there was no way I could sneak into the house without either of them noticing. Escape routes and excuses flooded my mind, but as I turned back towards my car, my shirt snagged on my sideview mirror, sending me tripping into the driver's door with a bang.

I winced, knowing that I'd likely have a bruise and that there was no way Livvy and Ridge hadn't noticed me now. I took a deep breath and turned, my lips stretched in more of a grimace than a smile.

Livvy waved me over, a huge smile stretching across her face. Ridge raised his hand in greeting as well, though his smile didn't reach his eyes. He looked about as excited to see me as I felt. I was pretty sure it was similar to the smile I forced whenever a tenant called for help unclogging the toilet, one for politeness that attempted to hide the disgust and dread building in my stomach.

As I walked over, I kept my gaze focused behind them to avoid making eye contact with Ridge. I doubted he'd be able to read the turmoil in my eyes, but why risk it?

"Mal!" Livvy ran over and hugged me as if we hadn't seen each other in years, her dark ponytail bouncing in time with her enthusiasm. "Where have you been? I was just about to call when I ran into Ridge. He's home for the entire summer. Isn't that great?"

"Livvy, you've got to let me breathe," I rasped. She released me but watched my face for a moment too long before leading me over to Ridge.

"It's so good to reconnect with old friends. All the memories we shared," Livvy rambled, making it impossible for me to focus on the awkwardness and tension coiling between Ridge and me. Suddenly she gasped and grabbed his arm. "Ridge! You should come to the rehearsal dinner. It's essentially a massive party for David and me to celebrate before we separate for the bachelor and bachelorette parties."

A bit of spit lodged in my throat, spurring a coughing fit. *Why couldn't I go two seconds without looking incompetent in front of this man?*

"I don't know. That seems like the kind of thing for—"

"Close friends and family, and who's a closer friend than one of my best friends growing up?" Livvy turned to watch Ridge, and I did not envy him having to say no to the full force of Livvy's pleading stare.

"I'll think about it," Ridge hedged. "I might have plans."

"Just let me know. Better yet, let Mal know. She's planned the whole thing, and it's going to be amazing."

"That might be difficult since I don't have Mallory's number. Not that she would respond if I reached out." Ridge gave a shrug as if he didn't care, but I could hear hurt in his tone. He was talking about the letter.

"I would respond, especially since you'd be contacting me directly. After all, communication goes two ways," I said, stung at the venom in his voice.

"I wouldn't want to inconvenience you, throw off your plans."

"Don't worry about it. I don't run away from my commitments and responsibilities." I gave a sugary smile, before turning to Livvy. "Do we have much more to do before calling it a day? I had a small issue and need to—"

I broke off as a familiar dented blue sportscar pulled up to the curb across the street, Amber stepping from the car. She looked up long enough to verify that there were no cars coming before crossing the street, looking at her phone as she walked.

"Oh my gosh, Rigdon! I'm sorry I'm late. I had an unexpected mishap, thanks to Ella's tailgating tendencies. That girl is going to cost my parents more in insurance than it would cost to just hire her a driver." Amber gave a small shake of her head, her blonde waves bouncing as she stood on tiptoes, wrapping her arms around Ridge's neck and giving him a kiss.

Apparently, Ridge was not single, and I'd already met his significant other. Who knew the universe had such a mixed-up sense of humor?

After a moment, Ridge broke away, a slight pink tingeing his cheeks.

"Um, Amber." Ridge cleared his throat and ducked his head. "We're not exactly alone, honey."

Amber waved her hand, as if it was no big deal to kiss a guy in front of complete strangers. "I'm sure they'll understand. After all, it's been almost a month since I saw you last."

"It was two weeks." Ridge corrected under his breath as Amber turned around, the smile on her face freezing before growing into a full grin when her eyes landed on me.

"Oh, my gosh! You're the girl from the crash. Are you really okay?" Amber grabbed my arm in a tight grip as she looked me over.

"Mallory told you about that?" Ridge choked out, paling at Amber's words.

Livvy just stared at me.

It took me a moment to digest Amber's words and Ridge and Livvy's reactions and then what Amber had said hit me. They must have thought I had told her about the accident in high school, the only car accident in my life that the two of them were aware of.

"It's not what you think!" I rushed to assure them. "On my way over, I was in a bit of a fender-bender."

Amber rushed to fill in details. "My sister was following her too closely and rear-ended her at a stop sign. Also, I just realized I don't even know your name."

"Clearly, we're all missing import information." Livvy stepped forward, taking control of the moment. "How about we back up and start this conversation from the beginning? I'm Livvy." She thrust her hand out in front of Amber, who took it with a practiced smile. "I'm Ridge's childhood friend and the bride at the wedding Saturday."

"Nice to meet you! Rigdon has told me so much about you and your group of friends. I'm Amber." She wrapped her arm around Ridge's waist, giving him an adoring look. "I'm Rigdon's girlfriend."

I watched Ridge for his reaction to Amber's use of his full name. Growing up, no one had called him Rigdon. That is, no one except his parents—when he was in trouble. Apparently, a lot could change in ten years, more than I'd ever imagined possible.

Livvy cleared her throat, pulling me out of my thoughts and back into the conversation.

"I'm Mallory, Livvy's cousin." *And one of Ridge's childhood friends.* "Nice to officially meet you."

"Likewise. Sorry again about Ella. She can be a bit...dramatic."

"That's an understatement." Ridge gave a laugh, breaking the odd tension that had drifted into our circle.

"You should have heard her when we got home." Amber gave a shake of her head and joined in Ridge's laughter. "'Daddy, it wasn't my fault. The girl responsible was so mean. She stopped suddenly, and I couldn't avoid hitting her, and she completely ruined Amber's car.'" Amber said the words in a high, whiney voice remarkably similar to her sister's. "As you can see," Amber gestured toward the blue sports car across the street, "my car is mostly fine and, with a few repairs, will be as good as new."

Quiet filled the circle for a moment as we took in Amber's car. My mind scrambled to find something to say, coming up blank.

"Anyway," Amber stepped away from Ridge and gestured to the car, "we've got to get going. We're late for dinner with my parents. and I hate keeping Daddy waiting. He was hoping to discuss the law firm internship with you over dinner."

"Amber, I don't know if I've gotten the internship yet. Besides, I don't want to be a lawyer. I want to teach."

"Daddy talked to Bill yesterday, and he said you getting it was basically a sure thing. If that doesn't work out, I'm sure Daddy has some projects you could start this week that will help with your law school application." Amber gave us another smile and wave before tugging Ridge toward her car. "It was so nice to meet the two of you. Livvy, good luck with the wedding plans!"

Ridge glanced back at us as he followed Amber across the street. "It was good to see you, Livvy. I'll let you know about dinner Friday." Ridge waved at Livvy and ignored me as he and Amber climbed into her car and drove away.

"Well, that was..." I stopped, unsure what word best described the situation.

"Awkward? Uncomfortable? Strange?" Livvy supplied, looping her arm through mine and dragging me toward the house. "She is not who I pictured for Ridge. I mean *Rigdon*."

I snorted. "That's an understatement."

We reached the door and I pulled away from Livvy. She pretended not to notice as she led the way into the house. I made a beeline for the table, hesitating when I noticed my drink was gone.

"It's in the fridge. I wasn't sure how long you'd be gone..." Livvy trailed off, watching me.

I pulled my drink from the fridge, took a deep breath, and turned to face Livvy. Despite the distraction of earlier, it was time for Livvy and me to face the letter and the secret she had kept from me.

Chapter Seven

Livvy sank into a chair at the kitchen table, tapping her fingers on the tabletop. "On a scale from 'mild inconvenience due to a long line at the soda shop' to 'dealing with a flooding bathtub after a new renovation,' how angry are you right now?"

I took a swallow of my drink, buying myself time as I considered. "More than dealing with unobservant drivers cutting me off on the freeway, but less than finding my fiancé cheating on me with his receptionist."

"That feels like a wide range. Either that or you have more inner road rage than I realized."

I settled into the seat across from Livvy, using my giant cup as a barrier between us and the difficult conversation ahead.

"Livvy, I love you, but you had no right to keep that letter from me." I forced the words past the lump in my throat and looked up to watch my cousin and best friend.

She flinched at my words, a sad smile tugging at her lips. "You say that now, but I remember how hard everything was for you following the accident. You were in so much pain and barely left your house."

"I was dealing with a broken arm and multiple surgeries."

"It wasn't just that, though. It was like something inside you was gone, like everything that made you vibrant and exciting and energetic and *you* had been a casualty of that crash. It took weeks of me constantly pestering for you to finally come visit, and when you did, you didn't want to leave my house."

I shook my head at Livvy's words, shying away from the picture she painted. "It wasn't that bad."

She gave a sad laugh. "Time may make memories fade somewhat, but I'll never forget how hollow you were after that accident, after Ridge...left."

"That still doesn't give you the right to hide that letter from me." Even now Ridge's words ran through my mind, asking me to forgive him and give him a second chance.

"Maybe not, but I was doing what I thought was best for you. I'm sorry you don't agree with my choice, but I'm not going to apologize for caring about you and trying to protect you."

We sat in silence for a moment, each processing the hurt of the other person. The sound of a clock ticking filled the room.

Finally, I took a deep breath and reached for Livvy's hand, giving it a squeeze. "I get why you did it. I may not agree with your decision, but I understand, and I forgive you. Just promise me, the next time a man writes me a letter and gives it to you to deliver, you won't hide it in one of your yearbooks to be discovered years later when it's too late for me to do anything about its contents."

"Deal," Livvy said.

We pushed up from the table and gave each other a hug before returning to Livvy's room and the packing disaster awaiting us. I did my best to push the letter from my mind, though I could still feel it lurking just out of sight in my purse, like it wasn't quite done shaking up my life.

Chapter Eight

PACKING LIVVY'S ROOM TOOK longer than a single bedroom should. We took a break part way through our efforts for Livvy to make a food run and to call and touch base with David. I used the time to call my dad and to find a repair shop for my car.

"Kiddo! How's it going?" Dad's enthusiasm rang through the phone, making me smile.

"Hi, Dad. Things have been better, but they could be worse. How are you?" I wanted to put off telling him about the crash, but I knew I had to say something before Aunt Jenna let it slip to Mother the next time they talked. The last thing I needed was for Mother to have another excuse to call me, especially because she'd somehow manage to connect my minor car accident to my dating life or the fact that I lived an hour away instead of down the street.

"Great. I've started biking to work, and you'd be amazed at how much energy I have throughout the day. I might sell my car and try biking everywhere."

"That would make trips to Costco challenging." I tried to picture my dad making the trek from Kaysville to Bountiful and then back again with groceries on a bike. With his lanky frame, slight pot belly, and florescent green bike, it made a humorous picture. Maybe I could convince him to wear a Hulk helmet, just for added fun. It would match his bike.

"True, but we'd still have your mother's car." He hummed to himself a bit before continuing. "I'll have to think on it some more. But that's not why you called. What's up?"

I took a deep breath. "I was in a fender-bender today. I'm fine, though my car needs some repairs. It was the other driver's fault." I shared the highlights, hoping to downplay the event. No need to trigger memories from the past and the accident we all avoided talking about.

Quiet filled the line for a moment before he spoke. "Are you sure you're okay?"

"Totally fine. My car's a bit dented, but nothing insurance won't cover."

"And you weren't hurt? Because, you know, sometimes things go undetected. You could have residual—"

"I'm fine, Dad. Promise! It was as minor as I said."

"Good, good." I heard him expel a breath and pushed down the guilt that tried to surface. I was nearly 30 years old. At some point, my family would have to stop babying me over something that had happened over a decade ago. "What can I do to help?"

"Insurance should take care of everything, though I'll be carless for a few days while repairs are made. Can you tell Mom—I mean, Mother?"

"Of course. Though she'll call you anyway. You know how she worries. Do you want my car while yours is in the shop? I can drive it to you and have your mom follow me down to drive me home."

"And give Mother an excuse to visit before the wedding? No, thanks. She'd volunteer to help and end up sleeping at my place for the entire week. I'd rather take public transit." I hadn't taken a bus since I 'd been a carless teenager, and it was not an experience I wanted to repeat. I'd always managed to end up on the wrong bus. However, I'd make it happen if it kept my mother away.

"True." Dad paused for a moment before changing subjects. "That development company, Milton Corp, called me again."

I groaned. The new apartment complex had been hounding my dad for months, trying to convince him to sell. They wanted to bulldoze the existing building, expanding their project and adding to their parking lot. Dad had put them off for now, but it was a lot of money that could go a long way in helping him retire.

"What did they say this time?"

"Basically, the same thing as before. But, honey, it's a really good offer. Are you sure you want to buy that entire complex? It's a huge investment, and the time it would take—"

"I'm sure." I cut him off, not wanting to hear his doubts. I'd dreamed of managing that building since Dad had first bought it when I was in elementary school. I wasn't going to let it go without a fight.

"I know that's what you say now, but it's an old building. Sometimes I think it would be cheaper to tear it down and start over myself. Renovations cost time and money, both things a teacher tends to be short on."

"I appreciate the concern, Dad, but I know what I'm doing. This is what I want." I pushed down my few doubts and hesitations, focusing instead on my end goal.

Dad took the hint and moved to more general topics until the conversation wound down.

We said our goodbyes and hung up. How on earth my polar opposite parents made a relationship work I'd never know, but I was grateful they did. Now if only my dad's level-headedness could rub off on my mother. And if only my dad could stop being so level-headed that he couldn't see how much that apartment building meant to me.

I pushed aside worries about the apartment complex, the rest of the day flying by as Livvy and I worked. We even managed to drop off my car at a nearby shop despite our long list of to-dos.

Hours later, I walked through my door, trying to ignore the protest of stiff muscles. I hadn't left Livvy's house until almost 11:00 p.m. After packing the last few boxes and moving everything into the garage to wait for moving day, Livvy, Aunt Jenna, and I had talked for hours. I'd only been able to leave when I'd pointed out that I had to get up for church in the morning. Livvy had driven me home, gushing about wedding plans the entire drive.

My apartment was dark, and I did my best to slip into my room without making noise. Chloe was probably still out with friends, but Audrey would likely be asleep in her room. Since her breakup, she tended towards early nights and few social interactions.

As I fumbled for the light switch in my room, my purse snagged on my door handle, causing it to tip. I flipped on the light and saw Ridge's letter sitting on the carpet. I picked it up and placed it on my grey nightstand, before moving to get ready for bed. After our talk about the letter, Livvy and I had avoided any conversation topics related to Ridge. Instead, I asked questions about the wedding. It took little prodding to get Livvy to share about the centerpieces her friend was making and the wonderful venue she'd found. She even claimed to have ordered the perfect bridesmaid dresses. I'd encouraged the change of topic, grateful for the distraction it provided from my thoughts and the "what ifs" I'd been battling since reading Ridge's letter.

After brushing my teeth and changing into pajamas, I got into bed, the letter catching my eye once more as I went to turn off my lamp. I picked up the letter, examining the handwriting before opening it and reading it once more.

This letter didn't, couldn't, and shouldn't change anything. Ridge had a girlfriend. He lived in another state. And, if his reaction to me earlier today was any indication, he did not like me anymore. Then why couldn't I let this letter go?

I took a deep breath and stood, attempting to push the thoughts away as I paced around my room. So what if Ridge had written all of those years ago? It didn't impact things now. The past was over and done. This letter didn't change a thing. Or did it? I was afraid of the answer to that question.

I pulled up Ridge's social media profile on my phone, wanting to know more about him and Amber. Perhaps, if I saw more evidence of the happy life they were living together, I could convince myself to let go of the past and get some sleep.

Ridge's page revealed little. The only activity it had seen in the last several years were a handful of birthday wishes and an updated profile picture of Ridge standing in front of a waterfall. I had Amber's last name because I had taken pictures of her insurance documents, but adding her to my search efforts felt like crossing a line. Especially since I didn't need to compare myself more to the woman than I already was.

I continued to pace until I was dizzy before trying, once more, to go to bed, but my thoughts kept churning. I applied soothing lotion to my hands, hoping the smell would help me settle in for the night. Instead, the smell of lavender caused my stomach to roil, not bringing the peace I desperately needed. What-ifs continued to circle in my head until I turned on my lamp again and moved to pace some more. The past seemed to be on replay, leaving me on an unstable emotional foundation. The feel of Ridge's lips, the flash of headlights and crunch of impact, the antiseptic smell of the hospital, and the void left by Ridge when he'd disappeared without a word circled through my mind.

This continued for several more minutes until an old notebook with a faded green striped cover caught my eye. I grabbed it from the bookshelf, its weight reassuring in my hand, and stalked over to my nightstand for a pen. Settling onto my bed, I opened to the first blank page, about halfway through the notebook past college notes and doodles. I stared at the empty lines for a moment, gathering my thoughts. This whole thing had started with a letter. Maybe I could settle it with one too. Taking a deep breath, I began to write.

Dear Ridge,

I want to start this letter with some outrageous claim about how amazing my life is and that, in the decade since I last saw you, I haven't thought about you at all. But we both know, if that were the case, I wouldn't be writing this letter. I wouldn't care anymore because I would have forgotten the past and gotten over you.

Instead, I'm sitting in my room, your letter on my nightstand as I scribble my scattered thoughts into a notebook wondering where to start. I finally got your letter. It's years late, but I got it. And now I can't sleep. How dare you? What gives you the right to turn my world upside down with only a few words? You broke my heart. I should tear up your letter and let this all go. So why can't I?

I thought I had moved on. I thought I no longer cared. But the fact that I can't get your words out of my head proves I'm not over you. Despite everything, you still have a piece of my heart and I want it back. If only getting it back were as easy as writing the words. Or as simple as reminding myself that you have a girlfriend.

Mallory

Chapter Nine

I FELL ASLEEP SOMETIME after 1:00 a.m., the words I'd spilled from my pen finally freeing me from my turmoil. Unfortunately, my alarm for church came too early. I hit snooze a few times, before rushing to get ready. My roommates gave me odd looks as we hurried to Audrey's car in an attempt not to be late. They had seen my rushed, late-for-school hairdo of a bun and minimal makeup on many occasions, but this was the first time I'd worn it to church. I had yet to tell them about the letter and everything that had happened with Ridge. But I felt like the car ride to church wasn't the ideal time to surprise them with the reappearance of a past flame they didn't even know existed.

I battled to stay awake through the entire service, heaving a sigh of relief when it finally came time to leave.

Unfortunately, I was delayed by Erica, one of the tenants in my building. Erica, a student studying art history or some other humanities degree, dressed like she belonged in the seventies. She had been campaigning for some renovations in her apartment for nearly six months. She claimed that the current color scheme of white walls and tan carpet did nothing for her artistic vibe. While I agreed that some updating was in order, her proposed redecorations of brightly patterned wallpaper and shag carpet reminiscent of my grandparent's house weren't exactly what I had in mind. However, she seemed convinced that if she asked me enough times, I'd change my mind and agree to let her overhaul the apartment, her roommates' bedrooms included. One look at her ever-changing rainbow of hair colors was the only reminder I needed that Erica's style and mine were not compatible. Today it was a less-than-natural red color with green on the ends that reminded me of Christmas, but not in a good way.

"I'm so glad I caught you." Erica flipped her long hair behind her shoulder and gave me a smile that showed too many teeth. "I've been thinking about that apartment renovation you promised you'd get around to, and I've found an even better wallpaper that you should use. It's totally vintage." She pulled out her phone and began scrolling through photos.

I glanced behind Erica to see her roommates, Tara and Amelia, giving me sympathetic looks while vigorously shaking their heads.

"Aren't these orange flowers just perfect?" Erica thrust her phone in my face, and I had to crane my neck back to take in the disaster she was showing me. I was all for tasteful vintage, but this looked like something one of my fifth-grade students had drawn and then thrown away.

"You know, Erica," I said, taking a step back, "I prefer not to discuss business on Sundays unless it's an emergency. Text that to me tomorrow, and I'll send it to my dad for consideration." *Or I'll report the designer to the fashion police.*

"Fine, but it's on clearance, so who knows how long it'll be left?" Erica typed something into her phone, and I felt an answering vibration on my phone. "Maybe those new apartments will be more fashion-forward."

I winced at Erica's parting shot, though I wasn't convinced losing Erica to my newest competition would be a problem. In fact, it would be the first good thing to come out of the new monstrosity being built down the street.

"I'll keep that in mind." I gave Erica a small wave, snagged both of my roommates, and headed to the car before anyone else could stop me.

As soon as we walked through the apartment door, I rushed into my room. I slipped out of my skirt into leggings covered in math equations and pulled on a sweatshirt. I was reaching for my doorknob when my phone began to ring from where I'd left it on my bed. Livvy's picture filled the screen and curiosity filled me as I swiped to answer the call.

"Hey, Livvy. What's up?" I flopped onto my bed and tried to ignore my growling stomach. I'd skipped breakfast in my rush to get ready for church and I could hear clanging pots in the kitchen. I prayed it meant Audrey was baking. I was going to need some serious sugar to combat my lack of sleep. And a Dr. Pepper.

"Mal, everything's ruined!" Livvy's voice caught for a moment as if she was fighting back tears.

"What are you talking about? What's going on?" Even the clanging in the kitchen had stopped, as if my roommates could sense the importance of the conversation.

"Everything is falling apart. I'm getting married on Saturday and my reception venue is flooded, my bridesmaid's dresses are a disaster, and my friend who was doing the centerpieces just backed out." I could hear sharp, short breaths coming through the phone. "My wedding is ruined!"

"It's not ruined." I scrambled to reassure her, though it sounded like a mess to me. "Just take it one step at a time." I racked my brain, trying to find one suggestion I could give that might help with the pile of disaster that was her wedding plans. "What about using a church building for the venue?"

"My mom's working on that right now. They have a youth activity planned for that night, but she thinks she can get it moved."

"That's great. That's probably the biggest issue. What's wrong with the bridesmaid dresses?" Even though I was one of the bridesmaids, I had yet to see the peach dress that I was supposed to be wearing. Livvy had assured me that it was gorgeous, but I had my doubts.

"They're the wrong color. Online it said peach, but they arrived today and they are definitely pink. I'm not having a pink wedding. My colors are peach and silver. This isn't some tacky high school Valentine's dance."

I let Livvy vent for a moment as I processed the information. It had taken months for her to choose those dresses. Not to mention, shipping had taken an additional two weeks because Livvy's seven bridesmaids were all different shapes and sizes and the store hadn't had the needed stock at the time she ordered. Livvy's chances of finding a peach dress that would fit and flatter all of her bridesmaids before the wedding were next to nothing.

"Okay. Fixing that will be tricky, but not impossible." Maybe tackling the problem from a different angle would help. "What happened with the centerpieces?"

"Abby had a family emergency. Not only will she be out of commission as a bridesmaid, but she can't make my centerpieces."

For a moment I thought about pointing out the good news that Livvy would only need six bridesmaid dresses, but had the feeling now was not the time.

"They were supposed to be this combination of peach flowers and tea lights with a hint of farmhouse." Livvy paused for a moment, and

I was surprised by the sudden silence. I heard a small shuffling sound before Livvy gasped. "Abby was in charge of the flowers too. Now I have nothing and no one to make them. I have no time. I've got meetings with caterers, I'm moving, I have a final dress fitting. I'm supposed to be meeting David's family for a special dinner when his grandmother's flight lands. Not to mention going to the bachelorette party. What am I going to do?" Livvy's breaths came in sharp, quick gasps over the phone, reminding me of the dramatic moment in cartoons when characters breathed into paper bags to keep from hyperventilating.

Everything Livvy listed was an essential part of the average Utah wedding. While I considered suggesting that she could skip the reception after the wedding, I had a feeling it wouldn't go over well. Livvy had been planning her wedding for ages, and I doubted she would settle for anything less than perfection.

An idea began to form, but I pushed it away as I listened to Livvy spiral. I could help. My only plans for the coming week were to paint before my new flooring was installed and to try to stop the new apartment complex from poaching my future tenants. I could push my project back by a few days. I'd be cutting it close, but I had time. I could step up and save the day. But did I want to?

I picked up the notebook I'd scribbled my thoughts in last night, fingering its spine as I considered my options and the emotions I was battling.

Livvy had kept a huge secret from me in hiding that letter, and its reappearance had messed with my emotional equilibrium, stirring up memories I'd rather forget. However, I'd like to think if something in my life was falling apart, as long as it didn't involve a past love interest reaching out, Livvy would step in and help fix it.

My phone buzzed and I glanced at it to see a text from my mother, no doubt trying to set me up with another date or panicking because my dad had finally told her about the fender-bender. I ignored it, turning my attention back to Livvy.

I considered my options, fidgeting with the notebook in my hands. It was only for a week, less than a week really, and then the wedding would be over. I could help Livvy, while also having a valid reason for dodging my mother's texts and calls. After all, even she would be unable to say I had nothing going on when I was saving Livvy's entire wedding. I would be too busy keeping things running smoothly to even have a date at the wedding, or so I'd tell her.

Helping with the wedding would be a ton of work and I had a feeling that this was just the first of many meltdowns Livvy would experience before the ordeal was over. But it could be exactly what I needed to finally shake my thoughts of Ridge and get my mother off my back. I took a deep breath as I returned the notebook to my nightstand. I listened to Livvy's panicked rambling for a moment longer, building my resolve before I spoke.

"I'll do it. I'll make the centerpieces and flower arrangements. I'll even help find the bridesmaid dresses." Now I just had to figure out how to be crafty. And how to do all of this without a car.

Chapter Ten

As soon as I offered Livvy my services, she bombarded me with information. Livvy may not have had time to make everything herself, but she had a vision for her wedding. Considering that my floral arranging skills were nonexistent, I hoped that it wouldn't lead to disappointment. The last time I'd tried to hot-glue something I'd ended up burning all of my fingers and my countertop, and I still shuddered when thinking about the glitter-glue incident during my first year of teaching. Maybe this time would be different. Or maybe I'd get third degree burns and be excused from the wedding altogether.

"I want it rustic but modern. A mix of wood and sparkle, filled with romance and lights. You know, something that totally speaks to my style," Livvy explained. I decided she wanted something like every other wedding reception I'd attended for the last year or more, but in peach and silver.

Part way through the conversation, my phone rang again, indicating an incoming call. I glanced at my phone, and an image of my mother in all her feathered-hair glory filled the screen. I quickly ended the call with Livvy, promising to call her later to discuss everything further, and accepted Mother's call.

She'd learned about the fender-bender.

"Why didn't you call me? I would have been there to help. I could have—"

"Followed me to the auto shop and then driven me home? Mother, I was fine, and Livvy helped me take care of my car. There was nothing you could have done."

I pinched the bridge of my nose, hoping the pressure would counteract the headache I could feel building.

"Yes, but now you're carless, and Livvy definitely doesn't have the time to drive you around with her wedding in a few days. I could come down and help—"

"That's not necessary. With school done for the year, I don't have as many places to go, and my roommates can help me." I could also use ride share apps, though I wasn't about to discuss that possibility with Mother. She didn't trust ride share drivers.

After a bit more debating, she dropped the subject, moving on to her favorite topic: my dating life.

"Have you given more thought to your date for the wedding?"

"I'm not bringing a date. I'm going to be too busy helping Livvy."

"But I have two great possibilities and a third passable option who could go with you." She continued. I breathed in, counting to four before exhaling. Maybe *I* should give that paper bag trick a try.

"How about you send me their pictures and brief descriptions, and I'll let you know if I'm interested in any of them?" Who knew, maybe I could treat my mom's selections like an online dating service. Thumbs up means the guy's a legit possibility, anything else means no. It could work.

"I'd much rather you went on a date with each of them and then picked the best guy for the wedding. Some of them don't look good in writing, but I promise they're great guys."

"I really don't have time for three dates this week." *Also, what made someone not good in writing?*

"School just ended, and I know your little home projects can't take all of your time. What else do you have going on besides waiting on car repairs?"

I ignored her dig about the apartment complex, knowing she wouldn't care about the battle for tenants I was currently waging against Milton Corp. "Livvy needs a ton of help with her reception, and I promised to step in."

"That's so sweet of you. Maybe one of these guys could help you! It might be a great bonding experience, working together on a family event."

I needed to end this phone call now, before I said something I'd regret. "I'll think on it, but how many guys are going to want to put together a wedding for a first date? That seems like a whole new level of crazy."

"Good point, but surely there's something one of these guys can do. Just don't mention it's for a wedding. You think on it and let me know. Besides, it's not like you'll be doing wedding stuff 24/7, and the dates don't have to be long. Just long enough to find a real contender for the wedding. I could even come down and help Livvy. I could sleep on your couch. It won't hurt my back that much and you'll need your bed for optimal beauty rest so that you're ready for your dates."

I wished on so many levels that she was kidding, but I knew better. Images of the week when Mother had crashed at my house as a birthday surprise came to mind, making me cringe. I did not need another shoulder-padded-power-suit shopping spree followed by binge watching 80s movies I was better off never knowing existed.

I managed to talk Mother down for the moment. Though I had a feeling the discussion was far from over. After all, everyone had their hobbies, and meddling in my life was my mother's. Someday, if I ever did marry, I had no clue how she'd spend all her free time. Maybe she'd learn to knit. Or I could channel her energy into my growing list of refurbishment and renovation projects, just as long as I was good with 1980s chic.

I wrapped up the phone call with my mother before shooting a text to Livvy.

ME: *Mother suggested helping you with your wedding would make for great date activities. Haha*

LIVVY: *At least it would mean more hands on deck.*

ME: *If you're that desperate for help, I say just elope. It would be easier.*

LIVVY: *Eloping sounds more appealing every day...*

I finally surfaced from my room to the smell of freshly baked cookies. Audrey and Chloe were sprawled in the living room, buried in pillows and blankets, watching a movie.

I made a beeline for the fridge, pulling out a bottle of Dr. Pepper from the back where vegetables went to die but drinks came out slightly frozen, resulting in a delightful caffeine-filled slush. I took a big swallow, allowing the burn of carbonation to distract me from the disaster I'd just signed up for. I then wandered over to the living room where a plate full of cookies beckoned.

"Whatcha watching?" I sat on the couch, next to Audrey, and deposited my drink on the coffee table before snagging a cookie from the plate. It was still warm, the chocolate leaving smudges on my fingers.

Audrey paused the movie and both roommates turned to stare at me.

"What?"

"First off," Chloe raised her hand, ticking off her thoughts on each finger, "you almost make us late for church. And, while I love you, you looked like death warmed over. Then you're quiet the entire car ride to and from church, not even commenting when we discussed the hot new guy. Seriously, he could star in a Marvel movie, he's that gorgeous. On top of that, as soon as we get home you disappear into your room, not bothering to eat anything, despite Audrey having made pot roast. Now, you join us on the couch like everything's normal even though you've broken into the off-limits slushy Dr. Pepper stash, which we all know is for emergencies only. Spill."

I didn't know where to start, so I picked the least threatening item on the list. "How did I not realize you made pot roast, Audrey? Are there leftovers?" I moved into the kitchen, opening the fridge to find a covered plate, my name written on a sticky note stuck to the top. "Cookies and pot roast, you're the best."

I popped the food into the microwave, took another swig of Dr. Pepper, and leaned against the counter as I waited for my lunch to warm up.

"You're welcome, but just so you know, eating does not get you out of explaining yourself," Audrey called from the couch.

I finished warming my food, grabbed utensils, and settled back onto the couch. "Fine. I honestly don't know where to start."

"How about the reason why you were still awake when I got home at 1:00 a.m.?" Chloe leaned forward, pushing blankets aside to rest her elbows on her knees.

I took a bite of pot roast and then dug into the story, starting with my time helping at Livvy's, explaining my discovery of the letter, glossing over prom with minimal details, and ending with the awkward front yard conversation with Ridge, Amber, and Livvy. I interspersed the telling with bites of food and swallows of soda, not caring if it delayed the telling.

"Oh, and I volunteered to help Livvy save her wedding because it's either that or go on a spree of blind dates planned by my mother in a last-ditch effort to get me a date for the wedding."

"Wow. That's a lot." Audrey blinked at me, looking as exhausted as I felt.

"Can we see the letter?" Chloe asked.

I went into my room and grabbed the letter from its hiding place in my notebook. They didn't need to know that I had taken my crazy a level further by writing letters to the man who had blown me off ten years before. That secret was better kept to myself.

I let them read the letter, using the quiet to finish my food and place the dishes in the sink before settling back onto the couch. I fiddled with the cap on my Dr. Pepper as I waited for them to say something.

As she finished reading, Chloe broke out in a squeal. "This is so cute." She bounced on the couch, waving the letter in the air. "He obviously feels bad about that night and wants to make it right. I wish a guy would write me a letter. Letters are so much more romantic than texts."

Audrey, the voice of reason, brought her back to earth. "But it's years old. Who's to say he still feels this way? Also, he has a girlfriend."

Chloe waved this aside. "This is totally chick-flick worthy. I mean, just picture it, estranged love-interests from high school driven apart by social expectations brought back together by a letter from their past." Chloe sighed and ran her fingers through her hair, causing it to stick up in spikes.

I fought the urge to roll my eyes.

Audrey grew quiet as she listened to Chloe gush, her whole face scrunching in a look of concern. "Yeah, that's a cute movie idea, but these are real people with real feelings. Do you honestly want Mallory to try breaking up a relationship after everything we both went through this last year?"

Chloe looked chagrined. "I didn't even think about that, Audrey. I'm sorry!"

Audrey reached over and squeezed Chloe's hand. "It's okay. I know you didn't mean anything by it, but this isn't a romcom. Besides, even if Ridge wasn't dating someone, how would this change things? He wrote that letter years ago. How could it possibly mean anything for you now?"

"I don't know." I couldn't sit still any longer and moved into the kitchen, using the sink full of dinner dishes to keep my hands busy. Audrey and Chloe followed. "A part of me wants to explain things to him, apologize and try to rebuild our friendship. But the other part thinks that's a terrible idea. He hurt me. Why would I reopen that door? Especially when he clearly wasn't even interested in being civil yesterday."

"It's not a terrible idea." Chloe leaned against the counter next to me, her grin so wide, I wondered if her cheeks hurt. "I mean, he probably feels similarly. He might even be harboring feelings for you, and he's been unable to move on, wondering about the love from his youth who got away." Chloe read too many romance novels.

I pictured Ridge's expression when I saw him this morning. "Not likely. I think he'd much rather pretend like I never existed and move on with his life." A perfect life where he got to ride in blue sportscars with blonde, gorgeous Amber by his side.

I stared into my scratched, metal sink, adding it to my mental list of someday updates as I scrubbed a plate covered in gravy. An under-mount farmhouse sink would be perfect.

I continued working, the scar on my arm catching my eye. I rubbed my knuckles over the raised edges for a moment, lost in the past, before finally shutting off the water and turning to face my roommates. "All of this would be so much easier if I had never found that letter. Then he and I could go on hating each other and forgetting about the past."

"Is that what you really want?" Audrey asked in a quiet voice from where she leaned against the counter. "Because you can keep pretending. He doesn't have to know that anything has changed."

"And you know we'll support your decision, no matter how good of a movie this would make." Chloe added, settling onto one of the bar stools at the kitchen island.

"Yes. No. I don't know." I rubbed my forehead, trying to ease the tension I could feel building. "I don't want to hate Ridge, but I don't know how to live in a world where I don't hate him."

The admission burned my throat, making me cringe at how calloused the words sounded.

"Oh, Mal," Audrey said, pulling me into a hug that Chloe quickly joined. "You don't have to know how. You just have to know that you want to make the change. Let time take care of the rest."

After lunch I slipped into my bedroom, needing a quiet moment to process everything from the day. The revelation of earlier, that I didn't want to hate Ridge anymore, had shaken me more than I would ever admit to my roommates. I had spent so much time being angry about prom and how much he'd hurt me that I hadn't realized how closely I'd held the hurt. Maybe that was why, after all this time, his words had the ability to rock my world.

I sank onto my bed and reached for the notebook, fingering the edges before flipping to a new page.

Dear Ridge,

I never thought I'd write those words the first time, let alone a second time, and, yet, here we are. Me, an emotional mess, and you, completely oblivious to the turmoil your little slip of paper has caused.

I realized something today. I still haven't forgiven you. I claim to have moved on, to have let go of the past, but it's a lie. You hurt me that night, and I have hated you every day since.

What happens when I let go of that hate? What happens when I no longer have anger to hold onto?

I don't know the answer, but I am terrified to find out.

Mal

Chapter Eleven

I LIFTED THE PEN from the page and stared at the words for a moment, wondering at what point journaling went from a socially acceptable coping mechanism and crossed into the realm of crazy. The doorbell ringing pulled me from my thoughts, and I put the notebook away, curious which of Chloe's friends had decided to stop by. Most likely it would be Derek, trying to convince us to host a game night or join him for a movie marathon.

"Mal, Livvy's here," Chloe called through the door.

Confused, I hurried out into the living room, banging my elbow on my doorframe in my rush.

Sure enough, Livvy sat cross-legged on my loveseat wearing a long blue maxi dress, her legs tucked up under the skirt.

"What are you doing here?" I rubbed my arm, hoping to help the tingling sensation fade a bit faster.

"To help you save my wedding, of course! I may not have time to shop for and make everything, but I want to make sure you have everything you need to hit the ground running tomorrow."

It was only then that I noticed Livvy's laptop sitting on the coffee table. I settled next to her so that I could see the screen, my stomach clenching at the number of tabs that greeted me.

"You definitely came prepared. I'm just going to…" I hurried into the kitchen and grabbed my second slushy Dr. Pepper of the day before settling back onto the couch. We had a lot of work to do.

Livvy and I spent the rest of the afternoon looking over pictures and discussing her wedding plans. Aunt Jenna had succeeded in scheduling a nearby church building for the reception, and she'd found tablecloths to rent. Now we just needed to find bridesmaids' dresses, make the floral arrangements, and create centerpieces. My head pounded as I tried to nail down all the details, but by the time Livvy closed her laptop, I felt decently confident of my ability to at least purchase the supplies needed for her dream reception. I was going to need some help on the assembly part, but that was a problem for a different day.

"Thanks so much for saving the day," Livvy said as she hugged me in the doorway on her way out. I was careful to block Ruby from the potential escape route. "I don't know how you're going to get everything done without a car." Livvy's face scrunched in concern as she pulled away.

"I'll figure something out," I promised, trying to lessen the worry I could see in her eyes. Maybe I could recruit my roommates. Chloe was taking summer classes, and Audrey worked full time, but maybe we could find a solution that would keep me mobile. "Worst case scenario, you can have someone pick up an online order for me and drop it off here or something."

Livvy took a deep breath and forced a smile. "You're right. It'll be fine." She gave a slight shake of her head, her words doing little to disguise the panic I could sense coming off of her in waves. "It has to be."

"That's the spirit. Just remember that memories rarely come from moments when everything went according to plan. And your wedding is going to be unforgettable!"

Livvy's breathing evened out as she nodded at my words.

"And we get to spend Tuesday shopping together, so that'll be fun." I referenced our upcoming shopping trip for bridesmaids' dresses, trying to find a bright spot in the mess surrounding us.

Livvy just smiled and waved before heading down the stairs. I hoped all my promises and reassurances weren't lies.

I closed my front door and leaned against it, still reeling at everything I had to do in the coming week.

"What am I going to do?" I asked Ruby, who simply blinked at me before walking away when she realized I would not be letting her outside. "I have no idea how I'm going to get everything done."

"You're going to worry about the wedding tomorrow and spend the rest of today eating treats and watching movies with us," Audrey said as she stepped from her bedroom. "I've been doing homework all afternoon and need a break."

"Same!" Chloe said, poking her head out into the hall. "I don't care what we watch as long as it—"

"Has a happy ending." I finished for her, familiar with Chloe's one requirement for any movie we watched. "I think we can swing that, just as long as all wedding talk is outlawed for the rest of the night."

Chapter Twelve

THE NEXT MORNING, I woke to someone knocking on my front door. Rolling over, I glanced at the clock. It was 7:00 in the morning. Not an obscene hour, but still too early after staying up past 2:00 watching one romantic comedy after another. With images of Tom Hanks, Ryan Reynolds, and Matthew McConaughey still playing through my mind, I shrugged on a sweatshirt and stumbled to the door. Chloe and Audrey met me in the hallway looking equally confused.

I reached the door and glanced through the peephole, my stomach dropping at who waited on the other side. Ridge stood outside, the ready smile absent from his face as he squinted at the door, almost as if he could see me watching him. I took a breath and pulled the door open, careful to block the opening so Ruby couldn't escape.

"Ridge? What are you doing here?" My voice came out in a croak, and I cleared my throat to displace the rasp. Me and late nights did not mix.

"One knight in shining armor at your service." Ridge gave a sweeping bow with his arms outstretched before straightening with a smirk. His voice conveyed his lack of enthusiasm.

I stared at him, blinking in confusion. After all the romantic movies and what-if scenarios of the night before, I decided there was a ninety percent chance I was dreaming. Though the suggestion of frustration and anger churning in my stomach hinted this was real.

"Livvy didn't call you, did she?" Ridge asked.

I shook my head.

"Of course not." He gave a sigh. "Can I come in? This might take a second to explain."

"Sure." I stepped aside, careful to continue blocking Ruby's escape as Ridge entered.

Closing the door behind him, I looked around the living room and registered the disaster my roommates and I had left after our late-night movie marathon. Like any good girls' night, we'd used the evening as an excuse to binge on popcorn, chips, and chocolate. We'd also severely depleted my stash of slushy Dr. Pepper. However, none of us had felt like cleaning up after hours of movie watching. Instead, we'd shoved the food onto the coffee table and left our blankets, pillows, and empty bowls strewn around the living room. I'd seen abandoned construction zones that looked better.

Turning, I flinched as I also took in the cluttered kitchen and dining room. If I'd hoped to impress Ridge with how put together my life was, I'd completely missed the opportunity. At this point, he'd probably be thankful I'd never written him back.

"Looks like I missed the party." Ridge picked his way across the living room before clearing off a place on the couch and sitting down.

Audrey and Chloe had slipped back into their rooms, no doubt working to look presentable. Not wanting to leave Ridge alone, I settled on the loveseat, ignoring the crackling sound it made when I sat.

It doesn't matter what he thinks, I reminded myself. *He's just somebody you used to know, whom you're actively working to forgive, nothing more.*

"What are you doing here?" The croak had thankfully left my voice, and I sounded almost normal as I spoke. I still wasn't convinced that I was awake, but the state of my living room and the fact that Ridge hadn't disappeared yet was a pretty good indicator I wasn't dreaming.

"Livvy roped me into helping," he said with an eyeroll. "She claims it's the least I can do and that I owe her."

"What do you mean, 'you owe her'?" This conversation was making no sense.

"According to Livvy logic, since Amber's sister is the reason you're carless and I volunteered to help with wedding plans, if needed, that means I've now committed myself to being your chauffeur for the foreseeable future."

"Don't you have an internship or something that you're supposed to be focused on?" I thought back to yesterday's conversation and Amber's mention of Ridge's impending future as a lawyer.

"If I get the internship, it doesn't start until next week, so I've got time." Ridge paused, considering his next words. "Look, given our history, I would have said no, but apparently Livvy unearthed some photos in the move that I'd rather never see the light of day." He paused, as if considering what he just admitted to. "Though if anyone asks, I volunteered to pick you up so that we could get started on everything and so that I could get an idea of the area where I'll be interning if I get the position with Amber's dad."

"Of course. You were always happy to be the hero who swoops in and saves the day." *And then flies away as if nothing has happened or changed.*

"What is that supposed to mean?"

"Oh, nothing. Just some high school memories surfacing." I paused, the tension building as we stared each other down. "You know, you could have called or texted. It would have been nice to have a bit of warning." I gestured to my pajamas, a pair of sweats that I'd owned since freshman year of college and a free t-shirt I'd gotten at a football game.

"I would have, but I don't have your number. And if I did, I figured you wouldn't respond anyway." He leaned back against the couch, arms crossed over his chest, drawing attention to some muscles he hadn't had in high school.

"That's rich, coming from the guy who kisses and runs. I'm curious, how did Amber get you to stick around after the first kiss?" I knew the words were a mistake as soon as I said them aloud, but I couldn't stop them for some reason. Ridge truly did bring out the worst in me at the moment.

We stared at each other in silence, waiting for the other to blink or speak. The only sound in the room was my large wall clock as it ticked away the seconds of our staring contest.

The sound of a door opening broke the moment, and we both watched as Chloe emerged from her bedroom, her pixie cut perfectly styled and her makeup drawing attention to her green eyes. I resisted the urge to smooth down my hair as she walked over and joined Ridge on the couch.

"Hi, I'm Chloe, Mal's roommate."

"Nice to meet you. I'm Ridge." Ridge gave the first genuine smile I'd seen since he'd reappeared in my life, and I forgot for a moment that I was mad at him. His familiar grin took me back to happy memories, before the disaster of prom.

"Mal's talked about you. You're even cuter in person," Chloe said.

Just like that, the good, happy feelings were gone as I contemplated beaning Chloe with a pillow.

"What brings you over? Mal didn't mention you were coming."

"I'm here to help with wedding preparations."

"That's so nice. You can tell me all about it while Mal gets ready." Chloe gave me a meaningful look.

Taking my cue, I headed for my bedroom. "I'll be right back."

"Take your time," Ridge said. "I need to call Amber and let her know what's going on. She hasn't answered my texts."

I wonder why. I glanced at the clock, which now read 7:07. It was going to be a long day.

I took a quick shower and twisted my hair into a side bun. It wasn't the most flattering hairstyle, but sleeping through my alarm on multiple occasions had taught me to get ready quickly. Besides, it wasn't like I was trying to impress anyone. Within thirty minutes I was ready to go, though I did pause long enough to call Livvy and demand an explanation. When she didn't answer, I sent her a text, throwing in a few angry face emojis to help her understand my level of frustration.

ME: Why didn't you tell me Ridge was coming over?

I waited, hoping Livvy would respond quickly. Her phone was almost always attached to her hand. However, my phone remained silent. Maybe she liked to sleep past 7:00 in the morning too.

I walked into the living room to find the disaster from the night before, but no Ridge or Chloe. Continuing into the kitchen, I spotted Audrey standing next to the stove, spatula in hand, as she worked on a pan full of scrambled eggs. Ridge stood next to her, buttering a plate of toast.

"Wow. Looks good." My stomach growled at the sight of food.

Audrey glanced over her shoulder as she worked. "Sit down. Everything's almost ready."

I looked at the table and noticed it was set, with Chloe already occupying one of the chairs. I sat down next to her, confused at the sudden manners my roommates had adopted. We never ate breakfast together or set the table, but I had a feeling my roommates were looking for any opportunity to interrogate Ridge.

"Don't you have class?" I asked, trying to draw Chloe's attention away from the man in our kitchen.

"It can wait." She winked. "Also, pictures do not do Ridge justice." Chloe turned and smiled as Ridge and Audrey walked over to the table with the food.

"This looks delicious," Chloe gushed, once everyone was settled.

Somehow, Ridge ended up in the seat across from me, though we both refused to look at each other. Instead, we all dug in, and I marveled at the flavor of the eggs.

"As usual, this is amazing," I exclaimed, disappointed that the eggs were all gone. "Do you want to become my personal chef for the rest of my life?"

"Depends. How much do you pay?" Audrey shot back with a grin.

"You could live here rent free, and I'd pay for all the groceries," I offered.

"I'd hold out for a bit more," Ridge said, looking up from his clean plate. "Make her throw in free utilities too."

I scowled at the suggestion.

Audrey tapped her finger on her chin as if considering the offer. She and I regularly bantered about her becoming a chef as opposed to continuing her career in business.

"Pass. I'd need benefits too." Audrey shrugged and then winked at me. "But I'll continue sharing my talents as long as I'm living here."

"Fine." I gave a dramatic sigh. "Do you think you have enough time to make a few more eggs?"

Three pairs of eager eyes stared at Audrey as she glanced at her phone. "Shoot! I've got to get to work." Racing to the door she snagged her giant purse and left with a wave over her shoulder.

Chloe finished off her plate and stood. "I've got to go too."

I looked at the time, noticing that it was after 8:00, and knew for a fact that Chloe was already late. However, leaving now got her out of doing the dishes.

I picked up the dishes I could carry and headed to the sink. "I guess that means I get to clean up."

Ridge followed me into the kitchen with the last few plates.

"I can help." He leaned on the counter next to me as I began rinsing dishes.

"Don't worry about it. I can stick most of this in the dishwasher."

"All right." Ridge continued to watch me, his blue eyes more intense than I remembered.

"What?" I asked when I couldn't take his stare a moment longer.

He shrugged. "Just wondering how you could go over a decade without talking to me and then be mad at me when I show up on your doorstep to help you."

"Excuse you? What about the fact that you ghosted me after prom? I thought we had fun. You even *kissed* me, which was my first kiss by the way, and then you disappeared without a word. I thought we were at least friends, if not something more." I paused, letting the words settle before continuing.

"Prom wasn't the only thing that happened that night. There was the accident and my dad and..." He trailed off before shaking his head. "It doesn't matter now. I tried to apologize, but clearly you didn't want to hear it."

We stood quietly for a moment, me finishing the dishes and Ridge watching, before I finally spoke. If I really wanted to forgive Ridge, I had to start somewhere.

"I didn't get your letter."

"What? What do you mean you didn't get my letter?" Ridge grabbed my arm and turned me to face him, confusion puckering his forehead.

"I didn't get your letter until a couple days ago. I found it while helping Livvy move."

"Wait, what? Livvy never..." Ridge's eyes widened as realization dawned. "All these years of radio silence, and it's because Livvy refused to pass on a stupid piece of paper?"

"Yep. I didn't know I was ignoring you. What's your excuse?" I turned back to the sink and scrubbed the plate I held with extra vigor, not sure I wanted to know his answer.

"Will you accept stupidity and an underdeveloped teenage brain?"

I paused, considering. "Only if it comes with an apology and the promise of a milkshake."

"Deal. But you have to promise to forgive me and not ignore me if I ever write you another letter."

I looked over to find Ridge, a slight smile curving his lips, hand extended to shake on our agreement. I wiped my hands on a dishtowel and accepted his handshake, a small jolt of electricity shooting up my arm at the contact.

"Deal." The words, the gesture—it all felt too easy. But we had to start somewhere, at least that's what I told myself. I just hoped opening this door with Ridge didn't lead to even more scars.

Chapter Thirteen

DECIDING I COULDN'T HANDLE sitting alone with Ridge in my apartment, waiting for Livvy to call back, we left before most stores opened. Despite our truce, this whole thing felt like a loaded situation. Unfortunately, I didn't have much choice. Hopefully, the awkwardness would be more manageable in his blue sedan that smelled like stale fast food than it would be in my apartment.

As we drove out of the parking lot, I tried to ignore the construction equipment that lined the street, workers in yellow vests and hard hats working to tear down the houses that I'd driven past for years.

"Looks like a happening place to live, lots of progress," Ridge remarked as we drove.

"Growth is happening everywhere in Utah, especially Utah County. Whether it's a sign of progress is debatable," I muttered, trying not to think of the offer Dad had hinted at from Milton Corp and how supposed progress would lead to my dream being torn apart like these houses.

Ridge ignored my barbed comment with a shrug and kept driving.

An awkward silence filled the car, the soft static of the radio doing little to ease the tension.

We pulled into the craft store parking lot ten minutes before it opened, the discomfort intensifying as we continued to sit in silence. There was a lot between us, years of neglect that I wasn't sure how to tear down. I continued to draw a blank as I stared out the windshield. I'd passed the craft store a hundred times but never entered. The bright orange sign was meant to be welcoming, but I felt dread building in my stomach as I took in the tan building, its large windows filled with red, white, and blue home décor.

Ridge pulled the keys from the ignition and turned towards me. "How about we have a do over from Saturday? Let's pretend this is the first time we've seen each other in over ten years. Where did life take you?"

"Many exotic and faraway places." I leaned back into my seat, relieved to have something to focus on. "I went to college in Provo, graduated, and found a job in Pleasant Grove. I've stayed put ever since. About a year ago, I started saving to buy the building I live in from my dad. I might as well put down roots somewhere, and having the other apartments as income opportunities will help with the whole starving teacher thing." *Assuming Dad doesn't sell to someone else.* I pushed the thought out of my mind. I couldn't focus on that on top of everything else. "What about you?"

"That's great." Ridge's excitement made my life sound interesting. "Since you did get that letter after all"—I flinched, but he kept talking, seeming not to have noticed—"I'm guessing you already know the highlights. I worked in Florida for a couple of years, came back, and moved up to Idaho for school. I'm still there and will be for at least two more semesters. Basically, my life has been slightly more exotic than yours." He winked and I turned away, trying to ignore the pull of his blue eyes and refusing to let that simple gesture completely erase my hurt.

"Given the temperature, humidity, and wildlife, I'd say Florida qualifies as 'exotic and faraway.'"

"I was talking about Idaho. It's hard to be more exotic than Rexburg." Ridge kept a straight face as he spoke.

I pictured the growing college town with its legendary winters, surrounded by farmland and mountains, and grinned. "True. But Idaho doesn't have alligators."

Ridge steered the conversation back to me. "Tell me about work. You mentioned being a 'starving teacher.'"

"I teach fifth grade." My cheeks lifted in a small smile, like they did every time I thought about my students. "It's not the most glamorous job, but I love it. The kids are great, and we have fun together."

"That's awesome. I'm planning to teach history when I finish school."

I whipped around to face Ridge, the seatbelt restricting my movements.

"Surprising, I know. I always swore I'd never be a teacher, but after trying so many other options, it just feels right." He shrugged and ducked his head as if embarrassed by his career choice.

I absorbed his words, trying to reconcile this new piece of Ridge with the boy I'd known growing up.

"I bet you're an amazing teacher." Ridge's smile made my stomach flip before it disappeared, a sad look stealing into his eyes. "Is it worth it? Really worth it? I love the content and the idea of helping kids. Not to mention, I could coach basketball. But Amber..." He trailed off. "Amber doesn't see it that way. She calls it a dead-end job."

I took a deep breath, trying to reconcile the woman I'd met on Saturday with her attitude towards the career I loved. "It's a lot of work and you'll never be rich, but I don't think I could do anything else. I love my job."

"Amber comes from money, and living off a teacher's salary does not appeal to her."

"There's more to a job than money."

"That's what I tell her, but..." He gave a small shake of his head. "The whole reason I'm here for the summer instead of taking classes is because she wants me to do this internship with her dad's company. I went to one orientation meeting, and I'm already dreading it. She wants me working with the legal team, but she'd be happy if I did anything in property development so I could one day work for her dad's company. Honestly, I'll probably spend most of the summer handing out flyers and trying to attract tenants to her dad's latest development."

I didn't know how to respond. I was a firm believer that you should follow your interests and dreams. But I could also understand Amber's hesitations.

"You can also do a second job during the summers."

"Like what? Be a temp? Work construction? Amber would love that." He expelled a small, humorless laugh. "Do you do something?"

I thought of my apartment and smiled. "Not really, though I'll own my place soon. Once I buy it, Audrey and Chloe will help with my mortgage, as will the other building tenants. After I've paid it off, I'm hoping to invest and buy more rentals, become a property manager. My own real estate empire."

"Sounds like you've got your future figured out." I heard a hint of jealousy in his voice and turned away as a blush stole into my cheeks. He was probably the first person I'd ever told my dream to who sounded genuinely impressed as opposed to skeptical. Even now, I could hear Matt's criticism of my "unrealistic" plan ringing in my ears. "Maybe *you* should get this internship with Amber's dad. Property management and development are a big part of it."

"Maybe, though I'd much rather do those things for myself."

The moment stretched uncomfortably between us, and I reached up to adjust the air vent. As I did, I noticed the dashboard clock. The store was open.

"We can go in now." I unbuckled my seatbelt and got out of the car. I was almost to the store doors by the time Ridge caught up to me.

"I know we're on a deadline, but that's no reason to leave me in the car." He nudged my arm as he caught up. "You've ignored me for years. Don't ditch me now."

"I figured it was my turn to leave you behind. Don't worry, I'll make sure to write you a letter in about five years to fully express my feelings."

"Ouch! Remind me not to write you any more letters."

"Only if you promise not to kiss me in the moonlight after a dance." The words escaped before I could think better of them.

Ridge seemed to ponder the offer before letting out a puff of air with a laugh. "Fine. Ruin my backup plan if things don't work out with Amber."

I shrugged and located the floral department with its rows of bright petals, beelining for a section of yellows and oranges. Ridge trotted up behind me, pushing a cart. I stopped in front of some peach flowers, examining my options. The only ones I recognized were roses.

Ridge gestured to the wide range of flowers in front of us. "Does Livvy have a favorite flower? Somewhere we can start?"

"I tried asking her yesterday, and she kept insisting that as long as the color matches, she'll be happy." I picked up a peach rose, managing to pull out several others whose stems were intertwined. I gathered them all into my hand, pretending like the bouquet was intentional as I considered the blossoms. They would make for a beautiful, simple bouquet, but Livvy was not a simple girl. She liked classy and bold, a challenging combination considering the fact that her main color was peach. I put the roses back, a bunch of larger blooms catching my eye. Their colors transitioned from peach at the edges of the petals to a dark-orange almost pink color in the middle. I carefully extracted one of the flowers to examine. The label called them peonies. I liked how big they were without being overbearing. *But would Livvy like them?*

I glanced at my phone, frustrated to see that the only text I'd received was from my mother. It was a message referencing yet another "perfect" date option for the wedding. She'd attached a picture of a man in flannel holding up a fish for the photo. He was missing one of his front teeth. While I enjoyed the outdoors, I was not a fisherwoman, nor did I have time to make the two-hour drive to meet this guy for dinner. I sent Mother a quick no before texting Livvy again.

ME: I know last night you said you didn't want a particular flower, but are you sure? Also, why didn't you tell me about Ridge coming over?

"That one's nice." Ridge reached over and fingered the petals of the flower I held, pulling my attention away from my silent phone towards his amazing scent.

Was that cedarwood? Maybe some kind of spice, like cinnamon? I shook my head. It didn't matter what he smelled like. We had a job to do.

"What if we paired them with some white roses?" I moved to grab the flowers, desperate for a distraction from his scent. "I read that having different shapes and sizes is good for a fuller bouquet." Not that I knew what that meant, but I needed to think about something besides Ridge as I clutched the haphazard bouquet in a death grip. "But I think it's missing something." Glancing around, I saw a bunch of flowers similar to the roses but red and flatter. I checked their label and a snicker caught in my throat at the name, making me sound like I was choking.

"What is it?" Ridge asked. Concern filled his tone, probably at my sounding like a dying drill.

"I don't know about you, but I find this whole situation *ranunculus*," I sniggered, showing him the label.

He grinned. "Well, not everything is going to come up *roses*." He reached for the stem of white roses I was holding and waved them in front of me. I groaned before another laugh escaped, this one coming out in a snorting burst of sound. At that moment a worker walked by, giving us dirty looks, making me laugh harder and causing Ridge to join in. It took a few minutes for us to calm down.

I wracked my brain, trying to think of a comeback. However, my lack of floral knowledge made it difficult. Spying some small white buds that I happened to recognize, I reached behind Ridge and snagged them. "Don't hold your *breath* waiting for everything to come together."

"That was bad," he said, shaking with laughter.

"Maybe, but it was better than yours, and it's given me an idea." I walked back over to the peach section of flowers, noticing that it also contained some ranunculus. "What if we did an all peach bouquet for Livvy? It could have peonies, roses, and ranunculus. Then we could add some white baby's breath for a change in color and texture." I grabbed bunches of each flower as I spoke, careful to avoid the tangle of roses from earlier, and held the mass up for inspection. It was elegant and beautiful, if a little lopsided.

"Looks good to me." Ridge gestured to the flowers in my hand with a shrug. "Are you sure Livvy doesn't have a flower preference?"

As if conjured by his words, my phone buzzed with an incoming text. I glanced down, hoping to see Livvy's name on my screen but was disappointed.

MOTHER: Your brother said you turned down a date with his friend. Why? You need a date for the wedding! You might have just turned down your soulmate.

I ignored the text, deciding that I would respond later.

"Livvy hasn't given me any specifics on flowers. I guess anything goes as long as it fits the color scheme."

"Peonies, ranunculus, roses, and baby's breath sounds good. Though maybe I should take a picture and send it to Amber. She's really good at this kind of thing."

I shrugged. Of course Amber would be good at flower arranging. She seemed like the kind of person who could use glitter without it infecting her home for the rest of eternity. I tried not to think about how it bothered me to have Amber brought into the moment, instead trying to be grateful to have help from someone who might have done this before.

Ridge snapped a picture and typed out a few words.

"Hopefully, she's more responsive than Livvy." Ridge lowered his phone. "Anything else we need?"

"Lots of stuff."

Ridge's phone buzzed and he smiled as he looked at the response. "She said the arrangement would be simple, but it should work."

"What a relief." I tried to keep my tone neutral, but thought I sounded a bit like a robot.

"How do we make it all stick together? Glue?" Ridge examined the flowers, his face scrunched in concentration.

"According to Pinterest, we use some kind of funky green tape." I glanced around trying to find it. "We're also going to need wire and ribbon." I had wire cutters and pliers in my toolbox at home.

"And what about the other arrangements? You said there were a lot." I considered the flowers in my hands. Ideally the corsages, boutonnieres, and centerpieces would somehow tie back into the bridal bouquet. However, I worried that the result would be too much peach, especially where we didn't know what the bridesmaid dresses would look like.

After a moment, Ridge picked up another bunch of peach roses. "I feel like all the flower things I wore to dances had roses in them."

"Those would be boutonnieres." I reached out to finger the petals of the roses he held. The one I'd given him for prom had definitely contained a rose, though it had been red instead of peach. I continued to ponder as an idea formed. "What if we used the peach roses to tie everything together?" I grabbed a few more bunches, not caring if they tangled together now. "We could do a single rose with baby's breath for the boutonnieres. It would be simple and, hopefully, easy."

"I like easy," Ridge agreed, adding the roses he was holding to the ones I'd placed in the cart.

"That just leaves the corsages and centerpieces."

"The corsages are those things girls wear on their wrists to prom, right?" Ridge questioned, his forehead furrowing.

I nodded.

"What if you just added a few more roses and made the corsages look similar to the—" he broke off. "What did you call them? Boot-in-scootins?"

I laughed. "Boutonnieres. They're a floral arrangement, not a line dance we did in high school." I thought about his suggestion. "It would make our jobs a lot simpler." I tried to picture the result. The image was hazy, but I was pretty sure I'd seen something similar online that we could base our design on.

"Then that's definitely what we're doing," Ridge said. "That just leaves the centerpieces."

"You say 'just' like it's no big deal. Those are the biggest part." I could feel a headache building behind my left eye with the thought of one more decision to make. *Where was Livvy when I needed her?* Despite the radio silence when it came to Ridge, I could really use her opinion on *her* wedding decor.

We stood, staring at the flowers for several moments, waiting for inspiration to strike again. Finally, Ridge bent down and picked up the ranunculus.

"Do we have to use flowers in the centerpieces?" Ridge asked.

"Not necessarily." I drew out the words as I considered his question. Most wedding receptions I attended used flowers on the tables, but that didn't mean Livvy's had to. It might even make our lives easier if she didn't. "But what else would we use?"

"My sister stuck a bunch of pictures of her and her husband on the tables at her reception," Ridge said. "They added other stuff, but that was the main piece. I remember having to stick all the pictures into frames the night before."

"I like it." It sounded better than trying to come up with 15 flower arrangements for the tables.

We spent the next several moments trying to guess how many flowers we'd need. Where neither of us had arranged flowers before we were clueless when it came to amounts. Once we'd piled all of the flowers into the cart, we tracked down floral tape, wire, and ribbon.

Next up were picture frames and the other "stuff" we needed for the tables. Ridge couldn't quite remember what had gone along with the picture frames at his sister's reception, but I figured we could find something that would work. We grabbed silver picture frames, lace, burlap, tea lights, mason jars, and various wood items, all things I'd seen on Livvy's Pinterest boards.

Throughout the process, Ridge and I joked and teased, something that was helped along each time I misjudged space and bumped the cart into shelves and displays. Ridge took over steering when I almost knocked a glass bowl onto the floor. It felt like we were back in high school. I hadn't realized how much I'd missed his friendship. Yet a part of me hesitated to jump in fully, despite our truce. *Ridge hurt me once. What is stopping him from hurting me again?* I pushed the thought aside, ignoring the twinge in my gut that came with it. Ridge and I were old friends reconnecting, nothing more. He had a girlfriend.

After a couple hours in the craft store, we called it good and made our way to the checkout. The woman assisting us looked to be in her late fifties with dark skin and dyed-blonde hair styled in a short, easy-to-maintain haircut. I glanced down at her nametag as we pulled everything out of our cart. Trudy. It seemed like a fitting name for the slightly plump smiling woman in front of us.

"Wow." Trudy grabbed the first items and started ringing them up. "Looks like you two are throwing a party. When's the big day?"

"Saturday." I checked the time on my phone. It was nearly noon, and I still hadn't heard from Livvy or the auto shop.

"Waiting to the last minute, then." She nodded. "You're lucky we just restocked everything. Last week we had a desperate bride in here trying to find wood stands like this," she said, holding up a piece of wood that looked like it had been sliced from a tree trunk, "but we were completely out."

"Good thing we came when we did." Ridge loaded the bags into our cart as she continued to ring us up.

"I'll say. We get engaged couples in here all the time, especially this time of year." Trudy scanned another item and slipped it into a plastic bag.

My head jerked up. "Oh, we're n—"

"You're such a cute couple," Trudy continued, stopping my response. "I can tell the two of you are going to make it. Most of the guys," she gestured at Ridge, "sulk around here looking miserable. But it's my opinion that if you can find a guy willing to brave the craft store, he's a keeper." She gave me a big wink and told me the total. I tried not to flinch as I reached for my credit card, but Ridge got his card out first.

"Let me take care of that, honey," he said as I looked at him in surprise. I felt my eyes widen further when he threw in a wink.

"Now, that's a gentleman!" Trudy wished us well as we walked away. Ridge looped his arm around my waist and pushed the cart one handed, ignoring my attempts to break free. As we headed toward his car, my stomach twisted and flipped in pleasure and consternation, making me wonder if it was trying out for a gymnastics team.

Ridge popped the trunk and I turned on him, flinching as I kicked the cart in the process. "What was that?" I asked as I hopped on one foot, trying to push past the pain in my toes.

"She was so convinced we were a couple. I didn't want to disappoint." He shrugged.

"Well, next time you're tempted to put on a show for someone, do it with your *girlfriend*." We may have called a truce, but that didn't mean my emotions had completely settled. I still felt a bit of hurt and anger lingering, not to mention some of the affection I had battled my teenage years seemed to be resurrecting despite everything. I wouldn't survive the week if he kept this up. My emotions were already running haywire, and we weren't even a day into wedding preparations.

Chapter Fourteen

WE LOADED UP THE trunk, and I put the cart in the return then got in the car. I used the moment to take deep breaths and clear my head before settling into my seat.

"I don't know about you, but I'm starving." Ridge put the car in reverse and backed out of our parking spot. "How about we refuel before getting our craft on?"

I agreed, eager for a break from the wedding to-do list.

Ridge pulled into the parking lot of a nearby burger joint, and we climbed out of the car. Leading the way inside, Ridge got the first door but didn't make a fuss when I reached for the next one. We both stopped to examine the menu. Deciding on a bacon cheeseburger and shake, I stepped forward and placed my order, making sure to ask for no ketchup or tomato.

I grabbed some napkins and headed to a nearby booth, where Ridge joined me a few minutes later.

"So, I know about your school and work life, but what about your personal life? Is there a guy I'll get to meet at the wedding?"

I laughed, trying to ignore how weird it felt to be discussing these things with Ridge. There was still a piece of me that wanted to hate him. "Much to my mother's dismay, no."

"Really?" Ridge leaned across the table, studying me.

"You sound shocked."

"I thought for sure you'd be married with kids by now."

"That makes two of us." I shrugged and gave a sad smile. "I've dated, but nothing's worked out. I was even engaged for a bit, but Matt decided he liked kissing other girls more than being faithful to me." I was surprised at how easily the words came out. Usually, I avoided talking about my failed engagement, but telling Ridge about my past felt natural.

"Ouch." Ridge flinched and gave me a sympathetic look. "For what it's worth, it's his loss."

"That's what everyone tells me, but it doesn't change the fact that he decided dating his receptionist behind my back, a total cliché by the way, was better than marrying me." I felt some of the familiar ache start to settle in my chest and opted to change topics. "It's old news now. I would return your question, but you're clearly dating someone."

Ridge gave a half smile, leaning back in the booth with one arm stretched along the back of the red-vinyl cushion. "Before Amber, I was basically a loner. I dated, but just a lot of first dates. There were only a few girls I felt like taking on second dates and none who made it past that. But then Amber waltzed in, and what can I say? She's hard to refuse."

Ridge's response sounded less than enthusiastic to my ears. His words weren't exactly a declaration of devotion and love, but it was hard to tell how he felt. We hadn't spoken in over a decade. Who was I to say his lackluster response proved he wasn't in love? Also, why did I care?

"So, does that mean you think Amber's—"

A worker showed up with our food, cutting me off. The amazing smells of fries and burgers filled my nose. After thanking the worker, I took a bite of my shake and let it melt on my tongue. Very few things beat the effects of chocolate and ice cream in times of stress.

"Good to know some things never change." Ridge's voice startled me from my moment of calm, making me realize my eyes had drifted closed as I'd lost myself in the rich goodness of chocolate, mint, and Oreo.

"'Scuse me?" I covered my mouth with my hand, trying to swallow. I hadn't realized that I'd taken such a large bite.

"You've always loved ice cream. I'm glad to know that hasn't changed." Ridge grinned, and I couldn't keep from smiling back.

"Well, ice cream does run through my veins," I quipped, remembering one of our old inside jokes.

"Is ice cream still a staple food group in your life?"

"Without a doubt." I laughed. "Though I do try to eat more fruits and vegetables than I used to."

I unwrapped my burger and took a bite, wincing as I registered the odd bittersweet taste of tomato. Pulling off the top bun, I removed the offending vegetable, relieved to see that the workers had at least gotten my "no ketchup" request right.

"And you still hate tomatoes." Ridge laughed this time, shaking his head. "I thought you'd have learned to like them by now."

"They're the devil's vegetable and should only be consumed in the form of pasta sauce, pizza sauce, or salsa." I worked hard to keep a straight face, but a smile slipped through with the last word.

"I forgot you called them that. What was broccoli again? Something about trees."

"A sad excuse for a tree." I grinned. "And they still are."

Ridge sat back, studying me. I reached up with a napkin to make sure I didn't have any ice cream on my face.

"I've missed you." He nodded his head, confirming the words. "Ten years is a long time."

My stomach tightened. I'd missed him too, but it hadn't been my choice to push him away. He was the one who'd left me.

My phone chimed, a welcome distraction, and I glanced down at the text.

MOTHER: I know you said no to the last guy, but I've found you a date for the wedding and it's not the flannel guy. Call me!

I managed to contain a groan as I tucked the phone between my thigh and the sticky red vinyl of my seat without responding.

"Everything okay?" Ridge asked.

"Fine. Just some family stuff."

"Anything you want to talk about?"

"Nope."

We ate in silence as I scrambled for a change in topic. Overhead, a song about summer love filtered through the speakers.

"Tell me about Amber," I blurted, scrambling to find words to fill the space between us. She seemed nice enough, though a part of me didn't like her and I couldn't figure out why.

"What do you want to know?"

"How did you two meet?" I figured it was as good a place as any to start.

Ridge filled the rest of our lunch with talk of Amber. They'd met through a common friend nearly a year ago, though it had taken six months for Ridge to ask her out. The details swam in my head as he talked about her, fleshing out the woman I'd only briefly met on Saturday.

"She's even helping her dad with that big development project I'll be working on during my internship. She'll be staging and decorating everything."

I nodded, staring into my melting shake, a bit overwhelmed at everything I'd learned about Amber. I'd wanted a distraction, and I'd gotten it.

We finished lunch and headed back to the car. I winced, climbing into the overheated passenger seat. While June made an excellent time for a wedding, it could heat up a car fast.

I felt my phone vibrate as I settled into my seat. I answered, hoping the unknown number would be the auto shop with good news about my car.

"Hello?"

"Is this Mallory Roberts?" a woman's voice questioned.

"Yes, it is." I looked up to see Ridge giving me a puzzled look. I shrugged.

"This is Heather Birch. I have an update on your car."

"I'm so glad you called. How long will repairs take?" I knew it was unlikely, but I prayed the repairs would be finished in a day or two.

"Unfortunately, we still don't have a timeline. We're waiting on some paperwork from one of the insurance companies as well as a part to make the repair. I apologize for the inconvenience. We may have more of an update tomorrow, but I can't make any promises." With each word my heart sank.

I finished the call and leaned back in my seat, staring at my phone. I had hoped that the repair would be easy and maybe even finished by tomorrow for bridesmaids' dress shopping with Livvy. Since she wasn't currently responding to my texts, I wasn't sure if she'd be okay to chauffeur me for the day. Deciding that it was time for a more direct approach, I called her. The phone rang for an eternity before it went to voicemail.

"Hey, Livvy. Call me back when you get this." I ended the call and sighed, trying to think. I couldn't help Livvy with bridesmaids' dresses without a ride, but she was strapped for time. When we'd talked about shopping, she had nearly burst into tears because she wasn't sure she'd be able to fit it into her schedule. David's parents were flying in from California, and his grandmother would be arriving from Japan a couple of hours later. Once they got here, Livvy's schedule would be filled with activities with her future in-laws, interspersed with last minute wedding appointments.

"Everything okay?" Ridge's voice brought me back to the present, and I looked up at him.

"Yes—no, but I'll be fine. I don't know how long car repairs are going to take, and I need to meet Livvy to go dress shopping tomorrow, but without a car..." I trailed off, gesturing in frustration. Ride share was always an option, but it didn't fit into my budget when I had flooring to pay for.

"I can drive you."

His words gave me pause. While Ridge had been a huge help today, I felt terrible asking him to give up more of his time just to act as my chauffeur.

"I can't ask you to do that."

"You didn't ask me. Livvy did when she called me in to save the day." Ridge nudged my shoulder and grinned. "I'm happy to help. I don't have anything going on until next week, and we both know that the less Livvy panics, the better it will be for everyone within a hundred-mile radius."

My eyebrows drew together as I processed what he'd said. "I've already taken over your entire day today. Won't Amber be upset?"

"Nah." Ridge waved his hand in the air, dismissing my concern. "She's too busy picking out paint for the new development and getting ready for a family trip. I'm actually dropping her off at the airport first thing tomorrow."

"What about your internship?"

"Don't worry about it. I promise I'm available. I wouldn't be offering to help if I wasn't."

I stared at his face, gauging his sincerity. "Okay, but I don't like it. And it would just be for a ride to the mall. Livvy will meet me there, and she should be able to drive me home."

"Duly noted. Now where to?"

"I guess my place. Let's get these arrangements started."

Ridge looked at me and laughed. "You look like you're preparing for a root canal. Or a firing squad."

We were about to spend an entire afternoon doing crafts. The comparison was close enough.

Chapter Fifteen

AT MY APARTMENT WE parked, and I grimaced as I noted flyers on all the windshields. If the colors were any indication, the new apartment complex was trying to poach my tenants again. I tried to ignore them, not wanting to draw Ridge's attention to my ongoing battle with the nearby development. We exited the car and loaded our arms with bags.

As we approached the multi-colored stone building, I noted the back of a white head of hair and a small black and brown chihuahua, sniffing at the lady's feet off-leash. My mouth curved into a smile as the little dog spotted us and came running, tail wagging fast.

"Hi, Cookie," I said as the little dog jumped around my ankles. "I can't really pet you right now." I lifted my bags a bit higher, noting that craft supplies became heavy in bulk. My comments didn't faze the excited dog. She continued jumping and twisting in a cute little happy dance I'd watched hundreds of times since moving into my apartment.

"Hello, Mallory." Mrs. Jeong walked over with a cautious smile. I had known the elderly woman and her husband for years, as I'd often helped my dad with repairs around their apartment. A slight accent lingered in her words, and she still spoke with hesitancy, despite having a better grasp of the English language than most people I knew. "We haven't seen you for a long time."

"I've been busy." I gave a shrug, drawing attention to the bags that grew heavier the longer I stood talking. "By the way, this is Ridge, my... friend from high school." I hoped neither Mrs. Jeong nor Ridge had heard me stumble over the words, but the small smirk on Ridge's face made it clear that was unlikely.

Ridge stepped forward with a nod. "Hello."

"Nice to meet you. You are busy. I won't keep you." Mrs. Jeong began to step back to let us pass, but something in her expression made me pause.

"Is everything all right?" I asked, knowing the Jeongs were highly private people and were often reluctant to ask for help, even when there were issues with their apartment.

"It's just, our toilet is having trouble again, and the grandkids will be over tonight. Do you have time to fix it today?" Mrs. Jeong fidgeted with her watch, her dark eyes pinched in concern as she waited for a response.

At this point, Cookie had given up on attention from me and wandered over to investigate Ridge's ankles. He was also unable to give the dog attention, but this didn't stop Cookie from licking at his toes as they peeked out from his sandals. I hid a smile as I watched Ridge try to escape the determined, curious little dog.

"I'd be happy to help. Let me get these bags inside, and I'll be right down." I gave a smile and took a step towards the stairs.

"That would be great." Mrs. Jeong ducked her head and walked towards her first-floor apartment, Cookie trailing behind.

"That was nice of you," Ridge observed as we started up the stairs.

"It comes with the job of property manager." I shrugged, adjusting the bags so that I could get at my house key where it hung from the lanyard around my neck.

"But most property managers I've interacted with make you submit a request and then take days if not weeks to get back to you unless it's a true emergency. A finicky toilet wouldn't qualify for immediate attention, if it ever got addressed at all."

"Well, I'm not most property managers. If I want my future properties to stay nice, I need to take care of them, and that means responding when my tenants have an issue." I echoed the words that I'd regularly heard my dad express over my years of helping him work on his various properties between Davis and Utah counties.

I unlocked my door and held it open so Ridge could slip past me. I followed him inside, and we both deposited the bags on the kitchen table. Ridge bent down to greet Ruby, and I moved to the hall closet to retrieve my toolbox.

I pulled the bulging purple canvas bag from the shelf, considering its contents. It had started as a basic purple fabric bag from Walmart, but with Dad's help and my efforts to renovate my apartment, it quickly grew to include an odd assortment of tools and supplies. I even had a few power tools in the locked outdoor storage off my patio, though I was always looking for opportunities to expand my collection.

Deciding that my basic toolbox should contain what I needed, I headed back to the front door.

"Let me get their toilet working, and then we can start on those floral arrangements. It should only take a few minutes." I called over my shoulder.

Ridge gave Ruby one final pat before following me to the door. "I can help."

"It shouldn't take long. If it's the same issue they've had in the past, I just need to plunge it and tighten a few things." I could also use the break from Ridge, though I wasn't going to tell him that.

"Then maybe you can teach me a thing or two about home repair. I really don't mind."

Deciding that it wasn't worth the delay to argue further, I nodded and allowed him to follow me downstairs to the Jeongs' unit. Mrs. Jeong greeted me with a large smile and motioned us inside once we'd removed our shoes. The house was clean and smelled like the amazing pho Mrs. Jeong had shared with me on multiple occasions.

"It's the toilet in the guest bathroom," she explained, leading me through the apartment, past pictures of various locations in Vietnam, to the tan jack-and-jill bathroom.

As soon as I stepped in the room, the constant sound of running water alerted me to the problem.

"Has it been running like this for long?" I asked Mrs. Jeong. She and Ridge both stood in the doorway leading to the hall, watching me.

"It started last night and hasn't stopped no matter what we try."

I nodded, grateful she hadn't waited to tell me about the issue. While an easy fix, the constant running of water would quickly drive up their water bill, an expense they could hardly afford since Mrs. Jeong had had to quit her job due to health concerns.

I lifted the lid on the toilet and got to work. Within a few minutes, I'd addressed the problem, giving the toilet a couple of flushes to ensure that the repair would last.

As I worked, Ridge and Mrs. Jeong talked. Mrs. Jeong was a quiet, private person and I was delighted to learn more about my reticent neighbor, including her favorite places to visit when her daughter came to town.

Satisfied with my work, I nodded and straightened. "That should do the trick, but if you have any issues, let me know."

Mrs. Jeong thanked us and walked us to the door.

"That was quick," Ridge said as we headed back into my apartment. "I think I even knew how to fix that."

I shrugged. "Most repairs I get asked to do are simple, but I'm happy to help, and it gives me a chance to get to know my neighbors better."

Ridge watched me as I spoke, his brows crinkling as he listened. "Most people would find it a huge inconvenience. Amber's dad regularly complains about the little repairs and side jobs his managers get forced into doing as maintenance."

"If I ever reach the point where helping people becomes too big of an inconvenience then I need to take a hard look at my life and make some major changes. I never want to be too busy to help a neighbor or friend."

I put away the tools and walked to the kitchen, not wanting to see the skepticism I was sure would be written on Ridge's face. When I'd told Matt something similar, he'd laughed and commented on how easily I would be taken advantage of with that attitude.

"I think that's an enviable perspective."

I turned sharply to look at Ridge to gauge his sincerity. The appreciation in his eyes warmed my heart, a blush traveling up my neck and stealing into my cheeks.

"Well, it does get me into some interesting situations," I said, needing a change of topic. "Like arranging flowers, for example." I gestured to the assortment of craft supplies awaiting us.

Ridge laughed. "True, but I know Livvy appreciates it."

I chose to ignore his comment. Instead, I settled into the nearest kitchen chair. Ridge dropped into the chair next to me, Ruby wandering over and looking for more attention. She sniffed his pants, but when he didn't bend down to pet her, she decided he wasn't worth the bother and made her way back to her perch on the couch. I wished my response could be similar, but somehow, he was worming his way back into my heart, and I didn't know how to stop it.

Chapter Sixteen

I TOOK A MOMENT to consider the sheer amount of stuff we had purchased. If we weren't able to create the floral arrangements and centerpieces with everything in front of us, I'd be amazed.

"Remind me when I get married that a wedding planner is worth the extra money," I said.

"Done," Ridge said. "But only if you promise to do the same for me."

"Deal. Though I'm guessing that day will come sooner for you."

"Sooner than you might think."

Before I could ask what he meant, Ridge's phone began to ring. He glanced at the screen before answering.

"Hi, Amber."

He paused and glanced at me. I took this as my cue to stare at my dinged, second-hand table and pretend like I wasn't listening.

"I'm helping Mallory get everything ready for Livvy's wedding." He paused. "I told you I'd be doing this all day." He listened a moment longer. "I don't have time to distribute more flyers." Pause. "Because I promised I'd help Livvy." Pause. "I ate dinner with your parents last night." Pause. "I know you go out of town tomorrow, but you told me yesterday with the new build, you wouldn't have time for anything today." Pause. "It's not like that. You know I love being with you." Pause. "If you feel so strongly, why don't you come here and help?"

At this I gave a small gasp, choking as a bit of spit lodged in my throat. Ridge looked over and I ignored his glance, walking to the sink for a glass of water. Though Amber seemed like a nice enough person, I did not want her in my apartment, making me feel like a third wheel as we worked. Also, after hearing Ridge explain her dreams to become an interior designer, I felt self-conscious about my apartment. I did not want to hear her pick apart my home, criticizing the space I was working so hard to improve.

"See you soon." Ridge's words drew my attention, and my heart sank. It looked like our craft party for two was about to expand to three.

"Amber's on her way." Ridge stuffed his phone back into his pocket. "She wants to hang out a bit before she leaves on her family trip."

"Great." I forced enthusiasm into my voice. "I guess we'd better get started." I did not want to spend my evening watching Ridge and Amber make puppy-dog eyes at each other. But maybe seeing them together would convince my traitorous heart to forget his letter and move on. One could only hope.

I moved to the table and began unpacking everything we'd purchased, sorting the different types of flowers into piles and stacking the center-piece materials out of the way on the kitchen counter.

Ridge took in the assortment on the table and whistled. "Good thing Amber's a wiz with crafts. I'm not sure we would ever finish with just the two of us."

I pushed aside my doubts about my crafting ability and grabbed my phone. There was another text from my mother that I ignored as I looked for one of the many tutorials I'd watched the night before. "That's good news. How do you feel about starting with the boutonnieres? Since they're the smallest, they might be the easiest."

Ridge agreed. I was grateful for my open concept floor plan so we could watch TV while we worked. Anything to avoid small talk or conversation of any kind. The witty banter and sounds of gunfire from a superhero movie filled the air as Ridge started cutting roses and I tried to figure out how to use the floral tape and wire. While Pinterest made it look easy, I realized that getting everything positioned just right before adding the tape could be tricky. Not to mention the tape was an odd texture, weirdly stretchy, and left a film on my fingers. My first attempt at a boutonniere looked like a first grader's art project and I gritted my teeth in frustration. Floral arranging was not my superpower.

"It could be worse." Ridge offered as he looked at the tangle of tape and flowers.

"How?"

A knock on the door saved Ridge from responding.

I answered the door, doing my best not to transfer the tacky residue from my fingers to the doorknob.

"Mallory!" I froze as Amber pulled me into a hug. "I'm here to save the day."

Not waiting for a response, Amber pushed past me, making a beeline for Ridge.

"Rigdon." She wrapped herself around him like a vine, pressing in close. I looked away before I had to watch another one of their kisses.

"Amber, I just saw you last night." I could hear the amusement in Ridge's voice and looked up in time to see him extracting himself from her embrace, substituting her hug for some hand holding instead. "I'm glad you're here. We could really use your help."

"Fine. We'll save the kissing for later," Amber said, her voice turning husky, before she gave a dramatic sigh. "But I refuse to work while watching another one of those movies." She gestured to the TV, which displayed an epic fight scene. "I'm so sick of these hero movies. Rigdon talked you into watching it, didn't he?"

"It was actually my—"

"He's always watching them. The first few were fine, but now they're all the same. How many times does the universe really need to be saved?" Amber trailed off and moved to the table.

Ridge gave a shrug and reached for the remote, turning off the TV and plunging us into silence.

I wasn't sure how to respond to Amber's immediate control of the situation. We needed her help, but a petty side of me stung as I watched her take over prep for *my* cousin's wedding in *my* home with *my* high school crush.

I froze as the last part of my thought registered and pushed it aside.

"It looks like I got here just in time. You have a good general concept, but your craft skills need some...help." She picked up my boutonniere and examined it.

"It's a good thing you're here." Ridge pulled out a chair for her, helping her get settled.

Amber got to work, pulling apart the arrangement that had taken me an hour to put together. Ridge sank into the chair beside her, draping his arm around her shoulders. This forced me to take a seat opposite them, but only after I managed to trip over my own feet on the way. *Just what I need. Front row tickets to flirt-fest.*

Instead of snuggling further into his arm, Amber gave Ridge a kiss on the cheek before pushing him away. "I can't concentrate if you keep touching me." She giggled. "We've got work to do."

While I hated to admit it, Amber knew what she was doing. In a matter of moments, she'd fixed my first attempt at a boutonniere, turning it into a work of art. She even organized Ridge and I into a semi-productive assembly line, cutting and matching flowers for her so that she could more easily pull together the arrangements. She made quick work of the boutonnieres and corsages, though she often made side comments about how she preferred real flowers. She had taken some flower arranging classes, and that knowledge shone through as she worked.

We continued working for the next several hours, most of the sound generated by Amber and her running commentary on her upcoming trip to California and how she wished Ridge was coming. I was grateful when my stomach growled audibly, quickly followed by Ridge's. The new sound was a welcome break from her constant dialogue and gave me an excuse to change the subject.

"I'm starving," I exclaimed, perhaps a bit too loudly.

"How do you feel about ordering a pizza so we can finish up while we wait for it to be delivered?" Ridge pulled out his phone as he spoke.

Amber shook her head. "I ate before I came."

"It's been a couple of hours. Are you sure you aren't hungry?" Ridge looked at Amber as if trying to understand how someone could say no to pizza.

"I ate a ton at brunch with my parents." Amber shrugged.

Of course she had brunch. I simply smiled. "I guess that means more food for us."

"How many pizzas should I order?" Ridge asked. "I'm hungry enough I could eat one by myself."

"How about we do two? One for you and then I'll split mine with Audrey and Chloe if they show up before it's gone."

"But what if I want some of your pizza?"

"I might be persuaded to share," I hedged. "If you get a kind that's worth eating."

Ridge put the order into an app on his phone, adding a side of breadsticks. Satisfied that we had a plan to address our grumbling stomachs, we got back to work until the pizzas arrived. Amber had just finished another arrangement when a knock sounded on the door. I jumped at the sound, bumping the table and causing flowers, tape, and wire to scatter. The movement knocked over my purse, spilling out my green-striped notebook. I quickly scooped it up before anyone else could grab it, stuffing it back into my bag. I then hung the purse on the back of my chair, praying no one had noticed my rush to hide the old notebook. The last thing I needed was for Amber or Ridge to read the words I'd been writing to help me process current events.

Ridge rushed to the door and answered it, leaving me alone with Amber and the mess. She shot me an annoyed look before returning to the arrangement in front of her, which I had disrupted.

After a mumbled conversation at the door, Ridge returned with the food. The smells of garlic and sauce filled my nose, making my stomach grumble louder. Ridge settled the pizzas in the one spot on the counter that hadn't been taken over by the wedding. He grabbed a slice, and I followed suit, not bothering to locate plates. My first bite of cheese, chicken, and alfredo sauce erased my stress for a moment, and I groaned.

"This is good." Ridge grabbed his second slice.

I nodded and felt something hanging from my chin.

"You've got a little something there." Ridge reached over with a napkin and dabbed at the spot.

Embarrassed, I reached for the napkin, our fingers brushing. The contact sent shivers down my arms. I mumbled a thank you and looked up in time to catch Amber glaring at me before she schooled her features into a forced smile.

"Hurry up. We still have a lot of work to do, and I'm not staying here all night," Amber said, her voice filled with forced cheer as she bent to her task and continued working. "By the way, did Ridge mention that his internship will be near here?"

I shook my head, still absorbed in pizza heaven.

"I have to get the internship first," Ridge said, reaching for another slice of pizza.

"You will. Daddy promised me. Besides, he needs your help with the new development. In fact, if things go according to Daddy's plan, this quaint little apartment won't be an apartment for much longer."

I froze at Amber's words, a piece of pizza lodged in my throat.

"I saw the signs for the new development when we pulled into the parking lot. I didn't realize your dad was working to buy this property too." Ridge continued eating, unaware of the turmoil his words were causing.

"He doesn't own it yet, but that's just a formality. With what Milton Corp's offered the current owner, there's no way they won't sell."

I seethed inside, remembering my dad's comments about the latest offer. Of course Amber's family was responsible for trying to take my apartment building away from me. She already had claim to Ridge, not that he was mine, but still, why not take my home too?

I set down my half-finished slice of pizza, no longer hungry.

"If I remember correctly, he's wanting this property to expand the parking lot and to make a dog park." Amber continued working, either oblivious to or not concerned with my sudden silence. "Mallory, you should move into one of the new units. I'm designing them, and they're going to be gorgeous!"

Ridge shot me an odd look but didn't comment. Instead, he finished his last slice of pizza and returned to the table.

"I guess we'd better get back to work," he said.

Amber's phone rang as we made our way to the table.

"Hi, Daddy." She answered and exchanged a few pleasantries before holding the device out to Ridge. "He wants to talk to you."

Ridge took the phone and disappeared out the front door, leaving me alone with Amber and my roiling emotions.

Amber and I worked in silence for a moment, waiting for Ridge to return and help us finish the flowers. I was ready to be done and for my guests to leave. I needed some time to think and process my day.

"I still can't believe I'm finally seeing the inside of one of these apartments. My dad has been trying for ages to buy this place. It's cute and cozy, though there's definitely room for improvement. Not worth the hassle the owner's been putting us through."

Amber stood and stretched before wandering into my living room. I fought the urge to escort her out the door and away from the space I'd worked so hard to make home. I knew it was a work in progress, and most of the time, I didn't mind, but watching Amber scrutinize the space put me on the defensive.

"I'm sorry?"

"It's just, my dad has been trying to buy this property for years. With how hard the current owner has made it, you would think the walls were plated in gold. But if you ask me, the value in this building is the land. It's worth more torn down so someone can build something else." Amber gave a small shrug.

"That's a pretty harsh assessment," I said. I knew the same guy who had purchased and torn down the neighboring houses had been pestering Dad to sell, but I hadn't realized Amber's father was the man behind the offers.

"Harsh, but true. Utah County is booming, and new development is where the real money is."

"I guess it's a good thing my dad is happy with income from tenants and not looking for a single big pay off." I muttered the words before I could think.

The next thing I knew, Amber was back in the kitchen, gripping my arm.

"What do you mean? Does your dad own this building?" She spoke quickly, excitement clearly written across her face, from her too-wide smile to her eager eyes.

"Yes. He bought this place as an investment when I was a kid. I moved in when I started college and have been here ever since." I didn't know why I felt compelled to tell Amber the building's history, but her eagerness made me wish the cue in my brain that told my mouth to stop talking would kick in.

"My dad has been trying forever to buy this place, and the whole time I simply needed to meet Ridge's friends. This is fate! Now I really can prove to my dad that I'm a great addition to the business. What does your dad want for the place? What will finally convince him to sell?" Amber's grip tightened in her enthusiasm, becoming almost painful.

I winced, prying her fingers from my arm. Gorilla Glue could learn a thing or two from that woman's grip.

"Nothing will convince him."

Amber scoffed. "Come on. Everyone has a price. Is it more money? The reassurance that his little girl will have a place to live once this building is torn down?"

Amber gave me a pointed look with this question.

"I could find another place to live. That's not the issue." I walked to the sink and grabbed a glass, needing space from Amber and her interrogation. I filled the glass with water and drank, hoping when I turned around, Amber would change topics.

No such luck.

"Then what is it? Because I'm sure my dad would be happy to provide you with a discounted apartment. I bet I could even sweeten the deal with a little extra something for you if you convince your dad to sell."

I turned around to find Amber, hands on the counter, leaning towards me in a power stance that must be part of the education of the affluent. Luckily for me, I had bigger dreams than discounted rent and a small payout.

"Thanks, but no thanks." I stuck the glass in the sink and walked back to the table.

"What's your price? I'm sure we can—"

The door opened and Ridge stepped in, cutting off Amber's question.

"Here's your phone back." Ridge offered the device to Amber, tension obvious in his stiff shoulders and furrowed forehead.

"Thanks, Rigdon! Did you and Daddy sort everything out?" She accepted the phone, apparently oblivious to Ridge's frustration.

"Something like that." Without saying more, Ridge returned to the table and began cutting roses with more force than before.

I followed, my thoughts rushing, and helped finish the flowers, working on autopilot. Amber was not the kind of person used to losing, and I had a feeling her father was similar. What chance did I have of saving my apartment building when up against them? The odds weren't looking great.

It took another hour, but with Amber's help, we managed to accomplish the impossible. As we worked, Ridge kept flashing me odd looks, as if he could sense my inner turmoil. I ignored him and kept working, grudgingly impressed with the flower arrangements when we finished. Amber might be trying to steal my home, but she knew her way around floral tape.

"I've got to get going. I have an early flight tomorrow." Amber walked to the door.

"Have a good trip," I said with forced politeness as I stood and stretched, my back popping after hours hunched in the same position.

"It was great seeing you again." Amber gave me another hug, this one stiffer and more forced than the first. She used the opportunity to whisper in my ear. "Think on our conversation about the apartment. I promise, I could make it worth your while to sell."

I gritted my teeth into a smile and nodded. Knowing who was on the other end of the offers for the building made me even more determined not to sell.

"Drive safe." Ridge walked her to the door. "I'll pick you up at 6:00 to take you to the airport."

"Aren't you coming with me?" Amber stopped with her hand on the doorknob.

"We drove separately." Ridge's tone conveyed his confusion. I bit back a snort at how oblivious he was to his girlfriend's wants.

"But I won't see you for a few days. The least you can do is ride home with me. We could spend some time saying goodbye." Her tone rose with the last words, hinting at what the goodbye could entail.

"I'll walk you to your car, but I'm not riding back to Orem with you. I'd be carless tomorrow."

"I'm sure Mallory wouldn't mind bringing you your car. You could borrow one of Daddy's to take me to the airport. He's letting me drive the Tesla tonight." Amber persisted. I wanted nothing to do with this

conversation, wishing they'd both leave so I could digest this latest revelation: that Amber's father was the one trying to take my home.

"I have a few more errands to run for the wedding tomorrow. I could
use your car and drop it off when I'm done." I offered, pleased by the
thought that maybe it could get me out of having to depend on Ridge
to drive me to the mall.

Ridge shook his head. "Amber, I'm not borrowing one of your dad's
cars when I have my own car to drive."

The debate continued for a few more moments before they headed
outside.

Taking advantage of the moment alone, I grabbed the notebook from
my purse and slipped into my room. I snagged the pen from my nightstand and started writing, ready to stop the second I heard the door open.

Dear Ridge,

*Today has been a rollercoaster. There's so much to process. You and I have
called a truce of sorts, and being with you has been...nice. I've missed your
friendship. It was fun catching up. In fact, if you weren't in a relationship,
I'd probably take you up on that date you wrote me about so long ago.*

*After the car accident, I liked Amber. She seemed nice, though definitely
from a different tax bracket from everyone I associate with on a regular
basis. But today, I feel like I've seen a different side of her, and I don't know
what to think. She wants to take my home. For her, it's just business, but for
me...it's my dream.*

Mal

Chapter Seventeen

Ridge was gone long enough for me wonder if he was coming back. Of course, if he was leaving, I would like to think he'd at least say goodbye and give me his keys, but who knew what his thought process was. After all, he was dating a woman whose family thought nothing of the word "no" nor of using their power to buy my dream right out from under me. I tried not to think about my plans to paint my bedroom or the new flooring that would be coming in a week.

Curious, I crept over to my window facing the parking lot and glanced out. Amber was climbing into a shiny black Tesla, no Ridge in sight. I heard the front door start to open and whipped around, trying to avoid being caught watching from the window. I managed to knock my knee into the coffee table, the pain radiating up my leg as I hobbled away from the window.

I made it to a bar stool and sat down, praying Ridge wouldn't notice as I rubbed the now tender spot on my leg.

Ridge stormed into the apartment, completely ignoring me as he settled back down at the kitchen table. Thunderclouds filled his expression, making me wonder if there was trouble in paradise and why my heart leaped a bit at the thought.

Still processing my latest discovery, I sat mute, rubbing my knee and staring at Ridge. His shoulders drooped and his eyebrows pinched in annoyance, making me want to run from the storm brewing in his eyes, though a small part of me wanted to fix it.

"It didn't make sense for me to drive Amber home. I'm her ride to the airport tomorrow, and I can't do that without my car." He let his breath out in a puff and began massaging his temples.

"Makes sense," I said, not sure where to take the conversation.

"Can we talk about something else? I care about Amber, really I do, but sometimes..." He trailed off, a strangled sound coming from his throat.

I had a feeling that those "sometimes" moments were more frequent than Ridge would ever admit.

"Sure. Like what? We're done with the flowers, so I figured we'd call it good for the day."

I waited, assuming Ridge would head home, leaving me to paint my bedroom ceiling and overanalyze the events of the day, maybe write a few more letters in the notebook. I also needed to call my mom and try to talk her out of buying me a shoulder-padded suit for the rehearsal dinner the night before the wedding. And there was always the task of trying to find tactful ways to dodge Erica's increasingly ridiculous renovation suggestions, like today's request to install neon orange mosaic tiles in the kitchen. Instead, Ridge walked to the couch and settled in. When Ruby walked over, he patted the couch cushion next to him and she jumped up, snuggling into his side. Apparently, she had decided he was worth bothering with after all.

"How about we finish our movie? A reward for all our hard work."

"I don't know. I need to work on my—"

"Come on, Mal. We've been busy all day. Let's do something fun."

A million reasons why this was a bad idea flashed into my mind. The fact that he had a girlfriend whose family was trying to take my home was at the top of my list, followed by the fact that I wasn't sure my heart could take more time alone with Ridge. It turns out, the distance between hate and love is small and my heart was trying to make the leap the more time I spent with him. Despite my better judgement, I settled on the couch and looked over, noticing that his discouragement still rested on his slumped shoulders. Taking a deep breath, I agreed.

The next few minutes dragged as I attempted to ignore Ridge and focus on the fight scene where we'd paused the movie. Instead, I counted the moments until Ridge would leave and my evening plans could return to normal.

When the movie finished, I sighed in relief.

"What should we watch now?" Ridge stretched his arm along the back of the couch, his hand coming dangerously close to brushing my shoulder.

"You've got an early morning. Are you sure you don't want to call it a night?"

"Are you trying to get rid of me?" Ridge grinned, sending my heart hammering.

My phone chose that moment to ring, saving me from responding. I glanced down, grateful, for once, for a phone call from my mother.

"Hello." My voice came out breathless, making me cringe.

"Mal-bear, I haven't heard from you all day. Didn't you get my texts?" Her voice rang through the phone, loud enough to carry, as evidenced by Ridge's raised eyebrow. He mouthed, "Mal-bear?" with a smirk.

I stood and paced into the kitchen as I decreased the volume on my phone.

"Sorry, Mother. I've been helping with Livvy's wedding."

"Which is so nice of you, but it's not helping you in the man department. Good thing I'm here."

If only you knew. I gritted my teeth. "You never know, maybe my dream man will be at the wedding."

Ridge made a choked laughing sound, and I glared at him from my place by the kitchen counter.

Thankfully, Mother didn't hear the background noise and continued talking. "You can always hope. Though I think you need to be more proactive. I know a few guys who would make great dates for the wedding, and every relationship starts with a first date, though you'll have to do it without that pantsuit I was going to order. It won't get here in time. You know your father and I—"

"Weren't even looking for love, but you kept yourself open to possibility and here you are." I recited the words, having heard them nearly every day since I'd first started dating.

"Exactly. Maybe you should go back to school, audit a class or something. It worked for your father and me."

My parents had met on the first day of college. To hear my mother tell the story, they locked eyes across a room and knew it was meant to be. Dad's version involved sitting next to each other and asking if he could borrow her notes, but either way, the stars aligned, and they found love. The fact that I'd graduated college without even a hint of a husband was devastating to my mother. Though I was considering expanding my education with a few property management classes as soon as I got a handle on my home repairs, I didn't dare tell her. I didn't need the "you never know where you'll meet your dream man" speech, again.

"I'll consider it. But I've really got to go. I still have a lot to do before Saturday."

It took another couple of minutes to convince Mother to get off the phone. When I finally hung up, I walked over and slumped back onto the couch. She was determined to find me a date for the wedding, even if it killed me. The problem was, even if I got married, I doubted her hovering tendencies would lessen. I had the car accident in high school—and the man currently sitting on my couch—to thank for that.

"You look like you need a distraction. I vote for another movie." Ridge's voice broke into my thoughts. I looked over to see him flicking through possibilities on the TV.

"What should we watch?" I gave in, hoping some fictional drama would distract me from the real-life drama that was my mother.

Ridge listed several options, each of which I rejected. Thanks to Chloe's movie watching habits, most of the recommendations consisted of chick-flicks, none of which sounded appealing at the moment.

"*That Thing You Do*?" He paused on one of the first movies I'd purchased when I'd subscribed for the streaming service.

"Yes! I will never say no to *That Thing You Do*."

Ridge pressed play and settled back onto the couch. "I haven't watched it in forever."

"It's so good."

"Who was it that had an obsession with that song about holding my hand and heart? Was that you?" Ridge settled next to me as we got sucked into the world of Guy Patterson.

"That was Kyle." I laughed, thinking about the song sung by a trio of Black women in pink dresses. "He used to act out the scene. He'd even do the hand gestures and hip pops."

Ridge joined in my laughter. I could still remember my tall, football-playing cousin acting out the song every time we watched the movie. "I'll have to ask his wife if he still does it."

"I bet it's how he convinced her to marry him. He flashed his pearly whites, broke out his sweet moves, and she couldn't say no."

We both became engrossed in the movie, laughing at witty lines and bobbing our heads to the familiar music.

"I still think 'Guys, Chad fell down,' is one of the most underrated quotes in movie history," I observed as that particular scene played out.

"What makes you say that?" Ridge turned to look at me.

"Well, if Chad hadn't fallen down, the entire movie wouldn't have happened. Chad wouldn't have broken his arm, Guy wouldn't have joined the band, and 'That Thing You Do' wouldn't have become famous." I gestured with my hands, trying to make my point.

"Or maybe 'That Thing You Do' would have remained a ballad and they would have gotten famous anyway, it just would have taken a bit longer." Ridge was playing devil's advocate, I could see it in his blue eyes.

"I don't buy that." I shook my head, rising to the challenge. "Faye has it right at the end when—"

"No spoilers!" Ridge held up his hand to stop me.

"But you've already seen it," I shot back with a laugh.

"It might end differently than I remember. I've got to be sure." Ridge gave me an earnest look, and I rolled my eyes but stayed quiet, my eyes growing heavier as I settled into the couch with the familiar movie banter surrounding me.

Chapter Eighteen

THE SOUND OF A key in the door jerked me awake and I looked around, disoriented. I was still on the living room couch; yet, something was off. It was dark outside, but I'd fallen asleep with the lights on, something I rarely did. Still tired, I snuggled down, ready to go back to sleep when my pillow shifted under me, engulfing me in the familiar scent of cedarwood.

Startled, I realized that my pillow was too warm and too hard. Looking up, I caught Ridge's confused gaze, his hair sticking up in spikes and his blue eyes blinking back sleep.

"What time is it?" he croaked, his voice husky.

I turned, trying to locate a clock, when Chloe walked in, staring at her phone.

"I'm glad you're awake. You will not believe what— Oops!"

Ridge and I were both sprawled on the couch, his arm still around my shoulders. I flushed, realizing what it must look like, and ducked away from him.

"Chloe," I rasped. "Ridge and I were watching a movie." I hoped she wouldn't notice that the TV was currently turned off, indicating just how long we'd been sleeping.

Chloe gave a skeptical look that I ignored.

"What time is it?" I repeated Ridge's question. Maybe I could pretend everything was normal and Chloe would buy it. Or the stars of my favorite home renovation show could turn up on my doorstep, tools in hand, offering me a free home facelift. Currently, the odds of either one seemed equally likely.

Chloe looked at her phone, a grin stretching across her face. "Just after midnight."

"Oh, man." Ridge sat up, moving his arm. I instantly missed its warmth and weight. "I've got to go. I was supposed to call Amber when I got home. She's probably freaking out."

"I'll walk you out." I moved to stand, wincing as my legs and feet tingled with the restoration of circulation. Ridge waved me back down.

"It's all good. I'll see you tomorrow…I mean, later today." He rubbed his jaw.

Ridge slipped out the door, leaving me alone with Chloe. She was fairly bursting with excitement.

"So," she drew out the word, "tell me everything. What happened? I'm assuming this means the two of you made up. Though, I thought he was dating someone. Did they break up? Did you comfort him? Did you kiss? Is he a good kisser? Does this mean you're dating? I knew you two would be perfect for each other."

"Shh." I tried to get Chloe to curb her excitement. "You're worse than my mother. Also, Audrey's asleep."

"Not anymore." Audrey shuffled from her bedroom wearing floral pajamas, her hair mussed and tangled from sleep. It was one of the few times I'd ever seen her without makeup. "Chloe's squeals could wake the dead."

"Sorry." Chloe looked chagrined but not enough to let the conversation drop. "I've just got to know what happened. Give me all the details." She plopped onto the couch next to me and clutched my arm, her eyes wide and pleading.

"Nothing happened." I shook her hand off and tried to rub the sleep from my eyes. "Amber helped with flower arrangements and left once we finished. Ridge wasn't ready to go home yet so we turned on a movie."

"You're no fun," Chloe huffed, sitting back. "You are my most likely friend to have a romance going, and all you did was fall asleep and wake up snuggling? I was hoping for at least a little lip action."

I noted her high heels, skinny jeans, and sparkly shirt. "By the look of things, you're more likely to have had some lip action. How was tonight's date?"

"Not even List-worthy, but you're changing the topic. I can't believe all you did was take an accidental nap."

Audrey stood in her door, a small smile lifting one corner of her mouth. "I wouldn't say that was all. You two looked very cozy when I got home."

"We took an accidental nap. It doesn't mean anything," I insisted, lifting a hand to my hair. My makeup was likely smudged, my hair tangled into a mess, and my face lined with creases. Not the most flattering picture in the world. "He's dating Amber and heading back up to Idaho at the end of summer."

"Idaho isn't that far away, and maybe things with Amber aren't that serious." Chloe ignored my attempt to change the subject, reaching down to pull off her shoes.

Audrey joined us on the couch, forcing me to scoot over to make room for her. The living room light highlighted the absence of makeup, and I was struck by the contrast between her put-together self and the casual look she only let Chloe and me see. "Maybe not, but breaking up a relationship shouldn't be a trivial thing. Be careful, Mal."

"Slow down, no one said anything about breaking up a relationship." I held up my hands in a placating gesture.

"Too many nights spent *just* snuggling and that's exactly what will happen," Audrey persisted. I could hear the pain in her voice and tried not to take it personally.

"Tonight was an accident. It won't happen again." As I spoke the words, my heart twisted, though whether in disappointment or embarrassment, I wasn't sure.

"Won't because you don't want it to, or won't because you're a good person who would never dream of breaking up a relationship?" Audrey's question gave me pause. My soft-spoken roommate cut straight to the heart.

I sighed and rested my head on the back of the couch.

"Forget about it. The wedding is in a few days, and after that, I'll be free of Ridge and all this drama." As I spoke, I couldn't decide whether I wanted my words to be true. Already, I could feel another letter to him niggling in my brain, my fingers itching to put it to paper as soon as I was back in my room.

Dear Ridge,

Tonight, we snuggled. That sounds so juvenile and cheesy, but it's what happened, and my high-school self is freaking out. It was accidental, so I'm not sure it counts. I was embarrassed when Chloe walked in on us; yet, I didn't want it to end. You're the only guy I've ever felt this comfortable around. Which is ridiculous. You broke my heart, and you probably make all the girls, especially Amber, feel this way. I can't forget that. I won't forget that. I won't be responsible for another girl's heartbreak.

Mal

Chapter Nineteen

THE NEXT MORNING, I woke to several texts from Livvy. She apologized for the late response and gushed over how much she loved the flower arrangements. Conveniently, she forgot to mention anything about Ridge and how he'd shown up to be my assistant yesterday.

My stomach twisted at the thought of Ridge, guilt clouding my mind for a moment. *What was I thinking, falling asleep on him? Why didn't I just send him home?*

Despite my attempts to go to sleep after my conversation with Chloe and Audrey, I couldn't push Ridge and the sensations of being so close to him from my mind. If it hadn't been so late, I would have avoided the thoughts with painting and other repairs on my home, but it wasn't an option at 2:00 in the morning. Instead, I'd paced and written my thoughts in the notebook. When that hadn't done the trick, I'd pulled out painters tape and prepped my bedroom ceiling and baseboards to paint later this week.

Luckily, today would involve limited Ridge time once he dropped me off at the mall. I needed distance from my high school dream guy and his welcoming arms. I also needed space from the revelation that his girlfriend's family was actively trying to steal my home.

I used my extra morning time to finish taping off my bedroom, promising myself that I would use my evening to paint, before taking a shower. I took the time to really look good, blow drying my hair and applying makeup. I told myself I was doing it because I wanted to look nice while trying on dresses, but that didn't change the fact that I thought about the ride with Ridge every time I changed my outfit.

My phone rang as I finished getting ready, Livvy's picture filling the screen.

"I'm the worst!" Livvy said in leu of a greeting.

"Hello to you too." I spoke slowly, a knot of dread starting to form in my stomach.

"I totally forgot that I'm supposed to meet some delivery guys at the new apartment. They're dropping off the couch David and I bought."

"But we're going dress shopping." I needed Livvy there. We'd been lucky with the flowers, that Livvy loved them so much, but I knew Livvy wouldn't settle for just any bridesmaids' dresses.

"I know, and believe me, if there were any other time they could deliver, I'd change it in a heartbeat, but it's either today or two weeks from now. And I need to be here to make sure everything's arranged just how I want it." Livvy's voice rose in pitch with each word.

"What do you want me to do about the bridesmaids' dresses? Shop for them alone?"

"Would you?" Livvy's relief at the offer was palpable.

"Livvy, these are your bridesmaids' dresses! I don't want to mess that up."

"You won't. I promise! Try on anything decent and send me pictures of your top picks. I'll just be sitting at the apartment waiting for the delivery guys, so I should be able to respond immediately."

"You seem to be forgetting one important detail." I hoped that my trump card would win the day.

"What's that?"

"I don't have a car. Ridge was going to drop me off at the mall, and then you were supposed to be my ride for the rest of the day."

She didn't even pause before responding. "Is that all? Ridge can be your ride."

"I can't ask him to do that." I'd already taken over one of his days this week. I would feel terrible taking another, not to mention the emotional whiplash of being around him was wearing me out. I pushed all thoughts of snuggling on the couch out of my mind.

"Maybe you can't, but I definitely can. It's my wedding, and I'm not going to let anything ruin it." With that, she hung up before I could protest further.

A few moments later, my phone rang. Glancing down, an unfamiliar number filled the screen. I took a deep breath and answered. Maybe, if I was lucky, it would be the auto shop. After all, why on earth would Ridge agree to go dress shopping? I highly doubted he would be interested in carting me from one department store to another in a desperate attempt to find a decent peach dress.

"Hello."

"Hey, Mal. Good news, I'm your new bridesmaids' dress shopping buddy." Ridge's voice filled my ear, and it took everything I had to contain a groan. "Bring on the peach."

"Are you sure you want to do this?" The words slipped out as I clenched my free hand into a fist at my side. "Best case scenario, which

I doubt will happen, you and I will spend an hour in one store while I try on dresses. You'll be the official photographer and middleman who sends all of the options to Livvy. In reality, we'll probably drive to several stores, spending an hour or more at each, trying to find something that works. I can't ask you to do that." I tried to paint a vivid picture, hoping to dissuade him. I could only take so much alone time with Ridge. Livvy would just have to find another time to go dress shopping on her own.

"Livvy warned me you might try to talk me out of it," Ridge said. "But you're not getting rid of me that easily. There's still the matter of some unearthed high school pictures currently in Livvy's possession that need to disappear when all this is over. I'll pick you up at 10:00. Maybe we'll find something with sparkles."

"That would be hideous—"

Ridge hung up before I could finish, leaving me sputtering and trying to adjust to the change in plans. How had this happened? Somehow, I'd gone from a twenty-minute drive trapped in the car with Ridge to another full day trying to keep my traitorous heart from giving him a second chance.

I glanced down at my phone to check the time and grimaced. I had 15 minutes until he'd be here. Knowing that it wouldn't do any good to try to talk him out of shopping with me, I rushed into my bedroom to change again, desperate to at least find the perfect power outfit for spending hours with the man who'd broken my heart. I would rather build and install my own cabinets than spend another day with Ridge.

A knock sounded on my front door right at 10:00. I answered, grateful that Audrey and Chloe had already left for the day. I didn't need more disapproving looks from Audrey and encouraging comments from Chloe. I was already struggling enough with the situation as I attempted, unsuccessfully, to read Ridge's reaction.

"You ready?" Ridge asked, a huge smile stretching across his face. He looked way too good for a guy who had probably gotten less sleep than I had.

Apparently, he was choosing to ignore the snuggling. Two could play that game.

"You really don't have to do this." I tried one more time to talk him out of it. "Livvy will figure something else out."

"And miss the opportunity to watch you try on one awful peach dress after another? Not going to happen. How do you feel about fringe?"

I cringed, thinking of all the peach disasters waiting for me. I grabbed my purse and followed him out the door, locking it behind me. "Let's get this over with."

Ridge held my door, and I settled into the seat as I waited for him to walk around and clamber in on his side of the car. He'd left the car running when he'd come to my door, and it was nice and cool inside, making me shiver.

"Where to first?" he asked as he backed out of the parking space. I suggested the first store, a place in the mall that specialized in bridesmaids' dresses, and he turned onto the main road, heading for the freeway.

As had become my habit on this street, I turned my head away from the left side of the road, refusing to take in the construction that was well under way.

"Looks like you'll have some new neighbors soon," Ridge said.

I refused to comment.

"Amber and her dad are both excited about that particular property. They think it'll fill up quickly."

"Sounds nice." I forced the words through my teeth, wishing for a change of topic.

Ridge seemed to take the hint as we turned onto another street, leaving the construction site and all it represented behind us.

"I can honestly say I've never been to this store before." Ridge attempted to reignite the conversation as he fiddled with the volume on the stereo.

"I can't imagine why not." I tapped my finger on my chin for a moment, pretending to consider his statement. The store we were headed to exclusively sold dresses for weddings and high school dances. "Good news! We're changing that today."

The first store was a bust. While they had tons of cute dresses, none of them were peach. They had a couple of floral options with peach in them that I tried on, but Livvy, via texts to Ridge, nixed them quickly, claiming that the floral arrangements were enough flowers for her wedding and that floral bridesmaids' dresses would just take things over the top. While I didn't necessarily agree with her, she was the bride, and her opinion took priority.

"We could revolt and buy the floral dresses anyway," Ridge suggested as we left the first store and made our way to a somewhat pricey department store. "By the time she realizes what we've done, it'll be too late to change anything."

"Do you really want that mental breakdown on your hands?" I walked to the dress section. "And does that mean you're done with shopping already?"

"I could do this all day." Ridge shrugged before reaching for a dress from a nearby wrack. "If flowers are out, how do you think Livvy would feel about animal print?"

I ignored his question, suppressing a shudder as I took in the peach snakeskin mess he was holding. "Hard pass."

The department store was even more disappointing than the first store. While they had a few peach dresses, each option was worse than the last, not to mention I'd flinch every time I caught sight of a price tag. The only somewhat promising dress resulted in a hysterical phone call from Livvy, panicking over whether we'd be able to find anything acceptable.

"We'll find something." I hoped my words would soothe Livvy. The phone call had already lasted several minutes with me repeating the same mantra.

"But it's my wedding! The dresses have to be perfect and—"

My phone was pulled from my hand, and I looked up in surprise to see Ridge press it to his ear.

"This is professional dress shopper Rigdon Ridge Ridge. Ma'am, rest assured that if we can't find something today, you get your money back, guaranteed. How do you feel about polka dots?"

Even I could hear the shriek that came through the line, causing him to flinch and pull the phone away from his ear.

"I'm going to take that as a no." Ridge hung up and handed the phone back to me.

"What was that?" I asked, my face frozen in shock.

"Nothing you were doing worked, so I figured we should try a different approach."

"Because sending her into hysterics is clearly a good idea." My phone started ringing and I grimaced as I saw Livvy's picture on the screen.

"You should probably answer that," Ridge said.

"And deal with an angry diva bride? No, thank you! This is your fault. You talk to her." I held out the phone to him.

"I know better than to poke an angry bear." He pushed my hand away.

"You already poked the bear." I thrust the phone out to him again.

"You don't have to answer it." Ridge started to walk away, a goofy grin on his face.

"But that'll just make her angrier."

"So? It's not like she's here. If she were, we wouldn't be having this problem."

Ridge's logic made a weird kind of sense. I glanced down at the phone one more time before taking a deep breath and hitting the ignore button. I hoped that I wasn't making a mistake by sending her to voicemail.

Chapter Twenty

THE NEXT STORE BROUGHT a bit more luck despite Ridge and I having to turn off our phones because Livvy wouldn't stop calling. While the store didn't have any peach dresses, they did have some peach tops that would work well with either a black or white skirt. The problem was the size selection. We needed something that ranged from extra-small to 2XL. We didn't even bother sending Livvy photos, deciding it wasn't worth the potential panic attack.

By the time we reached store number four, I was hungry—on the verge hangry. Ridge had alternated between helping me keep my sanity and increasing my frustration, pushing me further towards the end of my rope with his commentary and suggestions.

"What do you think of this?" Ridge held up something peach that made me flinch. I couldn't quite tell if it was an extra-long shirt or a super short dress. Either way, the fringe at the bottom was a no.

"Absolutely not." I moved to another rack of clothes that looked semi-promising. "What do you think of this?" I held up a lacy peach top that I felt was tasteful.

"Does it come in all of the sizes?" By now, Ridge knew the drill.

I looked through our options. "It's missing a few." I sighed, putting the shirt back and pinching my nose between my fingers, trying to stave off the headache I could feel forming. I was going to need an IV of slushy Dr. Pepper when we finished.

"Maybe we could get rid of the bridesmaids whose sizes are missing."

"Very funny. Do you want to tell them they're out, or should I?" I could only imagine that phone call, though maybe the missing sizes could get me out of playing bridesmaid Saturday.

"If you could do it, that would be great," Ridge said, a smile quirking his lips. "After all, thirteen bridesmaids seems excessive."

I shook my head and turned to look for more peach options among the racks of clothes. The department store smelled faintly of floral perfume, the acrid aroma worsening my headache.

"Do all the dresses have to match?" I could hear the frustration in Ridge's voice.

"What do you mean?" I turned to face him, my curiosity piqued.

"What if all of the girls wore peach, but they weren't wearing the same outfit?" Ridge gestured at the shirt I'd just put down. "One girl could wear that, another could wear one of the tops from the other store. You could even have someone wear that peach scarf we passed earlier."

"Livvy would not go for that." If polka dots sent her into a panic, I could only imagine what mismatched outfits would do. But something Ridge said stuck in my mind. "What peach scarf?"

"It was back that way." He thumbed over his shoulder, gesturing to the accessories.

I strode toward the shelves, cases, and racks filled with belts, purses, scarves, and jewelry. After a moment of scanning the racks, my gaze landed on a beautiful peach scarf. It was solid peach, made of soft fabric, and thin enough that I could imagine wearing it in the June heat without sweating to death.

"What are you thinking?" Ridge's voice came from over my shoulder. I turned to find him right behind me, standing with his hands shoved into his pants pockets. My stomach flipped as I took in his tousled hair.

That shirt really did do amazing things for his eyes and arms and...He's got a girlfriend. I reminded myself as I tore my gaze away from how Ridge's eyes popped thanks to the blue polo he wore.

"I think this"—I held up the scarf between us in an effort to create distance and shook it slightly—"might just work."

I snagged a black skirt and white blouse and headed towards the dressing room with the scarf still in my hands. I changed quickly, taking a moment to gauge my appearance in the three-way mirror. It was simple, but classy. I came out to model my ensemble for Ridge, striking a pose with hands on hips as I spoke.

"What do you think?"

Ridge gave a small wolf whistle.

"Be serious. I can't take much more shopping. Also, I can't believe those words just came out of my mouth."

Ridge schooled his features into a serious expression as he tapped a finger on his chin. "Well, in that case, it is my opinion as your shopping partner that this outfit looks awesome."

I glanced down, smoothing the skirt with my hands. It had a high waist and flared out in a way that made me feel flirty. "You're not just saying that because you're sick of shopping and want to go home?"

Ridge laughed. "While I am sick of shopping, I really do think it looks good."

"It's easy and I'm assuming most of the girls already own a black skirt and white shirt, so it should be inexpensive, too." I stood, pondering for a moment.

"Not to mention size isn't a factor."

"But the black skirt and white shirt wouldn't be exactly the same," I pointed out.

"True, but the scarf would be."

I stood in thought a moment longer. "It might be enough to pull everything together. Now we just need Livvy's approval..." I trailed off. "Dibs on not calling her."

"Oh, no, you don't. I'm here as driver and photographer only."

Ridge's expression told me this was one argument I would not win. With a sigh, I pulled my phone out and turned it on. I ignored the barrage of texts and voicemails filling my screen and opened my camera.

"Fine," I said. "But you have to take a picture first."

Ridge took my phone and snapped a few pictures with me posing, including one of me tripping while I worked to shift positions, which I made him delete. I hoped that my love for the outfit would translate into the images. Though I worried that I would just look fed up and mildly irritated after spending so much time shopping.

I texted the pictures to Livvy and then hit the call button, deciding against a video call.

"Where have you been?" Livvy's voice rang out, causing me to flinch and pull the phone away from my ear. She continued ranting, talking about her panic and stress.

"Did you get the pictures?" I finally broke into her tirade, ready to move the conversation along. Even if she hated the scarf, I needed to know so we could keep looking.

Livvy paused for a moment before responding. "What pictures? All I've had is radio silence for the last *hour*."

"I just sent you our latest find. I love it, and I think it would make everything easier." I kept my tone light and persuasive as I paced in small circles in front of the dressing room, the skirt swishing around my legs.

"Let me look."

I held my breath and looked over at Ridge as I waited for the verdict. If Livvy didn't like this, I wasn't sure what we would do. Maybe I could talk her out of having any bridesmaids after all.

"It's just a scarf," Livvy said, her voice confused. "I mean, it's a cute scarf, but—"

I broke in, catching the hesitation in her voice and hoping that I could talk her into the outfit. "It would be classy and unique. Think about it: size isn't a problem, it's inexpensive, and all the girls likely already own a black skirt and white shirt." I ticked off our reasons quickly, wanting to list them all before she could rule out the scarf.

"But it's June. Who wears a scarf in June?"

"You would be a trend setter." I forced as much enthusiasm into my voice as possible.

"True." Her voice trailed off. "But what about the skirts and shirts underneath? They wouldn't be a perfect match."

"But the scarves would, and at this point, I'm not sure we have many other options. I've already visited all the stores you and I talked about."

Livvy was silent for a few moments, and I prayed for good news. I looked over at Ridge, who was staring at me, waiting for the verdict.

"If we had more time I'd keep looking, but since we don't..."

I held my breath, waiting.

"I say get the scarves."

"Yes!" The cheer burst out as I pumped my fist in the air, excitement and relief filling me as one more item was checked off our list. I looked over to see Ridge doing a touchdown dance surrounded by women's clothing, his arms flailing as he jumped in circles. "We'll buy them right now. Bye." I hung up before she could change her mind.

"She said yes!" I did a victory dance of my own, managing to bump into Ridge. Instead of steadying me and backing away, he pulled me in for a hug.

Time slowed while my heart sped up at the contact. My body reacted, burrowing in closer while my brain tried to process everything and imprint it in my mind. I caught a whiff of his cedarwood-spice smell, the warmth of his embrace triggering memories of the night before. Then time caught up to me, and I snapped out of it, pulling from the hug a second too late.

"I'll just go change." I refused to make eye contact as I hurried back into the dressing room, knocking into a nearby clothing rack as I went. I rubbed the tender spot on my arm, my fingers encountering the familiar scar from the accident so many years before. Would my heart bear a similar mark when this week with Ridge was over?

Chapter Twenty-One

"WHAT DO YOU WANT to do now?" Ridge asked as we left the store, a bag containing the scarves hanging from his arm.

"I assumed we'd both go back to my place and start on the center-pieces," I said, a second bag containing the flirty black skirt swinging from my arm.

I tried to push the hug from my mind as I walked, but my brain seemed determined to dwell on the warmth and comfort of his embrace. Not to mention his smell. I would never think of cedarwood the same way. The sooner we finished the wedding prep, the better. I needed space from Ridge. My emotions were getting hard to understand and control.

"That's no fun." Ridge nudged me with his elbow, and warmth shot up my arm. "We finished another item on the wedding to-do list. I think we need to celebrate."

"So, you want to get food?" I asked.

"I think that should be part of the plan. But I was thinking of something more."

At this point, we'd reached his car. He held my door open and I got in and settled my bag on my lap, the moment alone giving me a chance to ponder what he was saying. He deposited the bag with the scarves in the back seat before climbing in and starting the car.

"More as in what?"

"More as in more than just food." Ridge pulled out of the parking lot and began driving in the direction of my condo.

"We could watch another movie." Even as I said it, I knew that would be a mistake. I didn't think I could handle hours of sitting next to Ridge with nothing to distract us. Too much more time at my apartment and I'd be happy to sell to Milton Corp just to escape the memories that would haunt me once Ridge was gone.

"Pass. We've done a lot of sitting lately. And I'm guessing we'll do more when we work on the centerpieces later." Ridge grew quiet for a moment, and I could tell from his pinched eyebrows that he was trying to think of something else to do. "How do you feel about going for a hike?"

I gestured down at my outfit. I'd worn my best jeans, a flowy top, and sandals. "I'm not dressed for hiking."

"But you can change."

I hesitated a moment. It had been a while since I'd been hiking, and time in nature sounded nice.

"Are you sure? We still have a lot of work to do." I tried one more half-hearted argument against it.

"I'm sure. We need some mountain air!"

I gave in, and Ridge drove to my apartment, following me inside and sitting on the couch. We both ate a snack before I slipped into my room to change. I quickly grabbed a t-shirt, tennis shoes, and shorts, changing in record time. Getting up into the mountains would be fun, and my body longed for the chance to stretch and move. I told myself that exercise was the only thing my body longed for and not the attractive guy coming with me.

I stepped into the living room to find Audrey and Ridge talking on the couch, Ruby snuggled on Audrey's lap.

"Hey. I didn't know you were home."

Audrey shrugged. "I just got here. I've been working late the last few days, so my boss said I could leave early."

"What are you up to the rest of today?" I asked, realizing that I might not have to worry about getting too close to Ridge after all. If Audrey came with us on our hike, I'd have a built in Ridge buffer.

"Undecided. Probably some grocery shopping and maybe a bit of reading. Though I noticed a few more flyers had materialized, so I was thinking about helping them make their way to the trash."

I groaned. How had I missed the bright slips of paper waiting on the cars outside? "Of course there are more."

"What are you guys talking about?" Ridge's eyebrows pushed together as he glanced back and forth between us, trying to follow the conversation.

"The new apartment complex down the street keeps trying to poach Mallory's tenants." Audrey waved her hand towards the parking lot.

"Is that allowed?" Ridge asked.

"No, but who's going to stop them? I've tried contacting the city, but I keep getting the runaround." I shrugged, slumping onto the other couch. "If this keeps up, we'll lose tenants and my dad will sell out for sure." My stomach clenched at the thought. All my money spent in revitalizing and updating this place would be gone, and I'd be back to square one. Dad and I had an agreement that everything I invested in renovating would go towards my efforts to buy the place, but what would that mean if he sold? I could feel my home slipping through my fingers the more Milton Corp pushed him to sell. Flipping properties was what Dad did. Why should this apartment building be any different?

Silence descended on the room as we became lost in our thoughts. A part of me wanted to shout at Ridge, pointing an accusatory finger and exclaiming that this was his girlfriend's fault, but I knew it wouldn't do any good. He had nothing to do with the development, even if he'd soon be interning for the enemy.

"I guess we'll be throwing away flyers before our hike." I stood up from the couch and made my way toward the door. I refused to dwell on the what ifs.

"Hiking will be fun!" Audrey latched onto the positive in my pronouncement.

"Want to come?" My eyes widened, trying to convey how badly I wanted Audrey to join us.

"I don't know..." Audrey trailed off, disregarding my pleading look. "I need to start apartment hunting, in case your dad decides to sell."

I flinched at her words, praying that she wouldn't have to move. I knew both Chloe and Audrey would have to find somewhere else to live, but I couldn't stand the thought of losing my roommates.

"We don't have to go hiking." Ridge joined in my crusade to convince Audrey to come along. "I'm open to suggestions. We could try something different, like going to an art museum. Or there's always bowling."

I inhaled sharply at the word "bowling," coughing and sputtering as I tried to regain my composure.

"Mal isn't a big fan of bowling." Audrey laughed, coming over to pat my back. "She recently had a...traumatic experience."

"It sounds like there's a story there." Ridge quirked an eyebrow as he paused, waiting for a response. Audrey and I looked at each other, grinned, and remained silent. "A story I apparently don't get to hear. Any other suggestions? You mentioned that you're in the process of painting your place, Mal. Want help?"

I shook my head. "We don't need paint fumes adding to our centerpiece party later." *And I don't need reminders of Ridge every time I look at a section of ceiling he might have helped paint, no matter how little time I might have left in this apartment.*

"If you're sure you wouldn't mind me joining, I'd love to go hiking. It would be nice to be outside for a bit." Audrey's words were hesitant, and I wanted to strangle Lyle, her ex. He had taken a shy but confident woman and turned her into a self-doubting, shrinking girl.

"Of course we don't mind! The more, the merrier. Though I get to pick the music on the ride," I teased.

Audrey smiled. "You have no respect for the classics, though I'll probably drive separately anyway so I can stop at the store."

"Are you sure Jovi can make it?" I would never know how Audrey's car continued to function.

"Let me worry about Jovi. She'll be fine. Which hike do you want to do?"

I considered our options, ignoring Ridge's puzzled expression. "There's always Battle Creek Falls. Or we could drive up the canyon a bit and try something there."

"As long as it's not too long, I'm in. You guys choose something while I change." Audrey rushed from the room, leaving me alone with Ridge once more.

"Is Audrey always so hesitant?" Ridge asked after she'd closed her bedroom door.

"She didn't used to be." I was surprised Ridge had noticed. "Her ex-boyfriend did a real number on her."

"That's horrible." Ridge looked outraged, something I could appreciate. "She seems like a kind, sweet person."

"Which was apparently the problem. Because she was so kind and sweet, she never suspected that he was cheating on her with her best friend."

Ridge gave a sharp intake of breath, and I could see fire in his eyes that I'm sure matched my own. Before he could respond, Audrey stepped into the hallway, ready to go. Her ponytail swished from its high perch on her head as she bent down to tie her running shoes.

"Did you decide where we're going?"

"Battle Creek," I said.

"That one's short enough Ruby can come along." Audrey moved to grab Ruby's leash, and the dog came running.

"I don't think I've hiked that one before. Sounds great," Ridge commented. "But I am confused about something. If the dog is Ruby, who's Jovi?"

Audrey and I laughed as we walked out the door.

"Jovi is Audrey's car. It's short for Bon Jovi." I locked the door after everyone had exited and began walking to the cars.

"I'm guessing you're a fan of classic rock?" Ridge asked.

Audrey shrugged. "That's one reason." She climbed into her old, battered car that I was pretty sure had more rust than paint, refusing to say more.

Ridge held my door, and I climbed into his car.

"I'm sensing there's more to the car name." Ridge pulled out of the parking lot, and I directed him to the trail.

"It's a bit of an inside joke between us. We dubbed the car Jovi because I'm pretty sure the only thing keeping it alive is luck and prayer."

"I get it!" Ridge laughed. "It's 'livin' on a prayer.'" He sang the song title, causing me to laugh at the out of tune song.

"Nailed it."

The car ride to the trailhead passed quickly, with Ridge and I catching up on lost time. I steered clear of questions about Amber. Audrey was waiting for us when we climbed out of the car, Ruby sniffing around the gravel of the parking lot. I had been laughing at something Ridge said, and I caught a look of concern cross her face. I simply shrugged, telling myself it was nothing. *She's wrong. I'm not getting too close. I'm not getting attached.*

It was about a mile hike to the waterfall, though the climb did get steep towards the end. The rocks and dirt crunched beneath our feet as we got moving. I listened to Ridge and Audrey talk, asking the get-to-know-you questions that surrounded introductions. They seemed to hit it off, and I was content to listen as we moved up the path, crossed the worn wooden bridge, and started the steep incline that led to the waterfall.

"You guys didn't tell me this trail got hard," Ridge panted as we continued to climb.

I laughed, though it sounded more like a gasp of escaping air. "For Utah, this is an easy hike."

"Do you guys want to go up or down?" Audrey asked, referring to the point where the path split up ahead.

"I vote down," I said. While the view was beautiful from the top of the falls, the climb up was even steeper than our current path, with shifting rock that was hard to walk on.

"Which is better?" Ridge asked.

"Probably down," Audrey said.

"Any way we could swing both? I'd love to see the view if we can," Ridge said.

"Probably. Let's see how we're all feeling after we rest at the waterfall for a bit," I said, panting with each word.

We took the turn for the base of the waterfall. The water flowed down the cliff face, making a peaceful rushing sound as it cascaded over the rocks into the pool at its base. I paused for a moment, taking in the sight. No matter how many times I hiked up here, I still loved seeing the waterfall.

"This is nice." Ridge maneuvered around the few people who were there to get closer to the falls.

"I think you need a picture." Audrey held out her hand for Ridge's phone.

Ridge patted his pockets. "Shoot. I must have left my phone in the car."

"You can use mine." I held up the device.

"Thanks." Ridge positioned himself on some rocks in the river, the waterfall providing a perfect backdrop for the picture.

I snapped a couple of photos, hoping that I would remember to text them to Ridge after our hike when I had better service. "These look great."

"Awesome. You should be in them too." Ridge motioned for me to join him.

"I'm all sweaty," I demurred, not needing photo reminders of my time with Ridge.

"Come on," Ridge insisted. "We need to capture this moment, a reminder of our hiking and wedding prepping success."

"Fine." I turned looking for someone to take the picture. Audrey held out her hand for the device, her lips curving down and her eyebrows crinkling together. "But don't you want to be in the picture too?"

Audrey just shook her head. "I'd rather take the picture."

I handed her the phone and reluctantly made my way over to Ridge. I stopped, a foot away from Ridge, and turned toward the camera.

"Closer than that," Audrey called. I stuck my tongue out at her and inched closer.

"Come on." Ridge grabbed my arm and tugged me in his direction. "I don't bite."

It took me a moment to register where on my arm he'd grabbed. The ridges of my scar were beneath his fingers, drawing his attention downward. While only a couple of inches long, the puckered edges stood out sharply against my skin. I had long since stopped trying to cover the mark, accepting it as part of me, but it was clearly the first time Ridge had noticed the line, a reminder of the accident and the night he ran away.

"What—"

Forgetting where we were, I jerked my arm back, causing my foot to slip on the rock. I gave a small shriek, working to regain my balance before I fell and soaked my shoes. Ridge grabbed my arm again and helped me onto the rock next to him.

"Careful," he said, once I'd gotten my balance. "We still have to hike back."

I nodded, pulling my arm from his grasp and turning to face the camera. Ridge settled his arm around my shoulders, and we stood there, grins stretching across our faces, as Audrey took the picture. My whole body seemed to come alive with his touch, but I tried to ignore it. Even conjuring images of Amber hugging him the night before couldn't fully dispel the pleasure I felt at his touch. Though if I focused on it enough, the shock on his face when he saw my scar might do the trick.

"Got it." Audrey called and we broke apart, moving back to the bank.

"Thanks." I took my phone from Audrey.

"You're welcome," Audrey muttered. "Just remember to be careful." She stooped down to pet Ruby, refusing to look me in the eye. Her words stung but served as a needed reminder for my traitorous heart.

"Make sure you send me all those pictures. I can't wait to show Amber." Ridge joined us, a giant smile stretching across his face. "You guys ready to head to the top?"

"Actually," Audrey paused and glanced down at her phone, "I've got to get going. I need to drop Ruby off and then get to the store."

"We don't have to hike to the top," I jumped in quickly. "We could hike back down…" I trailed off when I saw the look of disappointment on Ridge's face.

"I'd really like to hike to the top. I don't know when I'll get another chance to hike this trail. Amber and hiking aren't exactly friends," Ridge said.

"It's okay. I can head back now, and you guys can go to the top." Audrey's pitch rose at the end, making her statement sound more like a question. She watched me, eyebrows raised as she waited for my response. I could see the caution in her face and knew I should follow her down the trail, but I couldn't bring myself to disappoint Ridge after all he'd done to help me the last few days.

"I guess we're hiking to the top, then. Good luck at the store."

"I'll see you when you get home." With a wave, Audrey started the trek back down the mountain, leaving me alone with Ridge. I tried to ignore the look of concern she sent my way as she walked away.

"Let's go." Ridge began walking up the trail, turning to head to the top of the waterfall instead of following Audrey down. I hesitated for a second. It would be so easy to follow her, to leave behind my twisting emotions and embrace her words of caution, but I couldn't bring myself to do it.

I clambered up the trail, careful on the shifting rocks. Ridge waited for me at the top, taking in the view of the valley below.

"This is beautiful." Ridge nudged my arm. "Utah Lake even looks good from here."

I laughed and nudged him back. "This trail connects to another one several miles away. I hiked it once, and it was long but filled with views like this."

"Sounds nice." Ridge sighed and we stood there a few moments more before moving to let another group have our place. "Let's head back."

Ridge took the lead, and I carefully followed him, picking my way down the steep path. At one point, someone had installed rubber mats on this part of the trail. I assumed that the mats were meant to stabilize the rocks, but they were so worn and old that they did little good, making this section of trail the most treacherous. I was nearly back to where the trail branched for the base of the waterfall when Ridge spoke again.

"Too bad Amber isn't more outdoorsy. This would be a perfect place to propose."

I stopped at his words just as some overeager kids pushed past me. My feet shifted on the unstable rocks, and I slipped, falling in a not so graceful heap on the trail. A whoosh of air escaped my lungs, and I felt one of my ankles twist, twinging with pain.

Chapter Twenty-Two

"ARE YOU OKAY?" RIDGE was at my side in an instant. A small crowd was forming around us, and I felt heat creep into my cheeks.

"Fine, just clumsy," I lied. I wanted to scream. *What did he mean a perfect place to propose?* I knew he liked Amber, but they hadn't been dating long, and based on the interactions I had observed between the two, they didn't seem like a good fit. My world spun as my heart clenched at the thought. I obviously wasn't as indifferent to Ridge's romantic life as I had told myself and my roommates.

"Are you sure you should be—"

"I'm fine." I cut Ridge off and pushed to my feet. He grabbed my arm and held it as I stood. My ankle protested as I put weight on it, and I nearly fell again at the unfamiliar sensation combined with the light-headedness that had developed following his words.

"Careful." Ridge wrapped his arm around my waist for added support. My heart thudded at his touch.

He just mentioned proposing to another girl! I screamed at my inner self, but my heart refused to see reason as it sped up at the continued contact.

"I'm okay. Just twisted my ankle." I went to take a step, stifling a groan. My ankle was likely sprained, not the best state for hiking down a mountain, but I would live. It wasn't my ankle that I was most concerned about.

"Twisted ankles can be a serious problem." Ridge moved to help me through the small group who had stopped to offer assistance.

"But not serious enough to stop me from getting back to the car." I gritted my teeth. The sensation of walking on my injured ankle was uncomfortable but not unbearable. I tried to move out of Ridge's grip as we walked, but he kept his arm firmly in place.

"At least let me help you," Ridge insisted. "I can carry some of your weight as we walk."

The trip down the mountain was slower than normal. I told myself that it was because of my ankle, but the longer I walked with Ridge's arm around my waist, the more I slowed down and forgot about his almost-fiancée. We reached the car, and I hobbled into the passenger seat, Ridge carefully holding my door until I was settled.

"I want to look at that ankle when we get back." Ridge climbed in and started the car.

"It's fine," I grumbled, my tone curt. I hated being the center of attention, especially when injuries were involved.

"If it's fine, it won't be a problem for me to look at it," Ridge shot back.

"I'm not some damsel in distress. I can take care of my own rolled ankle."

"I didn't say you were a damsel in distress. Though, if you were, you wouldn't be making such a big stink about me checking on your ankle."

"No. If I was a damsel in distress, I would be passed out and suffering more serious injuries than a rolled ankle."

"Damsels in distress don't get rolled ankles?"

I paused for a moment, considering. "They might. But I feel like the focus is on more major problems. You know, curses, kidnappings by monsters, being eaten by dragons. Rolled ankles don't really rank on the distress scale." The words bubbled out as I tried to distract myself from the emotions I'd felt earlier. If I could ignore his pronouncement, ignore my emotions, maybe everything would be okay.

"Huh." Ridge was quiet for a moment before commenting. "I guess I've never really considered it."

"And it would be highly inappropriate to be discussing ankles with your rescuer anyway. In those days, a lady did not talk about her ankles." I'd kept a surprisingly serious tone throughout the conversation, but my last comment did me in. A laugh bubbled out, and I couldn't contain it.

"Good point." Ridge joined in the laughter as we pulled into my condo parking lot. "But since we're not in the days of knights and ladies, I'm still going to check that ankle."

I groaned but allowed Ridge to help me inside. Neither Audrey nor Chloe was home, and we had the place to ourselves again. I settled on the couch and watched as Ridge sat on the floor in front of me. He helped me out of my shoes before reaching out to gently lift my ankle and examine it. It was obviously swollen and it hurt when I moved it. However, the pain was overshadowed by the warmth of his touch. I tried to ignore the sensation but felt heat settle in my cheeks as I waited for his prognosis.

"I don't think it's anything major, but you'll want to ice it and elevate it," he said after a few moments of examination. Ridge joined me on the couch, and I stretched my leg out to rest it on the coffee table.

"I know the drill. I've had worse."

"I can tell." Ridge picked up my arm and fingered the scar. "How did this happen?"

"You already know the answer to that question." The words came out quiet, but he still flinched as I spoke, as if each word were a nail driven into his skin.

"I guessed as much, but I'd hoped..." He trailed off before taking a deep breath. "I'd hoped I was the only one left scarred after that night."

My stomach clenched, his words shifting my memories of the accident. "I thought you were fine. You weren't taken to the hospital, and then you moved to Florida so quickly after, I just assumed—"

Ridge held up a hand, stopping my rambling.

"Maybe 'scars' was the wrong word. I wasn't hurt physically, but I've been battling the memories from that night ever since. It's why I ran away."

After everything that happened on prom night, I deserve that. Ridge's words from the letter ran through my head.

"Ridge, what else happened that night? I mean, the accident was bad, but not something to run away from."

Ridge stared straight ahead, refusing to look at me. "It wasn't the accident so much as... what happened after."

I waited, sensing that there was more, knowing that the demon chasing Ridge was more than an accident he hadn't caused and the regret of ghosting me after a first kiss.

"My dad's...not a great guy. He's always had a temper. Usually, it was triggered by a bad grade or if I didn't play well during a game. He'd yell, maybe throw something at the wall. It wasn't great, but my family, we'd learned to cope with it. But that night...that night was different." Ridge spoke quietly, each word hanging in the room as he painted a reality I'd had no idea he'd been facing. I'd known his dad was intense, but this was more than I'd ever imagined.

"He'd been having a difficult time at work, and my mom had just quit her job, so finances were tight. Learning that my car was wrecked, even though it wasn't my fault, sent him into a tailspin. I'd never seen anything like it. He was yelling, storming around the house, throwing anything within arm's reach. He kept ranting about how irresponsible I was, but that he'd teach me responsibility. I thought he was starting to calm down when something shifted. Instead of throwing things at the wall, he started throwing things at me. I couldn't dodge fast enough. I made it to my room and locked the door, but he just kept at it. Yelling, pounding on the door, calling me worthless, ungrateful. I...I couldn't take it anymore. And I realized I was eighteen. I didn't have to take it anymore."

Ridge clenched his fists, his knuckles white and the tendons in his hands standing out. I reached over, resting my hand on one fist, wishing I could do more to provide comfort as he relived that night. His hand flexed then relaxed, as he opened his fist and laced his fingers with mine, searching for comfort.

"I packed a bag and waited until the yelling stopped and my parents were asleep, before slipping out. I texted Kyle, and while he didn't know everything, he knew enough not to question when I said my dad was having an episode. Kyle drove me to my grandparents' house, where I stayed for a couple of days until I could figure out a plan. I had an aunt who lived in Florida. She always told me if I ever needed anything, to call her. So, I did. By the end of the next week, I was on a plane on my way to stay with her. I got a job during the day and worked on my GED at night and didn't come back to Utah until my parents separated a few years later."

"Ridge, I'm so sorry. I had no idea." The words felt inadequate, but they were all I could think to say as I processed what he'd told me.

"No one knew. For the longest time, I thought it was normal for dads to act that way, but then I met Kyle and your Uncle Ken. Your family was more of a lifeline for me than you'll ever know."

We sat there in silence, the only sound the ticking of the clock on the wall and the occasional car driving past outside. My heart ached for Ridge and the nightmare he'd lived through.

Ridge gave a small shake of his head, expelling a deep breath, before letting go of my hand. "Anyway, lots of rest and ice, and that ankle should be as good as new."

I accepted the change of topic with a forced laugh.

"Thanks, Doctor Ridge." My voice cracked as I spoke. I cleared my throat before continuing. "Now can we eat something? I'm starving." In our rush to include Audrey in our hiking plans, we had forgotten all about the food part of our celebration. Not to mention, I needed distance between us, fast. My mind whirled with all I'd learned.

"Your wish is my command. What sounds good?"

I thought for a moment. "Honestly, fried chicken and potato wedges." I pictured the deli food and my stomach growled.

"Coming right up." Ridge got me settled on the couch with pillows and an ice pack before leaving for the grocery store. I used the time to scroll through the photos Audrey had taken. The waterfall in the background made a beautiful setting. I loved the pictures of Ridge and me together and knew that, despite the disaster my heart was heading for, I would treasure them after the wedding was over. Especially now that I better understood why he'd run. I selected my favorite few photos and sent them to Ridge before limping to my bedroom and grabbing the notebook and a pen then settling onto the couch to write.

Dear Ridge,

Thank you for being my knight in shining armor today. I can still fall down a mountain with the best of them, and it was good to know you were there to catch me.

I wish I had been there to catch you after the accident and the fight with your dad. I had no idea what you were dealing with at home. My heart aches, knowing the pain you must have gone through at the hands of the man who should have cared for you most. Please forgive me for not knowing, for not doing anything.

Mal

Chapter Twenty-Three

I FINISHED THE LETTER and hobbled back to my room, placing the journal on my nightstand before returning to the living room. I settled on the couch, scrolling through social media as I waited, my stomach grumbling and ready for food. By the time Ridge returned, Ruby had wandered out of Audrey's room and was settled on the couch next to me.

"Thanks for sending those pictures. They turned out great." Ridge distributed the food and sat on the loveseat diagonally from me. "Sorry the hike didn't end as expected. The waterfall was beautiful, though."

"I know it wasn't the best hike ever, but I'm glad we went. It was nice to be in the mountains." I paused to take a bite before continuing. "When I'm up there, I feel like I can actually breathe. I can let go of my stress and just enjoy everything around me." *As long as no one makes off-handed remarks about proposals.*

"I get that." Ridge nodded. "That's one thing I love about Rexburg. It's so close to trails and rivers and things."

"Where's your favorite place to go?"

He thought for a moment as he bit into his food. "Probably Island Park. It's a few hours away, but worth the drive. You can find a camping spot near Henry's Lake and spend a weekend exploring the mountains. It's gorgeous and not too far from Yellowstone."

"I've heard of it. Audrey has friends with a cabin up there, and she talks about it all the time. It sounds nice."

"It is." Ridge paused. "I wish I could get Amber to see how amazing it is. I took her camping once a couple of months ago, and I will never make that mistake again." His facial expression was comical. His lips and eyebrows scrunched, and he puffed his cheeks a bit.

"Not good?" I asked with a laugh.

"Horrible. She spent the entire time complaining about something. If it wasn't the dirt, it was the bugs. If it wasn't the bugs, it was the camp bathrooms." He sighed and then shrugged. "It was her first time camping, so I can't really blame her. I think our next outdoor adventure will be of the cabin variety."

At that moment, I wanted to grab Ridge and shake him, pointing out how wrong for him Amber was. But it wasn't my place. We may have been friends almost our entire childhoods, but we'd been back in each other's lives for only a few days, hardly enough time for me to have a say in his personal life.

I decided to change the subject. "So, you mentioned wanting to teach history. What era is your favorite?"

"That's a tough question. Probably World War II. It's a hard time to talk about, but I think there's so much we can learn from it."

Our conversation moved on from there, making the years of missed time fade away. It could almost make a girl forget how much she'd been hurt and how unavailable he was, especially now that I understood the past in a new light.

We finished eating in companionable quiet. I tried to draw out the meal, hoping Audrey would swoop in to help with the centerpieces despite the guarantee of disapproving glances that would come with her. A text, explaining that she'd gotten roped into something with Chloe, dashed that possibility. Not even my pleas for a Ridge buffer were enough to change her mind. *She must trust me more than I do.*

"Where do we start with the centerpieces?" Ridge stood, taking our trash and dishes into the kitchen.

"Probably with a table." I hated to get back to work.

Ridge glared at me with a shake of his head. "I kind of assumed that part."

I shrugged. "You've got to be more specific."

"Now that we have a *table*," Ridge gestured to my kitchen table, "what's next?"

"We sit here and pretend like we don't have more work to do?"

Ridge sat quietly, considering. "Do you think, if we sit here long enough, magic elves will come and make everything for us?"

"Not unless you're Santa Claus or a shoemaker," I said glumly.

"I haven't completely ruled out those career options, though I'm guessing they might pay about as well as a teacher, so I don't think Amber would be on board," Ridge joked. He paused for a moment longer before pushing to his feet and moving into the kitchen. "Come on. Let's get to work."

I groaned but remained seated. "If I never see a peach decoration, dress, or flower again, I'll be okay."

"What about peaches?" Ridge quirked an eyebrow at me as he walked back to the couch.

"That would be a tragedy! My disdain for peach extends only to the color. Peaches are in a completely separate category." I was full after our late lunch, but the thought of peaches made my mouth water.

"I don't know if the two are mutually exclusive. After all, the color peach has to come from somewhere."

"Notice I didn't include peach *fruit* on my list," I persisted, wagging a finger at him.

Ridge bit his lip and didn't reply. Instead, he sat back down on the couch next to me.

"Rustic-looking wood might be added to that outlawed list as well," I muttered as I thought about the supplies waiting to be made into centerpieces.

"What about tea lights?" he asked. "Or picture frames?"

I glanced around the room, taking in the few picture frames I had hanging on my walls. "My house would look kind of sad if I skipped the frames and put my pictures directly on the walls. But then again, it would make decorating significantly easier."

"That's true," Ridge agreed. "But regardless of your personal feelings towards the color peach and rustic wood, we've got to get these center-pieces figured out so we can help with set up in a couple days."

Ridge and I had been moving through Livvy's list faster than antici-pated, meaning tomorrow would give us a break from wedding prepa-rations so long as we finished the centerpieces tonight.

Ridge's words spurred me into action, and I pushed up from the couch, ignoring my ankle, and made my way to the table. My ankle ached a bit with each step, but not enough to indicate a serious injury. "Honestly, the easiest place to start would be to load the pictures into the frames, but since we won't get those from Livvy until we're setting up, we'll just have to make the best of what we've got."

Ridge moved around the table and retrieved the bags of picture frames, wood pieces, and mason jars that we'd purchased. Sticking them on the table, we began to unload everything. The hodge-podge of items was overwhelming but thanks to Pinterest, I had an idea of what to do. Leaving one section of the table open for our mock display, I got to work.

I stuck a picture frame in the center of the space and added a mason jar off to the side. I then took a couple of leftover roses from our flower arranging and stuck them in the jar. I put one of the wood pieces next to the jar and frame to create a grouping of three and stepped back.

"What do you think?" I considered my work. Somehow it didn't look anything like the pictures I'd seen.

"Uh, that's one idea." Ridge stood next to me, taking in the simple display. "Are the flowers supposed to lean like that?"

The roses I'd stuck into the jar were leaning away from each other, looking like they were trying to escape.

"I think their stems are too long. Maybe if I cut them..." I grabbed one of the roses and a pair of wire cutters that had been left out from the day before. Quickly, I snipped off the end of the rose and stuck it back in the jar, but the rose fell into the jar, disappearing below the lip. I'd cut it too short.

"Let's try that again." Ridge grabbed the wire cutters from me and picked up another rose, measuring it against the mason jar. He cut off the end and placed the resized rose in the jar, repeating the process with a couple more roses.

"It looks better, but it's still not great."

I looked over the pile of random craft supplies littering the table. We had ribbon, lace, tea lights, and the other leftover flowers from the wedding arrangements. Not a whole lot to work with. A small bag of polished peach and white stones caught my eye. They reminded me of something I'd find in a fish tank. I had grabbed them on a whim, thinking we could sprinkle them on the tables for an added bit of peach.

I pulled the roses out of the jar, picked up the stones, and poured them into the jar. They made a satisfying clinking sound that helped ease my tension. "What if we did something like this?" I held up the jar for Ridge's inspection.

"A jar full of rocks?" He gave me an incredulous look. "It seems kind of childish."

"Well, I am an elementary school teacher, but that's not quite the vibe I'm going for."

I set the jar next to the picture frame and wood stand and we continued to stare at the items in front of us. Ridge reached over and gabbed a tea light, setting it on the wood stand. It was a nice addition, but the arrangement still looked incomplete. I picked up the ribbon and toyed with it between my fingers. Finally, I reached over and wrapped a bit around the middle of the jar. It added a nice touch of silver that matched the picture frame. I quickly cut a piece of ribbon and did my best to tie a bow at the top of the mason jar. The result was a bit lopsided but gave the basic idea.

"I like that," Ridge said. "It's still simple, but I think it works."

"The question is: will Livvy be okay with it?"

"If Livvy doesn't like it, she can come up with something better."

I grinned up at Ridge. "I like how you think."

We snapped a couple pictures of the arrangement and sent them to Livvy before taking stock of our supplies. We would need more stones and ribbon but had enough of everything else for the tables at the reception. The day was catching up to me, and a trip to the craft store sounded like the worst form of torture.

"We can stop Friday on our way to help with set up. Shopping can wait." Ridge began clearing off my table and putting everything away.

"I never thought I would be so happy to not go shopping," I mused.

Ridge laughed and shook his head. "I'll never understand why girls love shopping so much."

"It's retail therapy. What's not to love?"

Ridge shrugged. "So, how do you feel about food and a movie? I'm beat."

"Sounds like a plan." I grabbed the remote and settled on the couch, making sure to prop up my ankle. "What movie?"

"Surprise me." Ridge continued to stand behind the couch. "What food?"

"Surprise me." I echoed, not wanting to move from the couch. My ankle was feeling stiff and achy after too long standing.

"I'll pick something up while you choose the movie. I need to call Amber while I'm out anyway. She'll be so proud to hear of our successful crafting." Ridge slipped out the door before I could say anything. I refused to examine the twinge in my stomach at the mention of Amber. I also ignored the reminder of the off-hand comment about proposing he'd made on our hike.

Scanning through Netflix, I quickly selected a movie and settled in to wait, dozing after a while. Nearly an hour later, a knock at the door startled me awake and drew me from the couch. I pulled open the door and found Ridge, arms full of takeout, waiting to be let in.

"You could have just walked in. What did you decide on?" I stepped back to let him inside, wincing when I put too much weight on my ankle. "And what took you so long?"

"Sorry. The conversation with Amber went longer than planned." He shrugged as he deposited everything onto the counter, changing topics.

"I figured we've already had French, American, and Italian cuisine this week. Personally, I don't have the stomach for Mexican food right now, so I thought Chinese would work nicely."

"French?" I questioned. Italian had been the pizza, American had been the burgers and fried chicken, but when had we had French food?

"French fries," Ridge said in a terrible imitation of a French accent, causing me to laugh.

"I don't think French fries are actually French." My stomach growled as I watched Ridge unload the food and I smelled the spices.

"Where do they come from if not France?" Ridge pulled out plates and utensils. When had he become so comfortable in my kitchen?

I pulled out my phone, doing a quick search. "The mighty Google says they're..." I paused for effect, "Belgian or French. Apparently, it's a matter of debate."

Ridge shrugged. "Either way, they're European and not Mexican or Chinese so we're safe to eat what I brought. Though to be fair, I've been told American Chinese food and real Chinese food are not the same thing."

"I'm starving, so let's dig in." I walked over and grabbed a plate, loading it up with rice, noodles, chicken, and veggies.

Once we had our food, we settled onto the couch and started the movie. Neither of us spoke as we ate, letting the movie do all the talking.

By the time the credits rolled, my eyes felt heavy, and it was getting late. The movie had been a random pick from Netflix that involved lots of miscommunication, but the main couple found love in the end.

"Hey, Mal."

"Hmm." The sound rumbled across my lips as I forced my eyes open to look at Ridge.

"Do you think that's possible?" The serious note in his voice gave me pause.

"What's possible?"

"Happily ever after, like in the movies."

"I guess so, if you're in love. I mean, people get married all the time claiming they've found that movie ending. Hence the obscene number of flowers on my table." I gestured to the floral arrangements, trying to keep the tone light.

"How do you think people know when they're in love? I mean, Livvy and David seem so sure, but...it's such a big decision. It certainly didn't work for my parents." Ridge's mention of his parents made me flinch as I remembered his revelation from earlier. How could someone trust in happy endings when that was the example he had to compare everything to?

"I'm probably not the right person to ask." My voice came out as little more than a whisper. "I'm good at knowing what I don't want. I'm not very good at deciding on what I do."

The two times I had been certain—prom with Ridge and my engagement to Matt—had gone so horribly wrong, a complete demolition of my heart. It seemed safer and easier not to commit to anyone, to keep them all at arm's length, rebuilding myself into someone strong and independent. Someone capable of building her own home, regardless of who else wandered into her life.

"That's a pretty heavy question for"—I glanced at the clock—"11:00 at night. Where's this coming from?"

Ridge shrugged and reached into his back pocket, pulling out a velvet ring box. My mouth fell open as he lifted the lid, exposing an extravagant diamond ring. "Because I thought I knew the answer, but now...now I'm not so sure."

Chapter Twenty-Four

RIDGE HELD OUT THE box to me and I hesitated before taking it and opening it.

This cannot be happening. The comment at the waterfall hadn't been so offhand after all.

"It's a ring. It won't bite, I promise." He joked, the words sounding far away, as if I was wearing ear protection.

I wouldn't be too sure about that.

My heart hammered at the sight of the ring. It was white gold with a large center diamond surrounded in a halo of smaller diamonds. The emerald cut jewel took my breath away while also making me question how much Ridge must have spent on it. It was hardly the ring someone on a teacher's salary could afford.

"You're proposing to Amber." The words felt like chalk in my mouth.

"Planning on it. I was thinking Saturday after the wedding would be perfect. We could go for a drive up Provo Canyon and stop at one of the parks to look at the stars. She loves it up there."

"Sounds like you've thought it all out, the perfect proposal." I handed the ring box back.

"So why doesn't it feel perfect?" Ridge slumped against the couch, snapping the box closed and stuffing it back into his pocket.

"I've never proposed before, but I would think that second thoughts are natural. I mean, it's a big decision." I scrambled, thinking about what to say. A part of me wanted to tell him he was making a mistake, that Amber was nice but not right for him. Yet, it didn't feel like my place. I'd only come back into Ridge's life a few days ago. Who was I to tell him what to do?

But he's asking you. Why not tell him the truth?

"You're probably right. I guess I needed to tell someone. That thing has been burning a hole in my pocket since I bought it." He blew out a long breath before shaking his head, as if hitting a reset button. "You know, once upon a time, I imagined giving you a ring. Funny how much things change. Now I'm going to be marrying an interior designer and becoming part of her family's business."

"Funny." My voice came out strangled.

Abruptly, he pushed up from the couch and headed into the kitchen, clearly closing the door on our previous conversation. "I think I hear some leftovers calling my name. Do you have any pizza left?"

"I've got a better idea." I followed him and opened the freezer. "How about a bowl of ice cream?" Personally, I could eat the entire carton at this point.

"How about both?" Ridge waggled his eyebrows at me.

"Fine. There are a couple of slices in the fridge." I pulled out the bowls while he got out the pizza.

"I have no idea how guys eat so much. If I ate even half of the food you do, I'd make myself sick," I joked, shaking my head to dislodge thoughts of Ridge's impending proposal. I started dishing up the ice cream, desperate for something to distract me.

"It just takes practice." Ridge winked at me as he stuck his pizza in the microwave.

The banter and laughter continued while we finished our food. Ridge decided to call it a night and I walked him out. As I closed the door, my thoughts and regrets surrounded me. *If only I'd gotten that letter sooner. If only Amber wasn't in the picture. If only.*

Desperate for a distraction, I grabbed my roll of painter's tape. I didn't care if it was after midnight or if my home would soon fall victim to Milton Corp's wrecking ball. I needed to work on something, and writing out my feelings wouldn't do it. Besides, just because I taped off the baseboards and ceiling in my bedroom, didn't mean I had to start painting tonight. There would be time later. After Ridge was engaged and out of my life, for good this time.

An hour or so later, I straightened at the sound of Audrey and Chloe outside the condo door. I'd made good progress and would be able to start painting tomorrow. If only I could repair my heart with a few yards of tape.

Maybe talking things out with my roommates would help, even if it meant Audrey's disapproval and Chloe's disappointment. As they pushed the door open, they stumbled into the apartment, giggling like crazy.

I waited a moment, certain they would calm down so we could talk. Instead, they took one look at my confused face and simply laughed harder.

"What is wrong with you two?" My tone was clipped and frustrated, something they seemed not to notice. My world was falling apart, and they were too busy laughing to notice.

"It was just—" Audrey choked off with another peal of laughter.

"At the restaurant, Derek—" Chloe kept laughing.

"He was saying something and then—"

This time Chloe cut Audrey off. "You forgot the part about the golf ball!"

"That came later," Audrey shushed.

I held up my hands, completely confused and annoyed. "Are you sure the two of you don't drink?"

Audrey and Chloe looked at each other, before bursting into laughter once more. With a sigh, I turned around and started for my bedroom. There was no way I could share what was on my mind when they were in this state, and it was late enough that I knew I would regret it if I didn't go to sleep soon. Morning came early.

"I'm calling it a night." I glanced over my shoulder to see the two of them trying to take deep breaths. "You can fill me in on everything in the morning."

"Man, I'm going to miss these moments if we have to move." Chloe's words caused my heart to ache, but I pushed them out of my mind. My dad hadn't decided to sell yet, and I had enough to worry about with the wedding and Ridge without anxiety over Amber's dad's offer.

Closing my door behind me, I walked to the bed and sat down. It had been a long day, and while my body was tired, my emotions continued racing. The time with Ridge had been wonderful. Seeing him again had reawakened feelings I thought were gone.

I reached for my notebook and opened the cover, pulling out Ridge's letter. The familiar words swam before my eyes as I fought back tears. The ring was a clear indication Ridge no longer felt the way he had when he had written the letter. So why should I keep it, a reminder of a moment lost? I should rip it to shreds and burn the pieces, slam the door on the broken-hearted girl whose life would have changed course had the letter come only a few years sooner.

Instead, I tucked it back into the notebook and turned to a blank page, pouring out my heart once more.

Dear Ridge,

I must be a glutton for punishment. Today was pure torture. You showed up on my door offering a ride and shopping advice, but after spending an entire day with you, I'm more confused than ever. I don't think I'm over you, a ridiculous notion given that you're basically engaged.

We had something years ago. You broke my heart. You walked away. I thought the best I could do was forgive you, but after this week...What I feel is more than forgiveness.

You're basically engaged. I've seen the ring! You told me your plans. You asked my advice. So why does my heart seem to think there's still a chance? That my high school dreams might finally come true. Amber is a lucky girl, and I hope she knows it. Because another girl's heart is breaking right now.

Mal

Chapter Twenty-Five

THE NEXT DAY I woke to a stiff, though less swollen, ankle, and a break from wedding prep. I enjoyed the opportunity to sleep in, though a part of me missed waking up to Ridge at my front door. I used the day to finally paint my room. The work was therapeutic, even if it gave me too much time to think about Ridge and how weird it felt not seeing him that day.

Friday I was wide awake by the time someone knocked on my door. I had slept fitfully the night before and felt exhausted. Thoughts of Ridge had danced through my head in the form of strange dreams, including one where I was helping with Ridge and Amber's wedding while my mother chased me around telling me that she'd bought me the house next door to her, dragging a bowling ball-toting mystery man who she claimed was my husband. The dream had left a cold knot of dread in my stomach, and I couldn't shake it off.

I lay in bed for a moment, hoping if I ignored them, whoever was at the door would go away. They didn't. Instead, another knock sounded, forcing me out of bed and into the realities of the day. Today was the rehearsal dinner and bachelorette party. After tonight, my reason for spending time with Ridge would be gone, and I'd go back to my lonely world of home improvement and trying to stop Amber's family from buying my apartment.

Rolling out of bed, I slipped on a sweatshirt and headed to answer the door, tripping on a roll of tape that I'd left in the middle of the living room the night before. Looking through the peephole, I wasn't surprised to see a smiling Ridge with a brown box in his hands. With an odd sense of deja vu, I opened the door.

"What are you doing here?" My voice rasped as I spoke.

"I was in the area and thought I'd stop by," Ridge shrugged. "Can I come in?"

"Sure." I moved out of the doorway and walked into the kitchen, Ridge following behind me. "You know, wedding prep isn't until later."

"I had to run an errand for Amber and stopped at a local bakery for donuts to share." He lifted the box in his hands, and I felt a smile forcing its way to the surface despite my dismal mood.

"A man bearing donuts is always welcome in this apartment," I responded, trying to ignore how those words caused my chest to pinch. I'd gotten a text from my dad sometime in the night mentioning he'd received another offer from Milton Corp. I couldn't help but worry that this apartment's days were numbered.

"Correction, a man in general is welcome." Chloe came from her bedroom completely dressed and looking beautiful. Her pixie cut was perfectly styled is short curls, making me conscious of my bedhead.

"Dig in, I've got plenty."

Chloe took the box from Ridge's hands and pulled off the lid, revealing a dozen square glazed donuts, a style unique to one of the better bakeries in the area. My mouth watered at the sight, and I moved to take one, doing my best to ignore Chloe's obvious attempts to flirt with

Ridge. Chloe was a perpetual flirt and usually didn't realize how her friendly gestures came across, even though we'd try to warn her.

"I see Chloe's in fine form," Audrey whispered from behind me. I turned to see her with Ruby's leash in hand, the dog trying to pull her master to the front door.

I just shrugged. "Want a donut?"

"Maybe when I get back." She slipped out the door, leaving me alone to watch the Chloe and Ridge show unfolding in front of me.

I snapped myself out of staring and walked over to snag a second donut. Its fried, sugary goodness revived me some, making me aware of all the questions I should be asking Ridge right now.

"Not that I don't appreciate starting the day with donuts," I paused to make sure I had his attention, "but what are you doing here? I thought set up wasn't until later."

"I was in the area and thought I'd stop by. I figured if I had donuts, you were less likely to turn me away. Besides, Amber doesn't get back until right before the rehearsal dinner, and I wanted company." He shrugged as if he regularly showed up at girls' homes with donuts in tow.

"I'll take it," Chloe chirped, drawing our attention back to her. I heard the front door open, announcing Audrey's return. The sound was shortly followed by Ruby taking her customary place on the back of my couch.

"Chloe, don't you have class?" Audrey walked into the kitchen and grabbed a donut of her own. "You don't want to be late and miss a quiz...again." Audrey tacked on that last bit when Chloe didn't move from her spot next to Ridge.

"Thanks, Mom." She drew out the words, an eye roll adding emphasis as she glanced at the clock. Panic soon filled her face. "Shoot! I've got to go." Chloe made a dash for the door, leaving us staring after her.

"What kind of cuisine does this qualify as?" I asked, remembering our conversation from the night before.

"I thought you might ask, so I did a bit of research. Any guesses?" Ridge quirked an eyebrow as he looked back and forth between me and Audrey.

Audrey shrugged. "French? Aren't they known for their pastries and desserts?"

Ridge shook his head and looked at me. "Your turn."

"Danish? I think the Danish are also known for their pastries..." I trailed off at the look of triumph on Ridge's face.

"You're both wrong. They're Dutch." His lips quirked in satisfaction as he made his declaration.

"So European, we were on the right track," I reasoned.

"Europe is a big area. The two of you weren't even close," Ridge insisted.

"Close enough. It's not like we guessed Egypt."

"Why would you guess Egypt? Did they find pictures of donuts when they discovered the pyramids? You guys were way off, and you know it." Ridge's words cued an epic stare-down, his blue eyes pulling me in, my heart pounding.

"On that note, I've got to get to work." Audrey grabbed her purse and slipped out the door, but not before shooting me a concerned look.

I glanced down at my feet, remembering that I was still in my pajamas, a pair of faded basketball shorts and an old sweatshirt that I'd grabbed from my floor on the way to answer the door. "I should probably get ready for the day."

I waited for Ridge to excuse himself and slip out the door, leaving me alone to get dressed or possibly return to bed and my wallowing. Instead, he walked over and settled on the couch.

"I'll wait here."

"You sure?"

Ridge let out a puff of air and grinned. "You're leaving me alone with half a dozen donuts. I think I'll be fine."

I quickly showered and got ready, choosing to wear something comfortable for wedding setup.

"What's first on our to-do list?" I asked as I stepped into the living room.

Ridge sat on the couch, typing on his phone.

"What?" His head jerked up, and he gave me a grin. "I wasn't paying attention. I was texting Amber."

"Just curious where we're starting."

"Probably picking up the supplies to finish all the centerpieces." His voice trailed off as his phone dinged and he looked at the screen.

I groaned as I slumped onto the couch next to him. "I hate the craft store."

Ridge looked at me with sympathy in his eyes. "We're almost done. You can do it!"

"Fine, but after this wedding is over, I'm boycotting craft stores for the rest of the summer." I sat a moment longer, trying to find the willpower to move. "Effort sounds hard right now."

Ridge laughed. "Come on, it's not that bad. You got a day off yesterday."

I grabbed a pillow and hid my face behind it. I didn't even bother commenting. Instead, I let my eyes close for a moment and listened to the AC kick on, the cool air making me shiver.

Ridge snatched the pillow from my hands. "No, you don't."

"I'm just resting my eyes." I made a half-hearted attempt to get the pillow back. "Besides, the craft store isn't open yet."

"But the grocery store is, and I have to pick up snacks for the bachelor party tonight."

"I didn't realize you and David were that close."

"We're not, but Kyle invited me to tag along and asked for my help getting ready."

"And that makes it my problem how?"

"Because you still don't have a car, which means I'm your ride. If you want to make it for wedding setup later, then you'd better get your behind in my car. Otherwise, I'm leaving you here, and you'll send Livvy into a panic attack with your absence."

"Fine, but I'm going to complain the entire ride to the store."

"It's two minutes away."

"Your point?" I pushed up from the couch and headed for the door, grabbing my phone from the table. A text from my mother filled the screen, reminding me that I had ignored her almost all day yesterday.

MOTHER: *Call me when you get a chance. I have great news!*

ME: *I'm going to be busy all day. Can it wait?*

MOTHER: *Fine. But call as soon as you can.*

The rest of the morning was spent running errands. Ridge had failed to mention that in addition to buying snacks, he also needed to pick up his suit from the dry cleaner and silly string and window chalk for decorating the car after the reception. I bit my tongue as he stopped at Milton Corp's site to pick up some flyers for Amber, their yellow color familiar from the number of times I'd had to pull them off my tenants' cars. Once we had all his supplies, we stopped at the craft store and grabbed our last few items. With everything loaded into the car, we headed to Orem for wedding setup.

We had just merged onto the freeway when Ridge's phone began ringing. He pulled it from his pocket, glanced down, and grimaced before answering.

"Hello?"

"Rigdon!" Amber's voice carried in the small space, making me flinch.

"Hi, Amber." Ridge kept his eyes trained on the road, though I could see his shoulders hunch towards his ears. "What's up? We just talked a few minutes ago."

I strained my ears to hear what she said, but apparently she'd learned to use a quieter tone of voice within the last thirty seconds.

"I'm busy helping with Livvy's wedding." He paused. "No, I do not have time." Another pause. "Amber, I told you a week ago that I wouldn't be able to pick you up." This time the pause was longer. "That may be true, but it doesn't change the fact that I don't have—" He cut off, and I could hear indistinguishable sounds coming from her end of the line. "Can we not talk about this now?"

After another pause, Ridge said goodbye and hung up. There were no terms of endearment, and the sigh that escaped as he set down his phone made me frown. What was going on? When we'd talked yesterday, he had been ready to propose despite his doubts, but there appeared to be trouble in paradise after all.

"So, Rigdon?" I finally asked, trying to break the uncomfortable silence that filled the car.

"Don't call me that." His voice was tense and not the slightest bit amused. "You know I don't like it."

"I didn't realize. Does that mean it's a special pet name reserved for your almost-fiancée and your mother when you're in trouble?" I was being nosy and I knew it, but the stress I saw on Ridge's face had me concerned.

"I've asked Amber not to call me that." He raised a hand and ran it through his hair. "She claims Rigdon is more professional. She thinks Ridge is juvenile, more the name of a high school jock than a world-class lawyer." His tone was acidic. "Not that I'm doing much as a lawyer yet anyway. My internship is essentially my chance to be a glorified errand boy." He waved a hand towards the box of flyers that I wished I could throw from the car.

I sat in silence a moment longer, considering his words. Taking a deep breath and gathering my courage, I spoke. "If you hate it so much, why do you let her call you that?"

"Dating involves sacrifice. It's about compromise," Ridge ground out.

"Compromise about where you go to dinner and who you eat with, not your name and other parts of your personality."

"I don't expect you to understand. It's not like your past relationships have worked out."

I flinched at his cutting words before responding, my words quiet. "Not that it's my business, but I do know that if the person you're dating doesn't respect you enough to accept your name and career choices, chances are good you shouldn't be dating them. Though maybe I'm wrong. After all, I just have a failed engagement to a cheating, manipulative jerk to base my observations on."

The silence that followed made me immediately regret my words, but I refused to take them back.

"You're right." His voice was clipped and cool, nothing like his usual teasing tone. "It is none of your business."

His words stung, and I bit my lip to keep from responding.

Ridge and I drove the rest of the way in silence. As he pulled to a stop in front of the church, a stone building not far from Livvy's parents' house, I unbuckled my seatbelt and clambered from the car, not waiting for him to put it into park.

Chapter Twenty-Six

I WALKED INTO THE church to find Livvy, wearing jeans and a floral blouse, wringing her hands and gesturing at the gym ceiling. Uncle Ben and Kyle were in the process of stringing lights and tulle in an effort to dress up the utilitarian space. From where I stood, they had their work cut out for them.

"It's not even," Livvy shouted as I walked over. "It needs to be even!"

"Livvy, we'll adjust. We need to get them hung first." Kyle tugged on a string of lights.

"Don't tell me what you need to do first. This is my wedding and—"

"And it's going to look perfect." A deep male voice cut in. I looked over to see David walking towards Livvy, his black hair perfectly styled and his dark brown eyes sparkling with laughter. He looped his arm around Livvy's waist before continuing. "You've got a good team helping you. Trust them to do their job."

I smiled at my future cousin-in-law and his ability to balance out Livvy. His calm counteracted Livvy's energy and tendency towards the dramatic. Not to mention his obsession with sports analogies helped him connect with Kyle and Uncle Ben.

Livvy leaned into him for a moment and sighed. "Everything needs to be perfect. My family will all be here, and your grandma flew all the way from Japan and—"

"Breathe." David rubbed her back. "Everyone is going to love it."

Not wanting to interrupt, I took a step back to give them some privacy.

"Mallory!" Livvy caught sight of me before I could turn and make my way back to the car to help Ridge unload. She stepped away from David and grabbed me in a hug that more resembled a choke hold. "Please tell me you've got everything. I need to know we're ready."

I struggled from her embrace, needing to take a breath before I could respond. "As long as you've got the pictures, we're good."

Her face paled at the words. "The pictures! I forgot the pictures. How could I forget the pictures?" She let go of me and whirled to face David.

"Breathe." David grabbed her shoulders and gave her a gentle shake. "There are several places that print photos within an hour or two. If we place the order now, we'll have plenty of time to pick it up before the dinner tonight."

Livvy took a couple of deep breaths before nodding. "You're right. We've got plenty of time. It's going to be fine." She caught sight of something over my shoulder and took off screeching, "What in the world is that?"

"How are you holding up?" I asked David, touching his arm to keep him from running after her for a moment.

"I can't wait until we're on the plane for Japan. We both need the break." He gestured toward Livvy's retreating back. "I just need to get her to calm down, and everything will be perfect."

"Good luck with that." I laughed slightly. "My advice, take her to pick up the pictures and don't bring her back until tomorrow."

"Good idea." David joined in my laughter for a moment before another screech from Livvy grabbed our attention. "I should check on her."

David took off in the direction of the kitchen, and I headed out to the car to see how Ridge was doing unloading everything. I probably should have stuck around to help him, but my frustration with him still festered. When I got outside, the car was empty and Ridge was nowhere in sight. Heading back into the church, I found our bags stacked against a wall and Ridge helping set up tables. I claimed a table and started unpacking everything.

Another exclamation from Livvy followed by a calming murmur from David had me shaking my head as I worked. David would be good for Livvy. If they could make it through today, the two of them could do anything.

"What are you laughing at?" Ridge asked, coming up beside me. His words were hesitant.

"Just realizing how incredibly lucky Livvy and David are to have found each other." I shrugged. "Is this everything?" I motioned to the supplies in front of me.

"It should be." Ridge rolled his shoulders and stretched for a moment. "You didn't tell me you were bringing me along to act as muscle. Had I known, I would have warmed up first."

I shook my head. "Of course, you're the muscle in this duo. I've got the brains and the looks. I can't provide everything."

"Hey, now. I have lots more to offer this partnership than just muscle."

"That's true." I nodded. "You've also got a car." Our joking felt stilted and forced. We stood for a moment, watching everyone work.

"If we're going to finish before the rehearsal dinner tonight, we'd better get moving." I stepped to the table, ready to assemble the centerpieces. Maybe work would distract me from the strain between us.

Ridge helped me finish unpacking without comment before he left to help Kyle and Uncle Ben.

"Mallory."

I turned to see Aunt Jenna, her hair falling out of its bun, making her way over to me.

"Livvy mentioned you were here. The tablecloths haven't been delivered yet, so you've got a bit of time before we need you."

"Is there anything I can help with?" I gestured to the chaos around me.

"Not unless you have a magic wand that can transform a Pinterest board into reality." She gave a helpless smile and shrugged.

"I wish. That would have made this last week easier."

"You've helped so much."

"I'm glad to do it," I promised, thinking of the time it had given me to spend with Ridge. Despite my recent frustration with him, I'd enjoyed it for the most part. "Are you sure there's nothing else I can do?"

Aunt Jenna thought for a moment and then smiled. "There is one thing."

"Name it." I hoped to find something to distract me from my attractive, infuriating, unavailable assistant.

She reached into her purse, digging around for a moment before pulling out some money and handing it to me. "You can go and take that young man," she gestured to Ridge, "to get ice cream. My treat."

My mind scrambled for a way out. "Are you sure? There's so much to do. You guys clearly need—"

She cut me off. "We clearly need for you to take a break so you can come back here and put together some amazing centerpieces. You've done so much for Livvy this week. Take a break. You deserve it." She patted my arm and walked away, leaving me holding the money.

"What was that about?" Ridge asked as he walked over carrying a bundle of tulle.

"I think we just got kicked out until later." I continued to stare into space for a moment before snapping myself back into reality. "Aunt Jenna gave me money for ice cream and said not to come back until they're ready for us to do the centerpieces."

Ridge forced a smile. "I don't know. It looks like they could really use the help." He gestured to the gym in its state of disrepair.

"That's what I said. Maybe we should—"

"Mallory Ann Roberts, why are you still here?" Aunt Jenna called from across the gym where she stood, directing table placement. "Go! Before I tell your mother you missed out on a perfectly good opportunity to get ice cream with a boy."

"But—"

"No buts. Go have fun." Aunt Jenna made a shooing motion, and I turned to gauge Ridge's reaction.

"I guess that settles it. Ice cream it is." Ridge moved towards the door, not waiting for me to follow. I had a sinking feeling that staying to help with setup might be the more enjoyable activity.

I followed Ridge out to the car, hesitating before climbing in.

"Where do you want to go? There are a couple of places by the mall." Ridge pulled onto the main road and started driving towards University Mall.

"Clarifying question: In your book, does frozen yogurt qualify as ice cream?" I forced enthusiasm into my voice, hoping to lighten the tense atmosphere in the car.

"I think frozen yogurt qualifies."

We decided on a place and the conversation died, the silence as heavy as concrete. If I was lucky, we would get the ice cream to go and get this outing over with quickly. I would not be the first one to apologize. This wasn't on me.

Ridge finally let out a breath. "I'm sorry that I snapped at you." His tone was clipped and made me question its sincerity.

"Me too."

We sat in silence a moment longer before my mouth twitched into a sad grin as a memory flashed into my mind. "Is Amber a big enough Jazz fan that you can commit to her?"

Ridge gave a small chuckle before shaking his head. "A lot has changed since high school. My requirements for a future wife have shifted."

Back in high school, Ridge had gone through an obsession with the Utah Jazz. He watched them every chance he got and swore any girl he pursued would have to be just as committed to the Utah Jazz as he was.

"Apparently." I had a sinking suspicion that sports interests weren't the only thing that had changed for him to consider proposing to Amber.

"You know, I've never asked Amber if she likes the Jazz." Ridge continued to chuckle.

The tension in the car had dissipated some, though the doubts from before lingered in my mind. *Could I really let Ridge pursue a girl so obviously wrong for him?* I wasn't sure I had much of a choice. "In some ways, high school feels like yesterday, and in others, it feels like an eternity ago."

"Right?" Ridge just shook his head. "I feel so old."

"Watch it, Grandpa." I nudged his arm. "If I remember correctly, I'm a few months older than you."

Ridge just shrugged. "Well, if the geriatric shoe fits..."

If he hadn't been driving, I would have slugged him. Instead, I settled for a death glare.

"Do you remember all those trips we took to the rock?" Ridge asked, changing the subject.

"How could I forget? Kyle begged to go every chance he got." The rock was a large boulder in Provo River. The area around the rock was deep enough that you could jump in. Kyle had turned it into a sport, trying to splash people floating the river in inner tubes.

"I remember one time, Kyle splashed this huge, bearded guy. The guy was so mad he got out of the river and chased us all the way back to the car." Ridge was laughing again.

"I don't remember that." My eyebrows pinched together as I thought back to those summers filled with frequent sleepovers at Livvy's house.

"I don't think you were there. It was mid-July, and we still hadn't been to the rock yet. Kyle was dying to get into the water, and I finally agreed after a solid week of him begging to go every day. It took us a good month to get up the guts to go back."

I laughed, picturing Ridge and Kyle, two strong, buff teenagers, scared to return to their favorite place.

"We had a lot of good times. I never thought they would end," I said, as we pulled into the parking lot.

"Me neither," Ridge agreed.

This was my moment. I could tell him about how I'd hated him for so long, but how my view of him had changed and...And what? Ridge was going to propose to Amber and then return to Idaho at the end of summer to finish school. Even if Amber wasn't in the picture, we would still have hundreds of miles between us. Besides, what if we went on that date he'd asked for in his letter, decided we were better off friends, and called it quits? I would have muddied up his relationship with Amber for nothing. In some ways, everything had changed from high school, but really it wasn't that different. Distance and timing still stood between us.

So, I kept quiet, letting Ridge direct the conversation to safer topics that didn't involve risking heartbreak. Yet, I still felt something splinter with the decision.

Ridge pulled the car into a parking spot, and we climbed out, heading into the shop. I looked around and took in the bright pink and green decor in addition to the flavor options lining one wall. We were the only customers in the store. Grabbing sample cups, I gave the cashier a nod and headed for the soft serve machines, Ridge following behind me.

"Where to start?" I muttered to myself. The flavor options included the classics, chocolate and vanilla, in addition to some more adventurous flavors like lemonade and cotton candy. My eyes landed on cheesecake and brownie batter, and I smiled, knowing I'd found what I wanted.

Ridge had already used his sample cups and was reaching for his main bowl.

"What are you getting?" I filled one sample cup with lemonade frozen yogurt, just to try it.

"I'm going to get a little bit of everything." He moved to the first dispenser.

I watched Ridge put a small strip of frozen yogurt into his cup before moving to the next dispenser and working his way down the line. It resulted in a rainbow of colors, but made my stomach turn as I considered the mixed flavors. Brownie batter, mango, cotton candy, cheesecake—no thank you!

I tried a couple more flavors before filling my bowl with cheesecake and a little brownie batter. I then added my favorite toppings: crushed cookies, peanut butter cups, brownie pieces, and cheesecake squares. I smiled, thinking of all the sugary goodness waiting for me.

Ridge was waiting at the register, and I pulled out the money Aunt Jenna had given me, using it to pay for both bowls. We then settled at a table next to the window.

"This is heaven." I took the first bite of my yogurt.

"Agreed." Ridge nodded, and I cringed as I watched him spoon both chocolate and lemonade frozen yogurt into his mouth.

"Doesn't that taste funky?"

He continued to nod. "A little, but in a good way."

I made a gagging face, sticking out my tongue and widening my eyes. "It looks and sounds awful."

"Want a bite?" He used his spoon to scoop some yogurt from the middle where so many flavors had mixed that the yogurt came out a funny brown color.

I shuddered and shook my head. "I'll stick with my safe chocolate cheesecake combo." I raised my bowl for emphasis.

"But that's no fun." Ridge waved his spoon in front of me. "Be brave. You might find you like it."

"What is this, the frozen yogurt version of *Green Eggs and Ham*?" I laughed, trying to dodge his spoon as it moved closer to me. "I do not like mixed yogurt, man. I do not like it, I'm not a fan." I stuttered, trying to come up with a catchy rhyme to encompass my feelings.

Ridge burst out laughing. "That's terrible," he groaned. "But you know how that book ends, don't you?"

"I'm pretty sure he stubbornly refuses, and we're left with an appreciation for his determination," I fibbed, wishing I'd never mentioned the book.

"Nice try. What can it hurt? I can put a scoop in your bowl, if you'd prefer."

I snatched my bowl off the table, protecting my chocolate-cheesecake deliciousness. There was no way I was going to let him tarnish my perfection in a bowl.

"Then I'll just come over and..." Ridge made to stand, and I gave in.

"Fine." I surrendered, holding my hand out for the spoon. "You win."

Ridge gave a satisfied smile but refused to hand over the spoon. "Not so fast. I want to make sure you actually eat it and don't dump it in the trash. Now, open up."

I slowly opened my mouth and watched warily as Ridge spoon fed me the brown, melty disaster. I winced as the flavor hit my taste buds.

"That's awful," I choked out, standing to refill the water cup I'd grabbed earlier. I continued to gag as I waited for the cup to fill and then downed it before refilling it again. Ridge stayed at our table, laughing at my pain. "How could you do that to me?" I made my way back to the table, the taste finally gone.

"I don't think it's that bad." He shrugged. "Besides, now you know you don't like it. Isn't that better than stubbornly refusing to try something?"

"No, no it's not." I shuddered at the memory of the vile taste.

Ridge just smiled and took another bite.

"How can you keep eating that?"

Ridge shrugged and continued spooning the disaster-in-a-bowl into his mouth. I settled back into my chair and picked up my bowl, grateful it was still half full. I was going to need every bite to erase the memory of that taste.

When we'd both finished, we sat a moment. The tension from earlier was finally gone, but I couldn't quite forget the hurtful words. Ridge had confirmed what I'd been telling myself all week, so why did it hurt so much? Why did I care if he wanted to marry a girl who wanted to change him and didn't see his value? It wasn't my problem. Ridge had made that clear.

I was debating if we needed to head back to the church when my phone rang. Glancing at the screen, I saw that it was the auto shop. I answered, fingers crossed that it was good news.

"Your car is ready for pick up." The cheerful voice on the other end informed me.

"Wow. I didn't realize it would be done so soon. I'll be right over. Thank you." I ended the call, a huge smile on my face. I was ready to be able to drive again and put distance between me and Ridge.

"Do you mind dropping me off at the repair shop? My car's done," I informed Ridge.

"That's great. Of course, I'll take you." Ridge pushed to standing, picking up our garbage as he went.

The drive to the shop was quick. In a few short minutes, I was walking to my parked car, keys in hand, ready to drive.

"It looks great," I observed as I circled to the back of the car and took in my perfectly shaped and painted bumper.

Ridge ran his hand along the bumper and nodded his head. "They did a good job."

"Thank you for being my chauffeur." Only an hour earlier, I would have hugged him as I spoke the words but felt I'd be out of line now. "But no offense, I'm so happy to be able to drive again."

"It was my pleasure." Ridge patted me on the shoulder in an odd side hug. "But does this mean I have to drive to the other wedding festivities alone?"

I shrugged. "Do you really want to drive out to Pleasant Grove and back every time you need to pick me up or drop me off? This will make things a lot easier for you." And for my traitorous heart. "Besides, won't Amber be back?"

Ridge dipped his head in a self-conscious gesture that looked strange on him. "I didn't mind. It was nice to catch up with an old friend."

His sincere words gave me pause and I looked up into his face, unsure of how to read what I saw there. He almost looked disappointed that our forced time together was coming to an end, despite our latest argument. I shook my head, sure that it was just wishful thinking.

"I've enjoyed being with you too."

An awkward silence filled the space between us, and I scuffed my toe in the dirt, unsure what to say next.

"Anyway." Ridge broke the silence. "I guess we'd better get back to the church. Those centerpieces won't assemble themselves."

I nodded and climbed into my car, surprised to feel a hint of disappointment mixed in with my celebration.

Chapter Twenty-Seven

THE CHURCH PARKING LOT had emptied, and I took the opportunity to circle the lot a couple of times, reveling in the ability to drive again. I kept rubbing my hands along the steering wheel as I blasted the AC and the radio, shivering as the cool air hit my skin. How I'd missed my country music.

When I walked into the gym, Ridge was looking over the stacks of centerpiece materials we'd deposited. I stood next to him, taking everything in. The gym looked like a completely different place, and it wasn't finished yet. Kyle and Uncle Ben were still making adjustments, but the tulle and lights draped from the ceiling looked incredible, giving everything a softer feel. Tablecloths had been placed on all the tables, and Aunt Jenna was in the process of bedecking chairs with ribbon and tulle bows, giving the folding chairs a fancier feel.

"Wow," I breathed, shocked at how the combination of peach and silver made the room feel soft and romantic. "This is beautiful."

Aunt Jenna spotted us and rushed over, wrapping an arm around each of us. "Perfect timing. We've finished all the groundwork, and we're ready for your details. David even brought back the photos, though he had to lock Livvy in the car to keep her from coming inside. I promised she could review everything tomorrow before the reception, but she's not allowed back until then."

"We've got this," I assured her.

I decided to start by putting the pictures into their frames. I'd told Livvy that we would need one picture per table with maybe a couple extras. Instead of printing 12 to 20 pictures, Livvy had printed a huge stack that would take forever to sort.

Ridge and I sat at a table, trying to find a variety of photos that depicted Livvy and David's love. I propped up my ankle, trying to help with swelling. While it felt much better, it was still a bit stiff at times.

"Definitely this one." Ridge held up a photo of Livvy in her wedding dress, hands on hips, glaring at the camera.

I giggled. "Only if you want her to turn that look on you."

"Luckily, looks can't kill." Ridge put the photo in his top picks pile. We'd decided that we'd each take half of the stack and select our top choices. Once we had two smaller stacks, we'd work together to pick the best of the bunch to fill the 12 waiting frames.

As I looked through photos from Livvy and David's engagement shoot, my heart warmed. Seeing the obvious love and joy on both of their faces reassured me they were meant for each other. David looked at Livvy like she was his whole world, a look that the photographer had captured in a gorgeous mountain setting filled with spring growth.

I finished with the engagement shots and started in on the bridals, admiring Livvy's dress. It reminded me of a princess ball gown with a full skirt, lace, and sparkling beads. It was bold but still beautiful and classy. Her hair was curled and pinned up with a tiara, not a veil, resting on her head. She looked like a fairytale princess, and David, who'd joined her in later photos, looked like her handsome prince.

"Makes you think about getting married, doesn't it?" I thought of my desire for a family and home in light of my abysmal dating life. I thought I was closer to at least part of that, a home to call my own for longer than a few months, but I could feel it slipping through my fingers.

"For sure. If all goes according to plan tomorrow, this will be me and Amber in a couple of months." Ridge continued to look through his stack of photos.

I froze. I'd known it was coming, so why did it hurt so much?

"I wish you both the best." I couldn't keep a note of sadness from creeping into my voice.

"What are those misty eyes for?" Ridge's words made me jump, and I moved to dab the tears away that I hadn't realized were filling my eyes.

"Just thinking about how happy they are and how I hope to find that for myself someday." I hedged, not wanting to share my true thoughts.

"I know that feeling, but you'll get there. I promise." He gave my arm a squeeze and went back to looking through pictures. "If you're lucky, you'll find someone who can make this face." Ridge held up a picture of David, lips puckered with his cheeks puffed out and his eyes crossed, Livvy unaware and smiling at the camera. I laughed and grabbed the photo, adding it to my top picks pile. They needed a few funny pictures on the tables to balance out all the gushy, picture-perfect romance we would be using.

Ridge and I debated over photos for longer than necessary, knowing Livvy would examine everything with a critical eye. Finally, we had our top 12 photos, the one of David with his cheeks puffed out included.

Once the frames were filled, we arranged the centerpieces, getting Aunt Jenna's sign-off before calling it a day.

"They look perfect." She walked from table to table, looking over the details. At one table she stopped to adjust a picture frame before moving to the next table to straighten a tea light. She made a few more minor adjustments before standing and giving me a hug. "Livvy is going to love this."

"We stuck the floral arrangements in that box to keep them from getting lost." I gestured behind me against one of the walls. "I figure you can take it with you for photos tomorrow. The bridesmaids' scarves are in there too."

"Perfect." Aunt Jenna gave me another hug before turning to give Ridge one. "Thank you, you two. You've done an amazing job. I don't know what we would have done without you."

"You would have figured something out." Ridge shrugged before looping his arm around my shoulders. "But it wouldn't have looked nearly this good."

I laughed before stepping away. He needed to stop this casual contact. It was making my insides leap and jump like a gymnastics routine.

He's taken, I chanted to myself, over and over. Hoping that at some point my head would get the message through to my heart. I worried that I was headed straight for heartbreak, but I wasn't sure there was anything I could do to avoid it.

Glancing at her watch, Aunt Jenna gasped. "We need to get out of here if we're going to make it in time for the dinner. You two go ahead."

Leaving the church, I drove home to shower and change. My phone rang as I started up the steps to my apartment. I looked at my phone to see my mother's face filling the screen. In all the wedding excitement I'd forgotten to call her. She was coming down for the dinner tonight and I'd assumed she could talk to me there.

Taking a deep breath, I answered. "Hi, Mother."

"Don't be mad." Her voice rang out of the phone, and I immediately went on the defensive.

"That's a terrible way to start a conversation," I said, dread building in my chest.

"Do you remember Florence's nephew, Jefferson?" I didn't. I barely remembered that Florence was her next-door neighbor. Not that it mattered. She didn't wait for a response. "He just got back from a trip to Connecticut or Colorado or something, and he'll be in Provo tonight."

"That's nice. I hope he enjoys being back in Utah," I said, still unsure how this connected to me.

"He doesn't have any plans tonight, so Florence and I decided that he should come to the dinner, and then, if everything goes well, he could be your plus-one tomorrow."

I almost dropped my phone. My mother loved to interfere. She was a professional meddler, and I brushed it off because I knew she worried. But this was a new low for her. She'd set me up on terrible blind dates, given my phone number to complete strangers, and pushed me to ask out guys I wasn't remotely interested in, but in all those instances I'd had a choice. I could say no to the blind dates, ignore the phone calls, and refuse to ask the guys out despite her pestering. This was the first time she'd taken me out of the decision-making process entirely.

"Excuse me?" Maybe I had heard her wrong.

"I got you a date for the wedding." She sounded excited and completely unaware of just how big of a problem this was.

"No."

"What do you mean, no?"

"I'm not going on a date with him." I forced as much steel into my voice as I could.

"But I already told him you would." She sounded puzzled.

"That's too bad. I guess you should have asked me first."

After the emotional turmoil of the last week, I was done. I had no control over the Ridge situation, but I did have control here, and I would not give into my mother this time.

"Mal-bear, don't be ridiculous. He's planning on being there. What am I supposed to—"

"I don't know, Mother. I guess he can be your date. Good luck telling Dad." I hung up and turned my phone to airplane mode, knowing that she would call back.

I moved into the bathroom and stripped out of my clothes. I placed my phone on the counter, turned up the volume, and selected a playlist full of rock music with heavy beats. Audrey would be proud. Hopefully the hot water and angry music would dispel my emotions before the bachelorette party tonight.

Chapter Twenty-Eight

I PULLED INTO THE restaurant parking lot a few minutes late, but I felt the improvement in my appearance, with soft curls framing my face and eyeliner highlighting my eyes, was worth it. Smoothing my hands down my flowy teal skirt, I took a deep breath, trying to steady my emotions. Between my interfering mother, my bridezilla cousin, and my off-limits crush, my nerves were fraying, on the verge of snapping. Luckily, Audrey and Chloe were both good friends with Livvy and would be a part of tonight's festivities. Hopefully, they would help me keep my sanity.

I walked into the restaurant and followed the hostess to the backroom I'd reserved weeks before. The large room was filled with people visiting in clusters on the sides with a large banquet table down the middle. I was greeted with a variety of sounds, including a very loud, "Honey!"

I looked up to find my mother, her hair feathered to perfection, racing towards me. She was dressed to the nines in a shoulder-padded pantsuit I'd been begging her to retire since I was in high school. A neatly dressed young man in gray slacks and a green button-down shirt trailed behind her.

"Mother?" I stumbled back as she threw her arms around me, giving me a hug instead of the lecture I expected.

"I'm glad you made it. Better late than never, I guess. After you hung up on me, I wondered if you would show." She stared me down for a moment, but I refused to squirm. She was the one out of line. Finally, she turned to the man behind her. "Let me introduce you to Jefferson. I know you said you didn't need a date, but even Ridge brought someone." My breath hitched at her words. "You remember Ridge, right? He and Kyle used to be such good friends."

She grabbed my hand and tugged me in the direction of the guy behind her, not giving me time to process that Ridge was here with Amber.

"Jefferson, this is my daughter, Mallory. Isn't she gorgeous? And she's completely single. Hasn't had a boyfriend in over a year," Mother babbled, making me want to run away. Sanding all the paint off my walls by hand would be less painful than this. "Mallory, this is Jefferson. We were talking while we waited, and the two of you have a lot in common."

Jefferson gave me a smile, and I took in the attractive man in front of me. He was average height, maybe an inch or two taller than me, with thick brown hair, high cheekbones, and glasses. He had the build of an office worker and looked like the kind of guy I'd normally go for, if my head and heart weren't so tangled up in Ridge.

"Oh, there's Jenna. I've got to say thank you for the invite. Livvy will only have one pre-wedding dinner in her life, if she's lucky, and I'm glad to be a part of it." That was my mother, simultaneously celebrating and criticizing as she spoke.

"Mother, it will be her only pre-wedding dinner. She and David are perfect together." I tried to defend my cousin.

"Well, you never know these days. Especially when someone has a strong personality like Livvy. Any number of things could happen. But we'll all hope this will be the only one and act surprised if she has a second." My mother brushed my concerns away, acting as if talking about divorce was completely normal the night before someone's wedding. I was grateful Livvy stood on the other end of the room and couldn't hear my mother at this moment. "Anyway, got to go." With that, my mother disappeared, leaving me alone with Jefferson.

"So..." My mind drew a blank as I tried to find a way out of this situation. "Sorry for the unconventional introduction. Your mother assured me you knew I was coming, but based on that little exchange, I'm guessing that wasn't the case," Jefferson said, his voice surprisingly deep. He smiled as he spoke, confirming my perception that he was a nice guy.

"Unfortunately, that's how Mother works," I laughed, shaking my head at the absurdity of the situation. Not only had my mother brought me a date, if first impressions were any indication, she'd picked a good one.

"Mallory!" I felt an arm slide around my waist and turned to see Chloe standing next to me with Audrey right behind her. "I wondered where you were hiding. Who's your friend?" Chloe batted her eyes at Jefferson, going into full flirtation mode.

"This is Jefferson, my mother's neighbor's nephew. Jefferson, these are my roommates, Chloe and Audrey."

Jefferson gave them a friendly "hello" and the conversation began to flow naturally as we each discussed careers and hometowns. I played it safe, choosing "Davis County" as opposed to explaining how frequently my family had moved growing up.

"How do you know Livvy and David?" Chloe questioned when an opening presented itself.

"I don't," he said, looking sheepish. "I'm a little bit of a wedding crasher tonight."

"Oh." Audrey's single word was bursting with surprise.

"My mother decided I needed help finding a date tonight." I supplied with a shrug, pretending it no longer rankled. She and I would be having a serious conversation about boundaries when the wedding was over.

Audrey turned wide eyes my direction while Chloe continued to smile and flirt.

"Lucky for us, then! I love meeting people at weddings."

I looked around the room, attempting to listen to the conversation as I searched for a familiar head of curly brown hair and blue eyes that spoke to my soul. Ridge stood a few feet away looking gorgeous in slacks and a burgundy polo, Amber standing at his side. My heart hammered, picking up speed at the sight of him. I was in trouble.

A jab in the ribs from Audrey brought me back to the conversation in front of me.

"Earth to Mallory. I don't know if you noticed, but you have a very attractive, *available* man currently standing in front of you, and you're completely ignoring him," Audrey whispered, nodding towards Jefferson.

"I know, but—"

"No 'buts.' Ridge has a girlfriend, and for once in your life, it looks like your mom may have set you up with a good guy. Don't you think Jefferson deserves a shot?"

The earnest expression on Audrey's face brought me back to reality. She was right. I wasn't going to throw away this opportunity. I nodded, turning back to the conversation.

"Fascinating!" Chloe exclaimed. I had no idea what had warranted such enthusiasm, but Jefferson seemed to appreciate the attention.

"Um, Chloe, I think I need a glass of water. Walk with me?" Audrey slipped her arm through Chloe's, pulling her away and leaving me alone with my date.

"Your roommates seem nice," Jefferson observed as they walked away.

"They're the best." I took a deep breath and pushed on, committing to this moment and conversation. I would leave with no regrets tonight. "You mentioned that you're working on your master's. What are you—"

"Mallory!" Amber cooed, cutting off my question as she and Ridge rushed over. She gave me a hug, and I stiffened. "Who's your friend?"

"This is my date, Jefferson...I'm sorry. I don't think I know your last name." I laughed, trying to cover my embarrassment. I watched Ridge's eyebrows scrunch together as he looked back and forth between Jefferson and me.

"Miller." Jefferson shook hands with them, ever the polite guy. "I just met Mallory tonight, thanks to some family meddling, but I can already tell she's an amazing woman."

I felt my cheeks heat at the compliment.

"She is awesome. This wedding would have fallen apart without her." Ridge gave me a nod, staring at me, his eyes intense and filled with...admiration?

"It's great that you were able to make it back in time for the dinner, Amber. That was such a short trip."

"Well, I finished my business, and I couldn't leave this guy alone at a wedding. Someone might try snatching him up." She wrapped her arm around Ridge's waist, looking up at him with a smile. "When she heard I'd be back in time, Livvy was kind enough to invite me to the bachelorette party tonight too. She didn't want me to be alone since she'd talked David into inviting Ridge to the bachelor party."

"That's great," I lied, gritting my teeth into a smile. It wasn't enough that I had to navigate a blind date with my mother watching, but now I had to watch Amber and Ridge through dinner and then play nice with Amber afterward.

"I can't wait for the bachelorette party. Pedicures and pajamas are right up my alley." Amber gave me a huge smile, though it felt fake. Almost as if...she saw me as a threat. Which was ridiculous, wasn't it? Ridge was about to propose. How could I possibly threaten that relationship if he was ready to take the next step?

"I came home from setting up the reception to find her waiting at my mom's house so we could drive over together," Ridge commented, his lips curving in a smile.

Was it just me, or was that smile forced? I shook my head, certain I was reading too much into the situation.

"What can I say? I love my Rigdon." Amber stood on tiptoe and planted a smacking kiss on his cheek, leaving a faint pink spot from her lipstick.

Thankfully, Livvy chose that moment to tell everyone to take their seats.

Sitting through dinner was more torturous than watching paint dry. Sitting next to Jefferson proved the highlight. He was a great conversationalist, and had it been any other event, I likely would have given him my phone number and asked him to call. Instead, I was too busy battling my emotions to focus on the date next to me. Ridge and Amber sat across from us, the two of them the definition of a gag-worthy couple. She kept running her hands through his hair, laughing at everything he said, and sharing her food. I nearly begged them to get married tomorrow and make it a double wedding. Anything to end the spectacle. Interspersed through it all, Amber made comments about how cute a couple we made and how lucky I was to have found Jefferson in time for tonight. As the meal came to a close, I excused myself and slipped outside for some fresh air. I leaned against the restaurant's patio railing, taking in the warm June night, trying to tell myself that the evening could only get better.

"There you are." I looked over to find Jefferson walking towards me, his keys in hand.

"Sorry, I needed a moment. I was starting to feel a bit claustrophobic." I flipped my hair over my shoulder and forced a smile, attempting to at least not make *his* list of worst dates ever.

"Understandable. I don't know how I'd handle being blindsided by a date at a family wedding, especially with my ex, or whatever Ridge is, also in attendance." Jefferson leaned on the railing next to me, looking straight into my face. "Unless I'm reading that entire situation wrong."

I paused before shaking my head. Maybe, if I told someone my true feelings, they would fade and I could move on. "Ridge and I never dated, but he broke my heart once. We basically spent the entire week together and now...now I think he's stolen my heart again."

The words felt odd on my tongue after being bottled up for so long, but the relief I felt at saying them was intense.

"Wow, that is quite the blow. Does he know how you feel?"

"No. He's got a soon-to-be fiancée. It would just complicate things."

Jefferson reached over and squeezed my hand, a gesture of comfort more than anything else. "For what it's worth, sometimes our biggest regrets are the things we don't say as opposed to the things we do."

"It sounds like you know from experience."

Jefferson shrugged and let go of my hand. "You could say that."

I nodded, not feeling like I could push for more details. "I'll take that into consideration."

"I'm headed out. It was nice meeting you, Mallory. If you choose not to speak up or things don't work out with Ridge, give me a call. I think we could be good friends."

I gave Jefferson a hug and waved as he walked away. I'd just given up a perfectly good, available guy for an unavailable high school daydream. My mother was going to kill me.

Chapter Twenty-Nine

DECIDING THAT IF JEFFERSON was finished with the dinner, I could be too, I started the long walk to my car at the back of the parking lot. I could use a moment to breathe before the bachelorette party began.

"Mallory!" Mother's voice behind me forced me to stop a few feet from my car. "I can't believe you're leaving already. And where's Jefferson? Don't tell me you abandoned him back there."

"Jefferson just left, Mother."

"Why did you let him go? The dinner's still going strong. Did you at least get his number? If this is how you behave after I've provided you with a date, no wonder you're still single. And there's the perfect house for sale just down the street from your father and me." She stopped to stand beside me, grabbing my arm before dropping it like she'd been scalded. She'd grabbed my scarred arm, her fingers brushing against the bumps and ridges that she did her best to pretend didn't exist.

"Can we not do this right now?" I asked, exhaustion filling my voice as I pinched the bridge of my nose. I could feel the pressure building behind my eyes, an indication of an oncoming mother-induced headache if I didn't get a Dr. Pepper soon, preferably of the slushy variety.

"You're not getting out of this that easy, young lady." With her hands on her hips, Mother could have passed for an 80s professional despite her deflating hair. It had gone from a towering mass of blond to a lopsided lump.

"Are you talking about the date I didn't agree to and wanted nothing to do with?" I shot back.

"His name is Jefferson and—"

"And what? We 'have a lot in common' so he and I will make a 'perfect' fit? He'll rescue me from my life of singleness and give me a life of wedded bliss safely ensconced a few houses away from you?" My voice rose with each word. I glanced around, grateful to find we didn't have an audience. I'd never been so grateful to park far from the entrance of a restaurant before in my life.

"It's a possibility," Mother huffed.

"You don't get it. Did you actually talk to him? Ask him any questions and allow him to answer? I bet I know more about Jefferson from our first two minutes of conversation than you do, and you set me up with him."

"Then you're off to a great start."

"A great start for friendship, yes, but that's it. Though if we talk again, it can be about how we're both single with meddling family members who won't butt out of our lives." I let the words fly, reveling in the feeling of release. I couldn't fix things with Ridge, but I could certainly face my mother. "You think I'm some miserable, lonely, sad excuse for a person living an incomplete life in a rundown apartment. Ever since the accident, you've wanted to shelter me and protect me. You've wanted to shield me, something that you can't do, even if I marry the man you choose and move in next door. Life still happens. Accidents occur. People get hurt. You can't protect me from everything, Mom. No matter how much you may want to!" I folded my arms across my chest, hiding the scar she hated so much.

I had finally found the words to silence my mother. She stood motionless, mouth agape. I pretended that the sheen in her eyes wasn't tears and turned towards my car.

"Maybe if you took a minute to hear what I actually want in life and stopped trying to make my world picture-perfect, you'd know that I'm happy. That I love my life and don't need your protection."

I finished the trek to my car and climbed in, dashing the tears from my eyes as I backed out of my spot and drove away.

I drove to the nearest drink shop and ordered a Dr. Pepper filled with raspberry and cream. I focused on the burn of soda with each swallow as I drove down random neighborhood streets, careful to avoid a certain park with its swings and memories of first kisses, trying to cool off before the party. If I could have backed out and gone home, I would have, but I knew Livvy was depending on me to make the night special.

The street in front of Aunt Jenna's house was full of cars by the time I arrived for Livvy's bachelorette party. Grabbing my purse and pajamas, I climbed the porch steps and rang the bell. I'd spent so many nights in this house that it felt surreal being back for one more party.

"Come in," Aunt Jenna greeted as she opened the door. "The girls are all downstairs. I think I heard something about facials."

Laughter filtered up the stairs, and I headed towards the sound, pasting a smile on my face and hoping that a night with the girls would erase my personal drama.

"Mallory!" Livvy called as soon as I entered the basement. "Where have you been? I was worried you'd miss all the fun."

"I just had an errand to run." I didn't want to talk about the struggle with my mother right now, so instead I held up my Styrofoam cup as proof.

Audrey and Chloe gave me questioning looks from where they stood near the food table, and I shook my head. Tonight was about Livvy. My fight with my mother could wait.

"You're here now, and that's what matters." Amber called from where she sat on the couch. Her face was covered in a light blue face mask, her hair clipped up in a lopsided mess on her head. In my opinion, it was the best she'd ever looked.

I quickly changed into my pajamas and joined in the fun. I painted my toenails while I listened to the girls quiz Livvy about her honeymoon plans. They were flying to Japan for two weeks to meet David's extended family. The evening passed in a junk food, pampering haze, and the ache in my heart eased as I forgot about my mess of a personal life.

"Time for the best part," Livvy called as the activities wound down. "Who's up for Truth or Dare?"

Several girls groaned.

"We're not 12 anymore," one of Livvy's bridesmaids said with a laugh.

"Besides, what would we dare?" Chloe asked. "We're adults. Anything even remotely interesting would be illegal."

"Fine," Livvy replied, her lips still quirked in a grin. "How about we just play Truth?"

I hesitated, worried where the conversation might go, but when everyone, agreed I knew there was no way out. Instead, I settled on the couch between Audrey and Chloe and hoped the game would quickly lose its appeal.

"I'll go first, since I'm the bride." Livvy tapped her finger on her chin as she looked over the group before settling on someone. "All right, Cami," a red-headed girl I vaguely recognized from Livvy's high school photos jumped. "Who was your first kiss?"

Cami turned bright red before ducking her head. Finally, she responded. "Ian Evans."

A shriek escaped the group, more questions following. Cami simply shook her head. "I'm not giving details. It's someone else's turn to answer a question."

The game continued for several minutes with questions ranging from first kisses to worst dates and beyond. I had started to relax when Amber was asked a question.

The questioner was Kristy, a petite Native American girl Livvy had met in college. "We all saw you with the gorgeous Ridge Matthews. How serious are you two?"

The other girls nodded and turned to watch Amber as she answered.

Amber, who had since washed off the mask and returned her hair to some semblance of normal, smiled. "Well, nothing's official, but I have a feeling it's about to become a permanent situation."

The other girls gasped and clapped their hands. Amber beamed under the attention.

"You're so lucky." This came from a brunette whose name I couldn't remember.

"Any idea when it'll be official?" Chloe asked, shifting closer to me on the couch.

"It could happen any day." Amber gave a delicate shrug. "We did some ring shopping a couple weeks back. Ridge has excellent taste."

The other girls shrieked and cheered as I sat back, trying to forget the large diamond ring Ridge had shown me. A rushing sound, like the buzzing of a saw, filled my ears, drowning out the conversation.

"Mallory?" Amber pulled me from my thoughts.

All the girls were watching me, curious looks on their faces.

"Sorry. I wasn't paying attention. What did you say?"

"It's your turn to answer a question." Amber gave me a wide grin and I felt my stomach clench. "Tell us the story of your first kiss."

I paused a moment, debating. I could lie. I could write Ridge out of my life right now. Ignore the past. If he was marrying Amber anyway, did it really matter? But then Jefferson's words about regretting the things left unsaid filled my mind. Maybe it was time to live with one less regret.

I looked over to see Livvy watching me, her eyebrows pinched together in concern. She was the only person in the room, outside of my roommates, who knew the story. She understood my hesitation, but I wasn't hesitating anymore.

"It was prom, my senior year of high school." Each word brought me closer to the big reveal. The tension in the room built, as if the others could tell this was more than a simple first kiss story. "After the dance, we drove to a park and sat on the swings, watching the stars. When we stood up, he pulled me close and kissed me. It felt like a movie."

"You never told us his name," Kristy observed.

"Who was it?" Cami asked.

Looking right at Amber, I spoke. "Ridge Matthews."

Chapter Thirty

Hours later, after everyone left, I sprawled on the couch in Aunt Jenna's basement, Livvy sitting next to me. After revealing that Ridge had been my first kiss, the game of Truth had quickly lost its appeal, and we'd settled in for a chick-flick marathon. Audrey and Chloe stuck by my side the rest of the party, shielding me from Amber's double threat of death glares and whispered barbs. They refused to leave until Amber was gone. I'd kept my phone on silent, hoping to avoid my mother as well, a decision that proved unnecessary. Apparently, she had decided to give me the silent treatment.

Now I sat in the stillness of a basement I knew better than my parents' current home. The worn brown sofas and piles of homemade quilts had witnessed many a movie night and sleepover. It was weird to think that tonight would be our last one with Livvy as a single woman.

Despite the familiar setting, the events of the evening continued to play through my head. Amber's look of complete anger and betrayal played in my mind, bringing with it feelings of both triumph and trepidation.

"Did I make a mistake?" I muttered, turning my head to look at where Livvy sat next to me.

"By telling Amber about your first kiss?" A yawn accompanied Livvy's question.

"Yes, and by spending so much time with Ridge."

Livvy stayed quiet, long enough that I lifted my head to watch her. Her brow was pinched and her lips pursed as she considered her response.

"I don't think so. It's about time you let all these emotions out. You've kept your feelings about Ridge secret for so long."

I choked down a laugh. "That's funny, coming from you, Miss Hide-My-Letter-To-Protect-Me."

"I had the best of intentions!" Livvy sat up and threw her pillow at me. I managed to knock it down before it hit me in the face, but it knocked over an abandoned bowl of popcorn in the rebound.

"It still hurt. Didn't you trust me to make good decisions?" I rolled to the floor and began picking up the scattered kernels.

Livvy joined me in my cleanup efforts, pausing before responding. "It had nothing to do with trusting you. I wanted to protect you, especially after the accident."

Silence filled the basement as we worked. We finished with the popcorn, and I moved to the random pink plastic cups scattered around the basement.

"You don't know what it was like to watch you. When Ridge ghosted you...you turned inward and faded. I could barely get you to come visit, let alone go out and do things that summer, even after your arm was healed. When that letter arrived, you'd just started college, and I was getting you back. You started dating and going to movies and dances again, stopped hiding your scar. I was getting my best friend back. I didn't know what that letter said, so I stuck it in my yearbook and pushed it out of my mind." Livvy collapsed back on the couch, covering her face with her hands. "Please don't hate me. I thought I was doing the right thing."

I set the cups on a side table and settled on the couch, my arm around Livvy's back.

"I could never hate you. I'll admit, I was angry at first. There are so many *what-ifs* when it comes to Ridge. But I can't let my past continue to limit my chance for happiness."

Livvy leaned back, resting her head on my shoulder.

"When did you get so wise?"

I laughed at the absurdity of her question. "I guess it comes with time and heartbreak."

We continued to sit there, basking in the last few moments before we went to bed and everything changed tomorrow.

"Ridge was mad at me, you know. After he found out about everything. He stormed over here and called me out."

I glanced at Livvy's expression. Her face was carefully neutral, as if waiting for my reaction before showing any emotion.

"I can't really blame him. I was pretty angry myself."

"I tried to make it up to you! Why else do you think I bailed on almost all of our plans this week? I was giving you and Ridge a chance to talk."

I wanted to whack the earnest expression from her face with a throw pillow. "You mean you ignored all my phone calls and forced me to spend *hours* alone with Ridge so you could feel better about not passing on a letter? How was that supposed to fix anything?"

"I don't know. It seemed like a good idea at the time. And I really was busy."

I shook my head, uncertain how to respond. It seemed my mother wasn't the only meddler in the family.

"I found it interesting, though. If he's as committed to their relationship as Amber claims, it's strange that he would care so much about a missed opportunity with a high school flame." Livvy gave a shrug and stood. "I'm beat, and I need my beauty sleep. Tomorrow, I become Mrs. Olivia Okada." She gave a dreamy sigh, like an overly dramatic teenager from the movies we'd grown up watching.

I followed Livvy up the stairs, wishing her goodnight before driving home. As I drove, I couldn't help but wonder why Ridge, after all these years, would feel so strongly about a lost letter. Thoughts I wrote out in a letter before I called it a night.

Dear Ridge,

I should probably feel bad, but I don't. I told Amber you were my first kiss, that you were more to me than my cousin's best friend. If you told the truth in your letter, I was once more to you than your best friend's cousin. If that's true, could you feel the same way again? That's the big question, isn't it? Can you love me now like you once claimed to? It probably doesn't matter. You and Amber may be getting engaged tomorrow, but I have to ask. I have to know. I'm done living with regrets and leaving words unsaid.

According to Livvy, you didn't handle the news of her hiding the letter any better than I did. Is it possible you were as hurt by Livvy's betrayal as I was? When I learned about the letter, I was angry. I couldn't believe she'd withhold something so important. Now, I wonder if you felt the same way.

Mal

Chapter Thirty-One

THE NEXT MORNING CAME too early. I'd spent a good chunk of the night after the party pacing my room, unable to sleep, despite writing my thoughts out in a letter. I was sick of writing and watching and waiting. I wanted to act, but I feared that it was too late. Yet, I couldn't shake Livvy's revelation or Jefferson's advice.

I climbed out of bed when my alarm went off, not bothering to hit the snooze button. There was a lot to do, and I was going to need all the time I could get to make myself presentable.

I hurried to shower, style my hair, and apply makeup. I decided on loose curls, adding a touch of elegance to my appearance. Combined with the peach scarf, flirty black skirt, and white blouse, I looked good. I ate a quick breakfast, applied some lip stain, and headed out the door, pretending like I wasn't about to spend hours watching Ridge and Amber while avoiding my mother.

I parked the car at the wedding venue, grateful and sad to be arriving alone. Ridge had texted me the night before, saying that he would drive with Amber, freeing me from at least one awkward interaction guaranteed to happen today. Though, a part of me wished for a moment alone with him, a chance to really talk about the emotions I'd been battling all week, as evidenced by the letters filling my notebook.

Livvy and David had decided on an outdoor ceremony at a local botanical garden. The smells of roses and fresh-cut grass scented the air as the officiator spoke words of hope and love. Seeing David and Livvy's love for each other warmed my heart and helped me forget, for a moment, about Amber and Ridge who sat a few seats down the row from me.

Following the ceremony, I waited with the rest of Livvy and David's guests for a chance to congratulate them before driving to the reception. My family had arrived late for the wedding, sitting towards the back, Mother refusing to make eye contact as I stood with the other bridesmaids. She currently stood several feet away, avoiding me by talking to Chris and Sheila. My dad walked over, his suit jacket in hand.

"Hi, sweetheart." Dad wrapped me in a hug, and I closed my eyes for a moment, savoring the contact.

"Hi, Dad."

"Your mother was upset when she got home yesterday." He stepped back enough to look at my face. "Anything you want to talk about?"

I sighed. "Not really, but I'm guessing I don't have a choice."

"You have a choice. Just know, if you choose wrong, I'll keep pestering you until you change your mind."

I grinned. "Then I guess I'd better pick right the first time. Mother is driving me insane."

"You say that like it's a new development. Don't forget, I was there for all the teenage years." Dad slung his arm around my shoulders, and we began walking the garden paths.

"This time she's reached a new low. She actually brought me a date for Livvy's wedding dinner. She didn't ask. She told me what she was doing, I said no, and she did it anyway."

A laugh of surprise escaped Dad as he stopped to look at me. "That's a new one. Here I was thinking she'd given you another lecture about how you need to marry and move into a house down the street so she can watch over you and slowly smother you to death with all her worries."

"I could have handled that." I shook my head and sat on a bench, looking around the gardens. "I shouldn't have snapped at her, but last night she went too far."

"I'm sorry. She's got tunnel vision right now. You know this time of year always reminds her of the accident."

"That's not my fault. Maybe she should try redirecting some of the smother energy to Chris and Sheila." I looked to where the rest of our family sat, jealous of the easy, comfortable relationship my brother and mother had always shared.

"I think Sheila scares her too much." Dad's chuckle made me smile, easing the tension that had lodged in my chest. "But that doesn't fix things between you and your mother."

"No." I sighed.

"What will fix things?" This was why I both loved and hated conversations with my dad. He could nudge me in the right direction with only a few observations and the right question.

I gave a small smile, feeling like I was back in high school. "An apology. Though technically it could come from her side too."

Dad sat next to me and slung an arm around my shoulders. "True, but we both know that if you want this to end in this century, you're going to have to say the words first."

"But she was out of line."

"But you're the bigger person."

I sat a moment, accepting the steps I needed to take, knowing that he was right.

"Fine, but if she even mentions dating, I'm blocking her number and avoiding all family holidays for the next year."

"I'll tell her to back down. She loves you, Mallory. We both do. She wouldn't meddle if she didn't care." With that, Dad kissed the top of my head. "By the way, I need to talk to you about the apartment building. I have to give Milton Corp a response by the end of next week. In fact, Mr. Milton mentioned his daughter was attending this wedding."

"Dad, I know the money is good, but think about the tenants. Audrey and Chloe need the cheap rent. And what about the Jeongs? They've lived there longer than you've owned the building. How can you just—"

Dad held up his hand, stopping my argument. "We'll talk later. For now, let's enjoy Livvy's wedding."

I nodded, my emotional bandwidth incapable of acknowledging what that conversation meant. Instead, I gave Dad one more hug and watched as he joined the rest of my family.

I leaned my head back and closed my eyes. Trying to block everything out for a moment. Family politics were exhausting, but Dad was right. I needed to forgive Mother, no matter how much I didn't want to. I just prayed the conversation Dad wanted to have would not entail selling my home, forcing me to move once again.

A throat cleared and I opened my eyes to find Ridge standing in front of me, ruining any semblance of peace I'd found. He looked handsome in his black suit with his hair slicked back. I felt my mouth go dry just looking at him.

"Hey." Ridge sat next to me, giving me a smile. "The scarf looks good." He winked at me and I smiled, hoping he didn't notice my blush.

"You look good too. Though, I bet you were wishing you could rock one of those awesome peach ties."

He shrugged, adjusting his green striped tie. "Only truly sexy men can pull off peach."

I laughed and shook my head. "Green makes a good backup."

Glancing around, I noticed we were basically alone. Now was as good a time as any to tell him. To stop hiding and dodging and regretting and tell him my heart.

I took a deep breath, wishing I hadn't left my notebook in the car. While my letters were far from eloquent, at least they were a starting place. Praying no one would wander over any time soon, I opened my mouth to speak only for Ridge to fill the quiet.

"I can't believe Livvy is married. Our ranks as single people are shrinking."

"It was a nice ceremony," I supplied, unsure how to redirect the conversation.

"After today, I should be taking a step closer to shrinking those ranks further." He patted his pocket, no doubt checking to make sure the ring was still there. "By the way, Amber had to go pick up her parents from the airport. Can you give me a ride to the luncheon? She took my car so I wouldn't miss pictures."

My breath escaped in a whoosh. Maybe waiting to talk in the car was a better idea. We'd be able to talk alone without the risk of interruption. "Of course."

Now I just had to get through pictures and figure out exactly what to say before my nerves did me in.

"Pictures, everyone!" The call came from across the grass, next to the gazebo where Livvy and David had said their vows.

"I guess that's our cue." Ridge stood and offered me a hand up.

We spent the next hour posing for countless pictures. It was my first, and hopefully last, time acting as a bridesmaid. My cheeks ached from all the smiling. I had no idea so many different photo combinations could exist as different groups came forward and posed. I was in more pictures than I could count, and if I wasn't in a picture, I was holding Livvy's bouquet or tracking down a missing family member. By the time we left the gardens, my feet hurt and I regretted my choice to wear heels, though thankfully my ankle had stopped swelling enough that I no longer had to worry about keeping it elevated.

Ridge and I piled into my car and headed to a nearby restaurant for the family luncheon. My stomach growled at the thought of the pasta and breadsticks waiting for us.

Maybe confessions of love are better on a full stomach.

"My cheeks hurt." I reached up to massage my face trying to return feeling. "So much smiling! And we're not even done yet."

"Luckily, we should be done with the formal photos. Everything else should be candid shots."

"I'm not sure candid is a good thing either. I usually end up pulling a face or getting caught mid-chew." I shook my head, remembering the many embarrassing and awkward photos from my brother's wedding.

"At least you're wearing a stylish scarf to go along with your awkward faces." Ridge tried to look on the bright side, but it didn't do much good.

The luncheon was low key and fun. Livvy was on cloud nine, seeming to have forgotten about her desperate need to see the reception venue. In fact, we were nearly late leaving the luncheon for the reception. In order to get everyone there on time, my car was crammed full of cousins who needed a ride over, eliminating my chance to talk to Ridge alone.

The church gym looked even better than I remembered. One of Livvy's neighbors had set up a sound system and was playing a nice mix of romantic music that set a sweet tone for the event. Small desserts and finger foods filled a table along the far wall, next to an arch covered with lights for the bride and groom to stand under while greeting their guests.

"It's perfect." Livvy rushed over to give me a hug. David followed behind her, beaming at his bride. When Livvy let go, he stepped in to give me a quick, equally enthusiastic embrace. "The centerpieces are wonderful, and the scarves worked out flawlessly," she continued, pulling Ridge in for his hug. "I never should have doubted you!"

I shrugged, flustered at her praise. "We were happy to help."

"It was mostly Mallory," Ridge commented. "I was just the lackey and credit card."

"Not true." I smacked him in the chest, smiling up at him. "He was a huge help."

"And we can't forget Amber's part," Ridge added, causing me to deflate a bit. I really needed to talk to him. I patted my bag, reassured to feel the familiar weight of the notebook.

"I don't care who's responsible," Livvy broke in, looping her arm through David's and resting her head on his shoulder. "It's perfect, and you two played a big part in that. Thank you." With that, she and David walked away, leaving me alone with Ridge. Maybe now was my chance.

"We did good," Ridge said, looking around the room.

"I think so too," I agreed.

"Rigdon!" My heart sank as I turned to see Amber rushing over to us. She wore a sparkly red dress that did wonders for her figure and caused her red lipstick to pop. "How was the luncheon? I'm so sorry I missed it." Her voice oozed regret.

"It was nice." Ridge allowed Amber to slip her arm through his. "I guess we should give our congratulations before the line gets too long."

Ridge and Amber moved towards the line, leaving me alone in the middle of the gym watching my heart walk away.

Chapter Thirty-Two

NEIGHBORS AND FRIENDS WHO hadn't been at the wedding ceremony filtered into the gym, and I watched for a moment, unsure what to do. My mother was gossiping with some aunts, my dad was talking with a group of men nearby, and Chris and Sheila had conveniently disappeared. Audrey and Chloe would be here later, but for the moment I stood alone in a room full of people.

Aunt Jenna rushed up to me, panic written on her face. "Mal, I need your help. We have a small emergency in the kitchen." She grabbed my arm, pulling me in that direction. "We don't have anyone stocking the refreshments table, and I need to get in the line." She waved her hand towards where Uncle Ben, Livvy, David, and a Japanese couple—who I assumed to be David's parents—stood, ready to greet guests.

"I'm happy to help," I reassured, picking up my pace. "Don't worry about it."

Aunt Jenna gave me a grateful smile and headed towards her daughter.

I entered the kitchen to find empty trays sitting next to plates of cookies, cupcakes, and brownies. Everything needed to be moved onto trays and taken into the gym asap. Depositing my bag in a corner on the floor, I washed my hands and got to work, grateful for something to occupy my mind and hands. Anything to distract me from what I hoped to tell Ridge before the night was over.

I spent the next two hours patrolling the refreshments table. At some point, I slipped my shoes off, unable to pace back and forth in my heels. In between trips to the kitchen, my extended family attempted to snag me to catch up, but I used the kitchen full of sweets as my excuse to bow out.

In my pacing, my eyes were drawn to Ridge. Each time I found him, Amber was at his side, laughing and holding his hand. My stomach clenched, every time, driving home the words I needed to speak.

During one of my trips, both Ridge and Amber had disappeared. Praying they hadn't left, I deposited my empty tray in the kitchen and headed towards the entry. Maybe a miracle would happen and I would run into Ridge. I only needed a couple of minutes to share my heart.

"I know, Daddy," Amber's voice rang out, causing me to jump as I approached the bathroom door. I glanced around the corner to see Amber pacing, phone pressed to her ear. "He insists that teaching is the right career for him, but he's said that about other careers before. A little pushing and I'll have him on the fast track to law school. The internship this summer is crucial."

A pause followed, and I ducked back around the corner to keep from being seen.

"Let me worry about Ridge. How goes the apartment building acquisition?" Pause. "I don't care what it takes, my clientele wants that dog park." Pause. "Offer him more." Pause. "I've already got most of the tenants ready to sign contracts in the new building. Give it a year, and when contracts renew, we'll up fees and recoup our loses." Pause. "I don't care if they have nowhere to go. We're turning this town into the next hot spot in Utah."

It wasn't a stretch to imagine which apartment building Amber was talking about. I pictured the old stone building I'd called home for years. I could see it now, being leveled, tenants like Mrs. and Mr. Jeong without a home they could afford. Not to mention Audrey and Chloe. The discount my dad gave all three of us on rent made it possible for us to room together. Without it, both Chloe and Audrey would have to move home.

I had to find Ridge, tell him what Amber was planning. Maybe I could convince him to fight for my building—if not for me, then for my tenants. Maybe I could finally help him see how wrong Amber was for him. Maybe I could convince him to give me a chance.

Doubt niggled at the back of my mind as I remembered my argument with Ridge from the day before. I'd attempted to voice my opinion, but he hadn't wanted to listen. Yet I couldn't stand back and let Amber have her way. My heart wouldn't stand for it.

I headed back to the kitchen, grabbing my bag from where I'd left it in a corner to keep it out of the way. Digging through it, I pulled out my phone to find a text from Chloe. I needed to get back to the party.

Promising Chloe I would find her soon, I pulled out my notebook and returned my bag to the floor. The notebook seemed to call to me, begging me to finally write my full feelings, no longer hesitating or hiding.

Grabbing a pen and taking a deep breath I wrote four sentences.

Dear Ridge,

I've written so many of these letters this last week, but I have to get this one right. I have to finally spell out exactly what I'm thinking and feeling.

I love you. If only speaking the words out loud was as easy as writing them down.

  Mal

Chapter Thirty-Three

I ENTERED THE GYM, freshly stocked refreshment trays in hand. I would find Chloe and Audrey, let them know I was okay, and then track down Ridge. A microphone screeched, drawing everyone's attention to Aunt Jenna, who stood by the three-tiered cake covered in layers of peach buttercream.

"Thank you everyone for coming to celebrate Livvy and David's big day. We are so excited to have David join our family. If we could have everyone gather over here"—she waved to the cake table—"we're going to cut the cake, followed by dancing, in just a moment."

People pushed up from their chairs and moved towards the cake. I quickly deposited my trays of cookies and moved to join everyone, finding Chloe and Audrey in the crowd. Livvy and David carefully cut the cake and fed each other a bite, despite catcalls for them to smear the cake in each other's faces. The happy couple couldn't hold my attention as my gaze combed the crowd, searching for Ridge. As the couple finished, music began to play, and Uncle Ben stepped up to take Livvy's hand while David went to find his mother.

I watched for a moment, enjoying the joy and peace on Livvy's face. Then the song switched and David took Uncle Ben's place. Livvy's smile grew, and she snuggled into his chest. An involuntary sigh escaped my lips as I watched the scene. It was completely chick-flick worthy.

"They're so cute!" Chloe gushed, bouncing on the balls of her feet. "How do I find a love like that?"

"Beats me." Audrey grabbed Chloe's arm. "Do you think a slice of cake might be part of the answer?"

Chloe laughed. "Maybe. It's worth a try."

I bowed out of joining them, refocusing on my mission.

"They look happy," a deep voice rumbled next to me, and I looked up to find Ridge watching me.

"They do." I nodded my head. "I hope to be that happy someday."

The music changed once more, and a different slow song filled the air. I looked up to see multiple couples dancing in the limited space between tables while Livvy and David continued to sway as if nothing had changed.

"I guess that's our cue." Ridge gave a sweeping bow and held out his hand. "May I have this dance?"

"Where's Amber?" The words left my lips before I could think better of them.

"She had to take a phone call."

I bet she did. My mind flashed to the words I'd overheard.

"I don't see the point in missing out on a perfectly good slow dance because she's not here to share it with me." Ridge offered me his hand once more. "Though I promise not to kiss you in the moonlight when we're done."

I bit my lip, knowing I wouldn't protest if he tried. "Then I'd love to dance with you."

Ridge placed one hand on my waist and continued to hold the other as if we were about to break into a waltz or some other formal dance. Instead, we swayed in a circle, rocking back and forth to the music.

"You know, Mal, it's been good to see you again." Ridge spoke before I could. I looked into his face, watching as a grin toyed at his lips. "I forgot how much I liked being around you."

"I must not have made much of an impression if you could forget so easily," I teased.

"No, you definitely made an impression." He shook his head. "I used to beg Kyle to invite you over. Everything was more fun with you around."

"Ridge, I..." I trailed off, not sure where to start, but knowing that I had to get the words out before something else could get in the way. Pushing back slightly, I looked up into his eyes. "I lo—"

"Rigdon." Amber's voice interrupted me. I looked over to find her glaring at me, an expression that clashed so fully against the first time we'd met and her kindness following the fender bender. "I can't believe I almost missed dancing with you. Well, good news. I'm all yours for the rest of the night. Mallory, you don't mind me cutting in, do you?"

I opened my mouth to protest, but Amber didn't give me a chance. Instead, she pushed her way between us, wrapping her arms around Ridge's neck and pulling him down for a kiss.

"Amber." Ridge gasped when she finally let him up for air. "You just saw me not even ten minutes ago."

"But I missed you the entire time."

I stepped away from the couple, not sure how to reclaim the moment. I needed to talk to Ridge before my insides burst with anticipation.

"Mal!" An arm slipped around my waist, and I turned to find Livvy grinning at me. "I need a breather. Come with me?"

Nodding, I followed Livvy out of the gym back to the kitchen, only faint sounds of music filtering after us.

When the door closed behind us, Livvy leaned against the counter, careful to avoid the desserts. She gave a big sigh and closed her eyes, rolling her neck from side to side.

"Tonight has been perfect," she said before opening her eyes to watch me. "And to say thank you for everything you've done to make that happen, I have something for you."

She opened her hand, revealing a small box I hadn't noticed she was holding.

"Livvy, you didn't have to get me anything. I was happy to help. That's what cousins and best friends are for." I took the box, opening it to find a silver necklace with a small skeleton key pendant on it. "It's beautiful."

"I got it to celebrate when you finally buy your apartment building, but you deserve it tonight after all the work you did this week. Tonight wouldn't have been possible without you, and you definitely had every reason not to help me after what I pulled with that letter." Livvy wrapped me in a hug, and I held on to this cousin and friend who had seen me through countless moves and other hard times.

"Thank you," I whispered, tears burning my eyes.

We finished the hug and I moved to put the pendant in my purse, managing to knock the bag over in the process. Various items went flying, and I quickly gathered them with Livvy's help.

"Someday, I'll grow out of this clumsiness," I muttered as I returned things to my purse.

Livvy remained silent and I turned, wondering why she hadn't responded with one of her usual quips. Instead, she crouched on the floor, my notebook open in her lap to the last page I'd written.

"You weren't supposed to see that." I reached to grab the notebook, but Livvy pulled it back, flipping to my earlier entries.

"I had no idea you still felt this way," Livvy whispered.

"No one does, not even Ridge." I gave a small, self-conscious laugh as I sank to the floor next to Livvy. "I've been trying to tell him all night, but Amber keeps getting in the way."

"Then I guess we'd better fix that."

I slipped out of the church, standing in the parking lot as I waited for Livvy to put her plan into action. With Kyle's help, she was going to get Ridge to come outside with the promise of helping decorate the newlyweds' car for their grand send off. I had one chance to get the words right.

I paced the sidewalk right outside the doors, a single streetlight and the moon providing enough light to see by. The quiet night was a refreshing change from the noise of people inside.

"I've got this. I can do this," I mumbled to myself as I walked past the front row of cars one direction and then the next, trying to calm my nerves. It felt like someone was using a jackhammer in my stomach.

"Kyle, you out here?" Ridge's voice filled the night, causing everything inside me to freeze.

"Ridge?" My voice came out in a croak.

"Oh, hey, Mal. You helping to decorate the car too?" Ridge came to join me where I'd stopped next to an old pine tree in front of his car.

"Something like that." I took one more breath, before turning to face him. Mustering my courage, I said the words I could never take back. "Ridge, I think I'm falling in love with you."

Ridge, who was turning to look at me, froze. His mouth hung slightly open, and his eyes widened. I didn't wait for him to respond.

"I know this sounds ridiculous. I mean, we haven't seen each other in years and one week is hardly enough time to fall in love. After reading your letter and spending this week with you, it got me thinking about old times, and yes there was hurt, but there were also good times, and I've realized that I've let go of the past. I want you in my life. One week isn't enough." The words tumbled out, a jumble of thoughts and emotions that couldn't be taken back.

"Mal, I don't know what to say. I've told you, I love...I'm proposing to Amber." His words stung, but his hesitation gave me hope.

"But you don't love Amber!" I yelled the words, all the hurt and frustration spilling out.

"You don't know that," Ridge said, defensive.

"I do. You couldn't even say the words just now. You said you're proposing to her, but you don't love her, and I don't think she loves you. She wants a man she can mold into the perfect corporate lawyer to compliment her as a perfect interior designer. If you propose to Amber tonight, that's the life you're choosing. You'll never be a teacher or basketball coach. You'll never go camping. You'll be a man stuck in a stuffy suit, tearing down apartment buildings, wondering what would have happened if you'd said yes to kissing me in the moonlight."

Ridge stood silent, watching me, his mouth open in surprise. He took a step forward, arm reaching toward me, when the church doors opened again, bringing with them the sounds of the reception.

"There you are, Rigdon. Kyle said something about you coming out here to decorate the car. It's never been my favorite tradition, but I'm game to—" Amber stopped, likely noting the energy crackling between me and Ridge. "Am I interrupting something?"

"Mallory was just…" Ridge trailed off, an awkward silence between us.

"Let me guess, she was trying to use you to convince me not to buy her pathetic apartment building? Because that ship has sailed. Daddy's calling now with a deal no one would be able to refuse."

My heart clenched. I was too late in talking to Dad, but maybe it wouldn't be in vain. Maybe, creating this moment with Ridge would still prove to have been worthwhile. There were other properties I could buy, but I would cross that bridge later. For now, I needed Ridge's response. I needed to know my words weren't in vain.

"Not quite," Ridge said.

Amber looked between the two of us for a moment before her eyes lit with understanding, laughter bubbling out of her as she walked to Ridge, interlacing her fingers with his.

"This is just too much. She fancies herself in love with you, doesn't she?" Amber's laugh grated on my ears, the sound shattering my dreams. "I worried this had happened after she shared about your high school kiss last night. She clearly hasn't moved on, and you basically spent an entire week together. Sorry, sweetheart, but he's taken. He's all mine, isn't that right Rigdon?" Amber turned wide eyes on Ridge, blinking up at him as she waited for a response.

I rubbed my scar, bracing myself for the set down, for the words that would once again break my heart. At least this time he would tell me to my face.

But they didn't come. Instead, Ridge stayed quiet, looking back and forth between the two of us as if waiting for one of us to provide the words he should say.

"Tell her, Rigdon. Tell her that you love me. We're going to get married, as soon as you give me the ring I know is hiding in your pocket. Tell her!" Amber stood in front of Ridge, grabbing both of his hands.

Instead of agreeing, Ridge took a step back, shaking his head. "I don't...I can't...I..."

The church doors opened again, and this time a group of people came out to line the entryway, getting ready to send the happy couple off on their honeymoon.

"There you are, Mallory. I was worried you'd left and forgotten your bag in the kitchen." Aunt Jenna wandered over, handing me my purse. "You guys are going to join the send-off, right?"

I watched Ridge a moment longer, begging him to speak.

Instead, he shook his head and took another step back. "I need some time...a chance to process...I..." He stopped speaking, taking a deep breath. "I've got to slip out, Jenna, but give Livvy my best."

With those words, Ridge turned around and disappeared into the parking lot, leaving me alone with Amber, my heart crushed at my feet.

"Don't think this changes anything. He'll be back, ring box in hand, and you'll be a distant memory the two of us will laugh about years down the road." Amber spat as she walked past me, head held high.

I stood in the dark, remembering another night when magic had felt like a possibility. Little had I known the magic would fade in the light of dawn when kisses vanished and promises were broken as harsh realities crashed down around me. At least tonight, I had no illusions of magic continuing to exist when the morning came.

Opting out of the sendoff, I climbed into my car and sat a moment, trying to gain control. After a few minutes, I took a deep breath and pulled out of the parking lot. Looking back for a moment, I noted everyone assembled at the church doors, David and Livvy running through a tunnel of sparklers, huge grins on their faces. At least someone would be getting their happily ever after tonight.

Chapter Thirty-Four

AT HOME, I WAS greeted by a half-hearted head raise from Ruby. I kicked out of my shoes and headed for my bedroom, where I changed into sweats. Upon exiting my room, I found Ruby sitting outside my door, staring at me.

"Not tonight, Ruby. I'm having a pity party."

She blinked up at me, unimpressed by my busy social calendar.

"Fine." I walked to the front door and grabbed her leash. "But it's going to be a quick one."

Less than five minutes later, I was back inside my apartment. I grabbed a spoon and a carton of ice cream before settling on the couch and turning on a home improvement show, Ruby curled up next to me. If now wasn't the time for binge-watching and eating myself sick, I didn't know when was.

Ridge's look of shock following my declaration was seared into my brain, his silence echoing louder than all the home improvement tools I owned, combined.

Ten minutes into the show and half a carton of ice cream later, I got the itch to get back to work on painting my apartment. The tape had started to peel from my bedroom ceiling, but I could easily reapply it and get to work. It didn't matter that it was late. I wouldn't be sleeping tonight anyway.

I quickly changed into my paint clothes and replaced the falling tape. I then grabbed the paint supplies I'd stashed in my laundry room and got to work covering my furniture with plastic sheeting. It was while I was in the middle of this process that my roommates walked in, wearing equally concerned expressions.

"What are you doing?" Chloe's nose crinkled at the disaster in my room.

"I'm prepping to paint," I said, stating the obvious and hoping that was where this conversation would end. Too many questions would lead to tears, and I'd shed enough of those over Ridge to last a lifetime.

"We can see that," Audrey said, her tone reminding me of one I used when dealing with rowdy students. "But why are you doing it right now? It's 10:00 at night."

"It just felt like a good idea. I've been meaning to paint all week, and there's no time like the present." A strangled laugh escaped as I attempted to push past the pair to grab paper towels from the kitchen. Not that it would matter. If Amber was right, my dad had sold out and this building would be flattened in a matter of months.

They formed a wall, blocking my escape. Instead, two pairs of arms reached around me, locking me in an embrace. The warmth and comfort of that hug broke my barriers, and the tears began to fall.

"I just—" I broke off with a sob.

"It's okay," Audrey murmured, smoothing back my hair. "Let it out."

"I didn't realize I'd let him in until...and now he's going to marry Amber and—"

"We're here for you," Chloe reassured.

Together we made our way over to the couch where we collapsed in a heap of tears and talking. Chloe retrieved more ice cream from the freezer, and as we dug in, I finally let all the emotions of the last week free.

Chapter Thirty-Five

I woke Sunday to puffy eyes and a pounding headache. A glance at my phone confirmed that I had slept in, missing the start of church. Chloe, Audrey, and I had stayed up late talking and even later watching one of Audrey's cooking shows. By the time I'd climbed into bed, I could barely keep my eyes open, but my heart felt significantly lighter, though still broken.

I stumbled from my room to find the apartment quiet and empty. Someone had even taken the time to clean up the living room after our late night. I felt immense gratitude at having been left alone with my emotions. Last night I'd needed to release everything that I'd kept bottled up inside. Today I needed to move forward.

I ate breakfast and then took the time to shower before changing into shorts and a t-shirt. The clock showed that my roommates would be home soon, and while I appreciated their support, I wasn't ready to be around people just yet. I grabbed a slushy Dr. Pepper and some snacks before heading to my car, deciding that a drive up the canyon might help me clear my head.

American Fork Canyon was green and beautiful but did not bring the calm I had hoped for. Instead, the winding road made my shoulders tense with building pressure. As if on autopilot, I made my way along Alpine Loop, not fully realizing my destination until I pulled into the Aspen Grove parking lot.

I exited my car and moved to the pedestrian bridge. Leaning against the red-brown railing, I looked up at the mountains and tuned out the activity all around me.

Was it worth it?

I snorted as the question popped into my head. I'd spent countless hours grappling with my feelings for Ridge. And what did I have to show for it? An even more broken heart and a week of my life I'd never get back.

I should have known better. I should have learned my lesson after prom and the accident. But apparently, I was a bad student. Instead of protecting myself, I'd torn down my walls and given him the key to my heart, knowing full well that he was in love with someone else. Yet, I'd also found it in my heart to finally forgive him. There was a certain relief and lightness knowing that ghost would no longer haunt my past.

A shriek followed by laughter caused me to turn and watch as a family made their way to the bridge. A young child held hands with her parents as they swung her up into the air. Each time they did, she squealed and laughed, kicking her legs in pure joy. That image encompassed what I wanted: happiness and a family of my own. At the moment, between the fight with my mother and Ridge choosing Amber, that dream felt faraway. But a voice seemed to whisper that it wasn't entirely out of reach. If I could find it in my heart to forgive Ridge and love him again, maybe I could find space to love and forgive others. My mother included.

As soon as I reached the mouth of American Fork Canyon and gained service, I pulled to the side of the road and called my mother.

"I'm not talking to you." Mother's voice was irritated, but at least she'd answered.

"I understand, but that doesn't mean you can't listen to me." I took her silence as a good sign and continued talking. "I'm sorry. I lashed out at you, and I shouldn't have."

More silence.

"I guess," I paused, taking a breath. "I guess your constant pushing just makes me feel...smothered and inadequate. Like I've failed in some essential part of being human. When you push so hard, it makes me think I'm not enough, not on my own, at least. Like I need someone else to protect me and make me enough for you."

I heard a sharp intake of breath on the other end of the line but pushed through. Now that I'd started, I needed to get the words out.

"Every guy you've ever set me up with, every single one, has been a dud. Well, I guess until Jefferson, but you get my point. I've gone on dates with guys who wouldn't talk to me, guys who talked about their mothers the entire time, guys who wouldn't stop talking long enough for me to say anything. There have been guys who wouldn't stop staring at their phones, guys who lectured me for glancing at my phone. I even went on a date with a guy who took me to dinner and made me feel guilty about every single bite I ate. All because you said 'they were perfect for me' because they had a 'great personality' or something else along those lines. It makes me wonder, if those guys are 'perfect for me,' then what's wrong with me to make you think that?"

"Oh, honey," Mother breathed into the phone, and I knew in that moment that at least one hard conversation in my life would be worth it.

"Since my first year of college, I've felt like all we ever talk about is dating and when I'll finally get married so I can move into a house down the street, safe under your umbrella of protection. Did it ever occur to you that I want a family, though maybe not the house down the street? I've tried, so hard, to find someone to love, but it just hasn't happened. I even got engaged, and it didn't work out! I love my life, but it's lonely. I want someone to share it with, but I want the right someone. I want to be excited to come home at the end of the day, not because I'm done with work, but because I get to tell the love of my life all about it. I want what you and Dad have, a partnership. Sometimes you clash, but I can see that you love each other, that you watch out for each other, that no matter what, you're there for each other. That's what I want."

"That's what I want for you too," Mother said, and for the first time in my life, I believed her. "You just never talk about dating, and I worry. I worry about you being alone. Ever since the accident, I can't seem to turn off the worry."

I paused for a moment, giving her words a chance to sink in. We were making progress, and I needed to choose my next words carefully.

"I get that. The accident was scary and changed so much for all of us. But you have to let me live my life. Being married, living in your neighborhood, none of that guarantees I won't get hurt again. This is my life, and I'm trying to make it something wonderful. I love my students, my roommates, my apartment. It doesn't look like what I always pictured, but...that's okay." I paused, my mind filling with memories of Ridge, from high school and from the last week. Yet, amidst the pain and regret, there was a sliver of hope. I'd learned to be brave once, sharing my heart with Ridge despite past heartbreak. Maybe, someday, I could be brave again.

Chapter Thirty-Six

I'M NOT SURE HOW long I sat on the side of the road talking to my mother, but the relief I felt as our conversation wound to a close was palpable. We had actually talked, listening to each other instead of jumping to conclusions. For the first time in years, she hadn't lectured me on dating or tried to convince me to move home. Maybe there was hope for us yet.

The highlight of the conversation came when she handed the phone to Dad. I'd braced myself for his news, certain he was going to tell me he'd sold the building.

Instead, I got a reprieve.

"I couldn't sign the paperwork. Mr. Milton called me, at Livvy's wedding, telling me about how his development would improve the city and benefit everyone. But then I heard what you said. What about the Jeongs and all the other tenants who have been loyal to us over the years? I couldn't just sell their homes out from under them. They deserve someone who will fight for them and genuinely care what happens to them. They deserve you."

My throat clogged at the words, relief filling me as he spoke. "Just to be clear, you're not selling?"

"I am, but to someone who will do the job justice. I think it's time we formalize our agreement. I'm ready to hand the reins to you."

I finished my call and drove home, elated at all that had changed in such a short time. I hadn't gotten the guy, but I had begun repairing my relationship with my mother and saved my home. For now, it would have to be enough.

I parked and walked into my condo where I was greeted by the smell of cookies baking. My stomach growled, reminding me of the snacks I'd taken but forgotten to eat.

"Audrey, you're my favorite roommate," I called as I stepped out of my shoes and headed for the kitchen. If I was lucky, there would be some fresh cookies already cooling on the counter.

"What does that make me?" Chloe asked from where she sat on the couch, causing me to jump. I'd failed to notice her thanks to my cookie tunnel-vision.

"Unless you're responsible for the heavenly scents coming for the oven, you're my second-favorite roommate."

"If I hadn't tasted Audrey's chocolate chip cookies, I'd be offended," Chloe said, pressing a hand to her chest. "But I think my answer is the same as yours."

Chloe joined me in the kitchen. I was disappointed to see that no cookies graced the countertop, but the timer on the oven was quickly counting down. Only 30 seconds until fresh, gooey, chocolatey goodness.

"Who said you could have some?" Audrey came out of her room wearing a lemon-print apron. Ruby followed on her heels, tail wagging.

"I'm pretty sure there's a cookie clause in your housing contract. Something about the landlady reserving the right to sample all baked goods created on the premises." I shrugged as the timer went off.

"I think that same clause includes something about sharing with roommates," Chloe added.

"I don't remember that being in the documents I signed." Audrey pursed her lips, as if considering the possibility. "I might have hesitated to sign."

"Well, if it's not currently in your contract, I'll have to add it into your next one," I said, casually. The two of them froze, staring at me.

"Does that mean your dad's not selling?" Chloe trailed off. I could see hope in her eyes, and I couldn't hold back my good news any longer.

"He is, but he's selling to me. We're going to draw up the paperwork this week and get everything started."

Audrey and Chloe both shrieked in excitement, rushing to hug me as I laughed at their joy. At least single life came with the best roommates the world had to offer.

Audrey's timer beeped and she quickly turned it off before flipping on the oven light, glancing inside to check on the cookies. She straightened and added a few more minutes to the timer. I contained a groan, realizing that cookie time would have to wait a bit longer.

"The cookies are for Derek's game night later," Audrey said. "I'm not sure there will be enough if you two get to them first."

"We'll only eat one each." At my words Audrey gave me a look that I needed to add to my teacher arsenal. "Okay, maybe two or three each, but your cookies are so good."

"Which is why I'm going to use them as bribery to get you to attend the game night and support a friend."

"Or you could let us have some now and we'll go to the game night later," Chloe persisted. I had no intention of attending the game night, but I was willing to try any tactic necessary to get fresh cookies from the oven.

"Nice try," Audrey said.

The timer went off and Audrey looked in the oven once more, this time satisfied with what she saw when she flipped on the oven light. I watched her pull out the tray of golden-brown cookies and decided it was time for drastic measures.

"But I'm recovering from a broken heart." I let sadness leak into my tone, hoping for sympathy, yet the words made my heart twinge, and tears sting my eyes. I thought I'd gotten a handle on my emotions, but apparently not.

"Oh, honey." Audrey set the cookie sheet on a cooling rack and moved to my side, wrapping me in a hug, oven mitts and all.

"I thought I was over this part. I had last night to cry," I blubbered.

"You can't expect to heal from a broken heart overnight." Audrey soothed.

I felt another set of arms surround me as Chloe joined our hug.

"But we only spent a week together." And yet, I already missed Ridge's presence on my couch.

"You knew each other for years before that," Audrey reasoned.

"Not to mention, you loved him before this week," Chloe added.

We stood in a huddle for a moment longer, and I let my tears fall as I soaked in the love and support of my friends. I finally straightened and released them, grabbing a paper towel from the counter to dab at my eyes.

"I'm an emotional wreck." I laughed self-consciously and then grinned at Audrey. "So, does that qualify me for a cookie before game night?"

She laughed, pulling off one of her oven mitts and throwing it at me. "Only if you help me get these baked before game night starts."

We spent the next hour baking cookies. The task got my mind off Ridge and let me embrace the moment. I also took the opportunity to sneak several cookies when Audrey wasn't looking.

When it was time to leave for game night, I decided to attend. Chloe and Audrey promised to leave whenever I was ready, and I didn't want to spend the evening home alone on the couch, stewing. Between games of Uno and Nertz, I laughed and forgot, for a moment, that my heart was in shreds.

After a few hours of games, my roommates and I decided to head home. Audrey used Ruby as an excuse to bow out early, and I was happy to tag along.

"What should we do now?" Chloe asked as we walked into the apartment.

"Go to bed." I glanced at the clock, noticing that it was after 11:00.

"I second that." Audrey hooked Ruby's leash to her collar and made her way to the door. "I have work tomorrow."

"And I have a bunch of painting to do," I added, a thrill shooting through me as I realized that all my hard work wouldn't be wasted after all. I was improving *my* apartment.

"You guys are no fun." Chloe flopped onto the couch and grabbed the remote.

"Welcome to adulthood," I quipped, walking into my room. "Where you can stay up late whenever you like but still have to be functioning in the morning."

"Uh, Mallory," Audrey's hesitant voice called from the front door. "There's someone here to see you."

Puzzled, I left my bedroom, curious to see who was visiting this late at night. My heart froze in my chest as I took in who stood in the doorway: Ridge, his lips tipped into a hesitant smile, my faded notebook clutched in his hands.

Chapter Thirty-Seven

I BLINKED SEVERAL TIMES, certain I must be dreaming. When Ridge didn't disappear, I folded my arms and discretely pinched myself, hard. The pain shocked my system and convinced me he was real.

"Where did you get that?" I asked, dazed. "Also, what are you doing here?"

"Hello to you, too," Ridge said.

I didn't respond, just continued to stare at him.

He gave a shrug before ducking his head and responding. "I needed to see you, to talk and find out if this is true." He waved the notebook in front of me, and it took everything I had not to snatch it back and run into the apartment. I'd said some pretty harsh things in there over the last week and my most recent entry...My mouth went dry at the words I knew filled the last page.

"You didn't answer my first question." I continued to hug myself as I looked down, away from his gaze.

"Livvy gave it to me."

"Livvy? But how...?" And then it hit me. I had left the notebook in the kitchen during the reception. She'd read those few pages before I'd snatched it back, but she must have taken it when I'd been outside talking to Ridge. "Oh, that meddling cousin of mine." I shook my head, wishing I was surprised by her actions.

"It came with quite the talking down, too. You can imagine my surprise when I answered the door earlier today to find Livvy on my doorstep, notebook in hand, ready to chew me out. She called me the biggest idiot in the world for letting you go."

I could picture the moment all too clearly.

"After she gave me a piece of her mind, she threw the notebook at me and stormed away to catch her flight." He shook his head with a chuckle. "I've never been so grateful for a notebook before in my life."

I stood, waiting to hear what would come next. I needed to know that Livvy sharing my heart through that notebook hadn't been in vain.

"I called things off with Amber after the wedding, needing space to think. She was furious, promising me I'd come crawling back, but the second I read your letters..." He trailed off, swallowing before forging ahead. "I knew I could never go back to her."

I gave a sharp intake of breath, and the weight I'd been carrying seemed to lift from my heart as I watched his face, searching for the truth in his eyes.

"So, I'll ask you again, is what you wrote true? Did you mean it?"

I licked my lips, took a deep breath, and jumped into a future with no regrets. "And if it is?"

"Then I owe you this."

Ridge stepped forward, wrapping an arm around my waist while his other hand lifted my chin to look up at him. He paused a moment, giving me time to back away, and, when I didn't, he pressed his lips to mine.

His kiss was even better than I remembered. His lips were gentle but firm, causing electricity to zing throughout my whole body as he toyed with first my top lip and then my bottom lip before deepening the kiss. I melted into him, returning his embrace as my world collided and fused with his. And though we weren't in the park under the stars, somehow this time was also fireworks and magic.

When we broke apart, we were both breathing heavily, his forehead resting against mine.

"I think I love you," Ridge said, running his finger along my bottom lip. My skin tingled at the contact.

"That's good, because I think I love you too."

Epilogue

One Year Later

I tried not to pace in front of my door, wondering what was taking Ridge so long. For a guy who regularly showed up early, he was very late today. I glanced at the clock on my phone one more time. Where was he?

A year ago, he'd shown up on my doorstep, asking me to take a chance on loving him. Since then, we'd had a summer spent almost constantly together, a school year of long-distance dating, and now, with him moving back to Utah permanently, we were looking forward to even more time together.

A knock sounded on the door, and I jerked it open. There, in all his tall, blue-eyed glory, stood Ridge. My breath caught as it hit me again that he was there for me.

"Hi." He ducked his head and reached for my hand as he stepped into my apartment, closing the door behind him. "Sorry I'm late."

"You can make it up to me." I moved in close, tipping my face towards his.

"How's that?" He leaned in closer.

"You could—"

The front door swung open, and we jumped apart, Ridge narrowly avoiding being hit.

"Oops! Sorry." Chloe pushed into the entryway loaded down with groceries.

"It's okay, we need to get going anyway." Ridge grabbed my hand again and tugged me towards the door.

"Do you mind checking the mail on your way out?" Chloe called after us. "I was going to, but my hands are full."

"Sure." I shrugged and grabbed the mail key. "It'll only take a couple of minutes," I promised Ridge at the look he threw my way. "Besides, if you were so worried about time, you wouldn't have been late."

"Ouch. I blame it on construction. Now that a new developer has taken over the apartments down the street, the road's a mess." Ridge gave a shrug.

It still boggled my mind that, in taking my offer, my dad had made the better personal *and* business decision. About a month after he'd rejected Milton Corp's offer, the company had come under investigation for mismanagement of funds, having all assets frozen about the time he would have been signing papers. While Amber had been cleared of any involvement, the last we'd heard, she'd moved out of state, looking for a fresh start far away from the Milton name.

"I still say we have time to check the mail." I persisted, poking him in the side.

Ridge laughed. "Fine, but we have to be quick. We're going to be extra late for dinner tonight."

When we got to the bank of mailboxes, I let go of Ridge's hand so I could open my box. The key got stuck and needed a bit of jiggling. I'd have to remember to bring some WD-40 with me the next time I checked the mail. The mailbox finally opened, and I looked inside to find a wedding announcement-sized envelope. I pulled it out, trying to think of whom I knew who was getting married. The envelope felt lighter than normal, as if it contained regular paper rather than the cardstock typical of wedding invitations. I began opening it, curious to see who would be tying the knot next.

Inside lay a single sheet of lined paper. My eyebrows pinched together as I began reading the now familiar handwriting.

Dear Mal,

I wrote you a letter once, telling you how I felt, and it took years for you to respond. I hope you won't take that long to answer this time, but if I have to, I'm willing to wait. Mallory, I love you. Will you marry me?

Ridge

I gasped as the words registered and whirled around to find Ridge, down on one knee, holding a ring with a simple oval cut diamond on a gold band. My heart pounded and my eyes swam with happy tears as I took in the moment.

"Is this real?" I whispered, my throat tight as I battled my emotions.

"Absolutely. Mallory, I thought I loved you in high school when we kissed. I thought I loved you when I wrote that letter in Florida. But now, I realize that was a crush because what I feel for you in this moment doesn't compare. I love you. Will you share my life and my forever, and marry me?" Ridge gazed up into my eyes as he spoke, each word settling into my heart.

"Yes!" I kneeled beside him and threw my arms around him, sealing my words with a kiss.

The momentum knocked us both off balance, bringing us dangerously close to sprawling on the sidewalk. Ridge steadied me before pulling back enough to slip the ring on my finger. He then drew me in for another kiss.

I could have stayed there all day, kneeling in front of the mailbox kissing Ridge, but the sound of a clearing throat caught my attention.

"Can we come out now?" a voice called.

I watched as Livvy, David, Audrey, and Chloe stepped out from behind some nearby bushes, cameras in hand.

I pushed up from the ground and rushed over to hug my friends. They expressed congratulations, grabbing my hand to examine the simple and elegant ring Ridge had chosen.

"I had no idea mailboxes could be so romantic," I mused as Ridge held my hand and we continued our walk to his car for dinner.

"I'm glad my proposal got your stamp of approval."

I groaned but couldn't quite wipe the smile off my face.

"How did you time all of that so perfectly?" I asked as I waited for Ridge to open my door.

"Your roommates helped. Though I nearly strangled Chloe earlier. It was her fault I was late. She was supposed to open the mailbox so I could slip the letter inside, but she took forever getting here from school."

Now my time spent pacing in front of the door made sense. I waited for Ridge to walk around and climb into his side of the car before I spoke again.

"It was perfect. And it wouldn't be us if it didn't happen a little bit late."

Ridge laughed, nodding in agreement as we drove to the restaurant, contentment and happiness settling around us.

"Promise me two things," I said as we parked. Ridge turned to face me. "Promise that we'll have a future full of letters and love."

"I can do that. What's the second thing?"

"Promise me you'll kiss me in the moonlight, no matter how old we get."

"Only if you promise to be my date to every dance for the rest of our lives."

I nodded, a smile filling my face as Ridge leaned over, sealing our promises with a kiss. The future ahead was bright, and I couldn't wait to experience every moment with this amazing man by my side.

For a bonus epilogue, visit authorhillaryslaughter.com

Also by Hillary Slaughter

Lost Roommates Series

Love Letter Lost

Losing Sleep

Lost Daydreaming

Acknowledgements

This book would not be possible without my faith, family, and friends and I want to thank all of them for the role they played!

To my parents, you believed in me and encouraged me to keep going, regardless of the number of times I called in frustration. Thank you!

Thank you to Lindy and Landon for being the best siblings a girl could ask for in addition to built in best friends. You keep me sane, no matter the challenges life throws my way. Lindy, you've been my number one fan since I started this writing adventure, and I would not be here without you.

Thank you to Madey. I miss you every single day and will always be grateful for my guardian angel.

Thank you to my extended family for your love and support. Grandpa, thank you for helping with the business side of things and for your patience with all of my random questions. Ashley, thank you for the amazing logo. Riley and Jayme, thank you for listening to me talk about books constantly and for helping me get outside when I introvert too much.

To the ladies of the For the Love of Books book club and all my bookstagram friends, thank you for giving me a space to nerd out about books and for all the book recommendations.

To Annie Jakes, Karen Thornell, Amanda Schimmoeller, Aspen Hadley, Clarissa Kae, Jentry Flint, Raneé Clark, and the many other authors who have answered my questions along the way. I could not have done this without you.

To Lindzee Merrill Photography, thank you for the incredible headshots.

To Emily at Midnight Owl Editors, thank you for helping me polish and finalize this book.

To my beta readers, arc readers, and everyone else who has had a hand in this book, thank you. There are too many to name and even if I tried, I know I would miss someone, but your support is felt and so greatly appreciated.

Finally, thank you, my readers, for reading Mallory's story! I hope you loved reading it as much as I loved writing it.

About the Author

Hillary Slaughter is a crafting addict, avid reader, and hiking enthusiast. Born and raised in Utah, she loves exploring the mountains, especially if she can bring her dog with her. She has a Bachelor's degree in English from Brigham Young University and a Master's of Business Administration from Utah Valley University. She loves writing sweet contemporary romance with a dash of humor and is the author of the

Lost Roommates Series. You can learn more about Hillary and her books at authorhillaryslaughter.com.

www.ingramcontent.com/pod-product-compliance
Lightning Source LLC
Chambersburg PA
CBHW061947170626
46813CB00006B/2560